When people think about the Gout Ronald Biggs — the man who go ___ her men the Great Train Robbery v ___ left Leatherslade Farm with the equiva ___ on, and were never caught or even suspected.

Keep on Running is a novel that draws on the true events surrounding the Great Train Robbery. It gives a dramatic account of what may have happened to those three men before, during and in the years after the robbery. It also features the shadowy character known to some as the Ulsterman, and provides a dramatic solution to the puzzle as to whether or not there was a shipment of jewels on board the train and, if there was, why the owner never came forward.

With *Keep on Running*, Britain's most lovable rogue has produced a gripping, imaginative and highly entertaining novel featuring events and people related to the biggest and most daring crime in British history.

Ronald Arthur Biggs was born in London on 8 August 1929. He made his first appearance in court at the age of fifteen, for stealing pencils from Littlewoods. In 1947 he volunteered for the RAF, but two years later was dishonourably discharged for breaking into a chemist's shop and being sentenced to six months in prison. He spent the next fourteen years in and out of the dock and a variety of jails, but found time to marry Charmaine Powell and have two sons, Nicholas and Christopher.

Biggs appeared to have settled for life as a family man and a builder in Reigate, Surrey, when he received an invitation from an old friend, Bruce Reynolds, to join him in a 'little piece of business' which culminated in the Great Train Robbery — on his thirty-fourth birthday — in 1963.

After capture and a dramatic prison escape, followed by five years of being chased around the world by Scotland Yard (and the birth of a third son, Farley), in 1970 he settled in Brazil, where he still lives. He has been able to stay in that country because he has a Brazilian son, Michael. His autobiography, *Odd Man Out,* was published in 1994. This is his first novel.

Keep on Running

Ronald Biggs
with
Christopher Pickard

BLOOMSBURY

If you would like to write to Ronald Biggs, the address is:

Caixa Postal (PO Box) 234
Rio de Janeiro
20001–970
Brazil

First published in Great Britain 1995
Bloomsbury Publishing Plc, 2 Soho Square, London W1V 6HB

A CIP catalogue for this book is available from the British Library

ISBN 0 7475 2188 3

10 9 8 7 6 5 4 3 2 1

Typeset by Hewer Text Composition Services, Edinburgh
Printed in Great Britain by Clays Ltd, St Ives plc

Everyone has run from something or someone during their lives. This book is dedicated to those who had to keep on running.

Prologue

The last time I spoke with Freddie Birch was on 8 July 1995. I remember the date, because Freddie was calling from Spain to congratulate me on my thirty years on the run. A lifetime, he said, and he wasn't far wrong, because that's what the judge had wanted to take from us – a lifetime of freedom.

Me and Freddie are two of the survivors of what has come to be known as the Great Train Robbery, an event that is as fresh in the minds of many as if it had happened yesterday. But while I was caught, charged, sentenced and subsequently escaped, three members of the gang never had a finger laid on them. Scotland Yard may have had their suspicions, but they never had the proof. For Freddie, George and David, the Great Train Robbery was the perfect crime.

A lot of water has flowed under the bridge since August 1963 and however much we might want to change the course of the river, we can't. There is no going back for any of us.

Freddie had read my autobiography, *Odd Man Out*. He said he still felt clammy and uneasy every time the robbery was mentioned in the press. Like me, he could never stop looking over his shoulder.

'So, Freddie,' I said, 'what about your story? When are you going to tell the world what happened over those first tempestuous years following the robbery?' He thought for a while and then said, 'No, Ron, you tell the story. You know what happened and could tell it so much better than me. But no real names, Ronnie, not even the initials. We don't want Scotland Yard shaking the dust off those files, do we?'

Mum's the word, Freddie. I hope you, your wonderful family and all the others who were involved enjoy the story. It is a remarkable one.

Ronald Biggs, Rio de Janeiro, Brazil
March 1995

1

St Stephen's School, West Kilburn, London, February 1951

A chill wind blew across the bleak playground. It was another grey day in one of the greyer parts of London. But for once it was not raining, so the pupils of St Stephen's School in West Kilburn could enjoy their morning break and play outside.

Headmaster Peter Coates, who despite his advanced age was considered something of a maverick amongst those who made up the Local Educational Authority, stared out at his charges. The war had done much to soften his views on life. Like so many of his fellow countrymen, he was happy to have survived the conflict and happier still that the school and its pupils had withstood everything that Hitler had thrown at it. The fire power of Hitler, he reflected, was nothing compared with the destructive power of the average London schoolboy.

The headmaster's thoughts were interrupted by a slight tap on the door. This time it was not going to be the first in a long line of little boys, terrified at meeting the ultimate figure of authority in their small world. An authority who had the power to warm the seat of their pants with a cane or a slipper if he so desired. Today was to be different. Coates had agreed to meet a parent, a widow who could get time off work only if she came to see him in the morning. The boys would have to postpone 'judgement day' until four o'clock.

'Mrs Jenkins is here to see you, Headmaster.' The messenger was the headmaster's secretary. A grand title for a girl of seventeen who would have had problems holding an intelligent conversation with most of the boys in the lower fifth.

'Show her in, Daisy. And see if you can rustle up a couple of biscuits to go with the coffee. And best china, Daisy . . . no mugs today.'

Mrs Jenkins was a slight woman, probably quite a looker in her day. From his dusty files Coates knew that she was just thirty-three. She had been seventeen when she gave birth to her son. He decided it would be ungentlemanly to mention this fact, for while Mrs Jenkins saw David, at sixteen, as little more than a child, no doubt she had never considered herself anything less than a mature adult when she had married the late Gordon Jenkins.

'Mrs Jenkins, a real pleasure to see you again.' Coates meant it and extended his hand in welcome. Without loosening his grip on Marjorie Jenkins' arm he steered her into the leather chair in front of his desk. A chair which, like himself, had seen better days.

'Coffee is on the way, or would you prefer tea?'

'Coffee would be fine. I don't want to take up too much of your valuable time, Headmaster, but it's my son, David. I know your report says that he is doing well enough, but I can't understand this obsession of his for cops and robbers. What little pocket money I can spare him goes on detective books and magazines or trips to the cinema to see the films. He must have seen that *Blue Lamp* at least ten times since it came out. As you know, I lost my husband in the war. Not having a man around the house, I got my brother to have a chat with David, but not even he could persuade him that there are more things to life than cops and robbers.'

'Mrs Jenkins, you have to understand that all young men have an interest of one sort or another,' the headmaster said, trying to put Marjorie at ease. 'For some it is football, for others cricket. There are those who like to go train-spotting and then in your son's class, where most of the boys are fifteen or sixteen, there are many who are totally obsessed with the fairer sex – a hobby which, in my experience, is often the most detrimental of all to their school work.'

A knock and a rattling tray signalled the return of Daisy. 'Poor Daisy can tell you a thing or two about young men's infatuation with the fairer sex. Can't you, Daisy?' Daisy looked at Marjorie Jenkins and both blushed as the girl poured the coffee.

'In the short time Daisy has been with us, she has found herself the centre of attention of many a young man's first romantic stirrings. They have even been known to send her flowers. Flowers pinched from an allotment, but flowers all the same.'

Coates took the opportunity of Daisy's entrance to pace around the small office with his cup of coffee. Experience in the classroom had taught him to keep moving and not to get stuck in one place if he wanted to keep the attention of his audience.

'Knowing that you were coming here today, I spoke to David's teachers. Your son is a bright boy. Possibly university potential, if he puts his mind to it. His English teacher says his work shows a vivid imagination. He does well in maths and science. In woodwork and metalcraft he has shown a remarkably mechanical mind. I will not lie and say that my staff have not noticed his interest in crime, or 'cops and robbers' as you put it, but if I am going to have to talk to your son about anything, it will be about his frequent use in class – as red herrings – of the very latest crop of crime stories. It is human nature, Mrs Jenkins, including that of my teaching staff, to be fascinated by crime. A sad reflection on our society you can argue, but nothing new. Jack the Ripper, Dr Crippen, Al Capone and more recently Neville Heath and John Haigh have all captured the interest of our nation, not just of your son and my staff. On the positive side, it shows your son is well informed, at least about crime, because he devours the newspapers we leave out in our somewhat limited library. I think I prefer this to his poring over the sports pages or hiding in the toilets with some lewd magazine.' Coates was in full flow, his disquisition broken only by the bell signalling that his presence was required to teach history to the lower fourth.

'Mrs Jenkins, rest assured that I will keep an eye on young David and I will have a chat with him. His interest in crime should not be totally discouraged. It may blossom into an interest in the law of this fine country. The police force is a very solid career today, or, if we push David, perhaps he has what it takes to be a lawyer. Sadly, there appears to be enough crime in London to keep both the police and the lawyers gainfully employed for the foreseeable future.'

Lambeth Juvenile Court,
London, June 1952

Reginald Clough-Kirby, all five foot four of him in his stocking feet, had never met the headmaster. If he ever did, they were unlikely to see eye to eye. Clough-Kirby, a greengrocer by trade, loved the trappings of power his place on the magistrates' bench brought him.

Today was another of those special days for Clough-Kirby. The day he handed down sentences to the juveniles who had dared cross the law and his own bench. That Clough-Kirby did not have any children of his own did not cause him any doubts as to his fitness to administer the law, as he defined it. He adjusted his robe one last time and made his way back from the toilet to the magistrates' room where his two colleagues on the bench that afternoon, Maureen Crossley, a retired schoolteacher, and Jim Forsyth, an accountant, were waiting. Crossley shared Clough-Kirby's view that hanging was too good for the majority of the human race, especially the children who seemed to have been running riot in the streets of London since the end of the war. Like Clough-Kirby, she had no children of her own, but she had certainly never let the 'gels' at her school behave like the ruffians she now saw before her. Forsyth, a father of three, had a more liberal outlook on life, but more often than not found himself in a minority of one. He was already looking at ways to move to another bench to get away from the ghastly duo of Clough-Kirby and Crossley, but he knew it would not be easy. He was in exactly the right place, the powers-that-be had explained to him, to balance a bench which was clearly weighted in favour of a harsh and conservative view of law and order. For today Forsyth would have to swallow his pride and suffer the pomposity of Clough-Kirby, who would announce the sentences – many which he had personally disagreed with – in a manner more befitting the Old Bailey than a juvenile court.

5

KEEP ON RUNNING

Except for those who had to be there because it was their job, the dank and badly lit court was empty. Clough-Kirby made an opening address to nobody, an address which was duly recorded and filed away in some dusty warehouse, never to be read or looked at again. The first children, because children is all they were, to be brought before the bench were the lucky ones who got off with a stern warning or a small fine. Most were treated leniently because their parents had come to court and grovelled sufficiently – in Clough-Kirby's opinion – to be given 'one last chance'. It was often unclear whether that 'last chance' referred to the parents or their children.

Waiting to be called were two south Londoners, George Enoch Rawlings and John Frederick 'Darkie' Birch, better known as Freddie. Rawlings was a husky sixteen-year-old, big for his age and powerfully built. Birch, on the other hand, was slightly built, only five foot three, with dark good looks which were the product of a white English mother and a black Jamaican father. A father he had not seen for the last six years. Both boys were up on larceny charges and the one thing they had in common was that the articles they were charged with stealing were only a fraction of what they had stolen in total. Despite their tender years, George and Freddie were hardened and proficient thieves.

George was appearing before the beak for the second time in nine months. On the first occasion Clough-Kirby had warned him that if he appeared before that bench again he would be packed off to an approved school – that was the fate to which George had now resigned himself. It was bad enough that he'd been done for nicking four hundredweight of lead; when the beak got to hear that the lead had been ripped off the roof of a church . . . it was well known that 'Old Reg', as Clough-Kirby was nicknamed, was a right Bible-basher.

Freddie Birch, for his part, had been grabbed by a store detective as he left a shop with an expensive set of drawing instruments he had 'forgotten' to pay for. Birch had wriggled away from the detective and legged it down the road, but had run straight into the arms of a beefy copper. Done bang to rights he was led off to the nearest police station and invited to make a statement. 'Make a clean breast of the matter,' a detective had told him in a fatherly fashion and suggested that Freddie would be wise to have any other acts of dishonesty taken into consideration. 'You'll feel much better when you've got it all off your chest.' But Freddie had looked the detective straight in the eye and lied convincingly enough that this was the first and only time he had ever 'forgotten' to pay for something.

The question of bail arose and some hours later Freddie's mother arrived at the police station, where she promptly burst into tears at the sight of her young son in the hands of the law. Now she sat beside him on one of the hard wooden forms in the anteroom to the court, nervously twisting a handkerchief between her work-worn fingers.

George had arrived at the court with his street-trader father, Ernie Rawlings, who now sat studying the *Greyhound Express*. 'Big Ernie' was no stranger to police courts and had done time for burglary, receiving stolen property, obstruction and causing grievous bodily harm to a police officer. Ernie's sister, Rose, was also well known to both the police and the courts of London, but to date she had avoided prison.

It was not long before the two boys were chatting, introducing themselves and telling each other what they had been nicked for. Rawlings told Birch that there was a good chance the bench would send him to Stamford House Remand Home for a week or so for a medical report – a load of old cobblers, in his opinion.

As the court prepared for the next case Clough-Kirby took the opportunity to blow his nose and examine the contents of his handkerchief. Without looking up he asked the clerk of the court in a low voice for the name of his next victim. 'George Enoch Rawlings, Your Worship,' the clerk, another career sycophant, whispered back. Clough-Kirby fumbled with his files until he found the right one.

A uniformed police sergeant with a clip-board in his hand took his cue, opened the door of the courtroom and bellowed, 'GEORGE ENOCH RAWLINGS!' George winced slightly at the sound of his middle name. He hated it and it had involved him in more than a few punch-ups during his early schooldays. The bigger George got, the less the other kids had taken the mickey out of his name, but it still caused him embarrassment. George and Ernie stood up and were ushered into the magisterial *sanctum sanctorum*. The lead from the church roof had been brought into the courtroom and was piled on a canvas sheet at the side of the bench: four hundredweight and twenty-three pounds of mangled bluey.

Clough-Kirby's nervous tic was already working overtime when George took his place before the bench. With rich detail, Detective Inspector Bragg, CID, described the rooftop chase and rugby-tackle finale. Gratuitously, the detective added that George had not co-operated with the police in locating the other 'elements' possibly involved in the theft.

When called to give evidence, the Reverend Robin Doe meticulously itemized the extent of the damage to the roof of St Luke's. Bluff and Sons, a building firm, informed the bench that they had estimated the cost of repairing the roof at over a thousand pounds. A small fortune for the church.

The bench put their heads together and, after a lengthy conversation, Clough-Kirby cleared his throat and delivered a blistering diatribe against the 'wilful, outrageous and criminal vandalism' committed by Rawlings and 'others'. It was the others – who hadn't been caught – that gave the bench most reason to be indignant. Clough-Kirby glared in George's direction and then at the heap of crumpled lead. He remembered George and his father well, and he remembered his promise. After further mutterings and head-wagging with the couple on either side of him, he pronounced sentence: George Enoch Rawlings would spend the next three years in an approved school and would be confined in Stamford House Remand Home until a vacancy occurred at a suitable establishment.

Held firmly by the sleeve of his jacket, George was hustled out of the courtroom by the police sergeant and handed over to another copper. 'Another customer for Stamford House! Three of the best!' George looked pale, but he was defiant enough to give Freddie a grin and a thumbs-up sign as he was led off to a detention room.

Freddie Birch replaced George in the dock. Freddie was turned seventeen, six months older than George, yet in the dock appeared to be three or four years younger. The police had warned Clough-Kirby and his colleagues that Birch was a bit of a 'cheeky chappy' who enjoyed his own brand of humour. Little Freddie stood alone in front of the magistrates, a bit scared but trying not to let it show.

Agnes Birch, Freddie's mother, who had taken the day off from the biscuit factory to take her son to court, was clearly intimidated by the trappings of the courtroom and the trio on the bench. She started twisting her handkerchief around her fingers again as she perched on the edge of her chair.

Police Constable Arthur Drake, the bogey who had caught Freddie, was the first to give evidence. Less skilful with words, PC Drake did

8

his best to lay before the magistrates the events that had led to the apprehension of the diminutive defendant. He warmed to the subject when he described his own heroics as 'grappling with the accused'. The wide-awake shop assistant who had spotted Freddie slipping the wallet of drawing instruments inside his windcheater was called and told the court that he had given Trevor Ende, the store detective, a prearranged signal that a shoplifter was about to leave the premises. Mr Ende, an ex-copper, gave a concise account of what had happened when he stopped the boy outside the shop. When questioned about the theft, Freddie had tried to make a run for it, but the detective had grabbed him by the arm. A struggle ensued, Mr Ende told the bench, during which he sustained grazes and a sprained wrist. As Mr Ende left the witness box the magistrates joined heads for the usual whispered natter.

Next the fatherly detective who had taken Freddie's statement at the police station was called. He read the lad's statement to the court. Clough-Kirby then turned his attention to Freddie's mother and asked questions about her son's behaviour at home and at school. In a quavering voice, Mrs Birch told the court that her son was a good boy, very helpful and clever with his hands. A quick learner. She was at a loss, though, to understand why he had stolen the drawing instruments. She suggested that it might have something to do with the disappearance of his father. They had always been close, she explained. Clough-Kirby manifested fleeting sympathy and went into yet another huddle with his colleagues.

Then, 'John Frederick Birch,' thundered the magistrate without warning, 'you are a very fortunate young man not to be standing before the court on a charge more serious than larceny. The violent resistance that you demonstrated upon being detained indicates that you should be severely punished. Your mother has told the court that you are a good and helpful child and has asked that you may be "given a chance". But I am not entirely satisfied that you do indeed deserve this chance and so I am going to remand you in custody for fourteen days so that a medical report can be made before I make up my mind. She also says that you are a quick learner. Let us hope that this is one lesson you learn quickly and take to heart.'

A little later, Freddie Birch, George Rawlings and two other young law-breakers were locked in a van with barred windows and driven across London to Stamford House. George was the only one among them who had been there before and laughingly told the others what to expect.

'Don't bend down in front of any of the masters,' he said. 'They're a right bunch of brown-hatters and arse-bandits.' His stories did little to reassure the Stamford House virgins.

As George spoke, he fiddled in his pocket and before long produced a small pair of wire-cutters which his father had slipped to him just before saying goodbye. When the van pulled up at a red light George, who was still rabbiting on, went to work placing the tip of the pliers in the lock. In seconds he had the emergency door of the van open. His timing was perfection and as the light turned from amber to green he bolted out the side door and away, narrowly missing a passing car in the inside lane. In the confusion and heavy traffic there was little the distracted driver or guard could do but go on through the light. By the time the van was able to stop without risking a major accident, George was well gone. Freddie admired the big lad's bravado, but kept his mouth shut, head down and tried not to laugh. He hoped that the fact he had not tried to escape with George when he could have done would count in his favour at the end of his time in Stamford House.

London Sessions/Wormwood Scrubs, February 1953

After his fortnight at Stamford House, which he had found to be no holiday camp, Freddie Birch was granted his 'one last chance'. Less than eight months later, he was up before the beak again, this time at the London Sessions. After being found guilty on two charges of robbery, Freddie, now eighteen, was sentenced to three years' borstal training. Delivering a scathing tirade before passing sentence, Mr Justice Warrington told Freddie that he was lucky to be getting off so lightly – his recent record, which had come to light after further police investigation, qualified him for five years' imprisonment. The judge rattled on about the 'opportunity' that he was giving Freddie and how he should take advantage of it. At borstal, he was told, he would be able to learn a trade. It was a tune that Freddie had heard before.

In a chilly cell beneath the court, Freddie sat thinking about his situation. He was a fucking borstal boy! A chance to learn a trade – for fuck's sake! One of his mates, Tony Lucas, sentenced to borstal training a year ago, was going to have a laugh, he thought. It was only three months earlier – just before Freddie had his collar felt – that he had visited his friend at the borstal institution at Portland, close to Weymouth. Now here he was in the same boat. With any luck, he told himself, he might not be sent to Portland; from what Tony had told him it was a 'bugger of a place' and it wasn't exactly a doddle to have it away from either. Escape was now very much in Freddie's mind.

Christ, it was cold! Freddie turned up the collar of his jacket and breathed into his cupped hands. He moved around the cell, reading the names, sentences and obscene observations that had been scratched on the walls by the crooked and convicted down the years. A grumbling elderly gaoler unlocked the door of the cell and a tall, broad-shouldered fellow, about the same age as

11

Freddie, was pushed through the door. A voice cut through the gloom.

'Jesus, fuckin' H. Christ . . . I don't believe it! Darkie Birch! Got you again, did they?'

'George! Is that you, George? George Rawlings? Smack me in the mouth with a hockey stick, it is!' It was George Rawlings, all right, who after a number of close calls and a chase through the West End had finally been tagged by Old Bill's finest.

'What did you get this time?' George asked Freddie.

'Fuckin' borstal!'

'Me too! Join the club. What a choker and I'm not even eighteen! That judge should learn the fuckin' law. What did you get done for?'

'Robbery. Me and a couple of mates turned a bookie over – we had to take stoppo and I got lumbered, didn't I?'

From their brief previous encounter the two boys felt they would hit it off. They were both south Londoners, Freddie from Camberwell and Big George from Kennington. Both were from rough and ready working-class families. They sat on the hard wooden bench in the dark, dank cell, shooting the breeze and catching up on each other's recent villainous deeds. The eight months that had passed since their previous meeting had hardened them both. Neither showed any sign of remorse or fear of what lay ahead.

During the late afternoon they were taken out of the cell and handcuffed. A couple of burly officers marched on either side of George – they were taking no chances with him this time round. Then, with others who had shared similar fates that day, they were conducted from the cell area down the steps to a waiting Black Maria. They were the only two who had been sentenced to borstal training and were on their way to Her Majesty's Prison, Wormwood Scrubs, where they would be classified and eventually sent to the institution that was considered most suitable. After their experiences at Stamford House, prison was not exactly going to be a new adventure for either of them; they knew what to expect. What seemed to worry George more than anything was that as one of the 'boys in brown' he would have to wear short trousers.

'I'm going to look a right fuckin' berk in that borstal boy gear!' he said.

The journey from the London Sessions to 'the Scrubs', locked in the tiny cubicles inside the 'charabanc', as the coppers liked to call it, seemed all too short. The condemned men sat in gloomy silence looking out through tiny windows. Ordinary street scenes of people coming and going took on a new importance. Freddie saw a flash of white thigh as the Black Maria overtook a girl on a bicycle and found himself thinking about his girlfriend, Valerie. It might be quite some time before he could get between her legs again. She'd written to him several times while he'd been on remand, swearing 'true love' and all that bollocks, but now that he'd been weighed off she would surely blow him out.

The Black Maria turned off the road and into the driveway leading to the entrance of HMP Wormwood Scrubs. The driver stopped at the gates and beeped the horn a couple of times. Well-greased bolts slid from their keeps and a bespectacled prison officer threw the gates open, allowing the police van to enter. Behind them the gates were closed, locked and bolted. Then twin gates were opened on the opposite side of the gate-lodge and the Black Maria proceeded to 'Receptions'.

A uniformed police sergeant carrying a clip-board under his arm got down from the van and pressed a shining brass bell-push. The sound of rubber-soled boots on highly polished linoleum announced the arrival of the reception officer.

'What have you got for me, Sergeant?'

'Seven beauties from the Old Bailey, Mr Merryweather! Three for corrective training, two PDs and two for borstal training.'

'Right! Bring 'em in, Sergeant!'

In Receptions, the handcuffs were removed and the convicted men told to sit down on forms in front of the reception officer's desk and to keep quiet. 'You did all your talking at the London Sessions,' said Mr Merryweather, 'and you didn't make a very good job of it!'

In turn they were called to the desk, where they emptied their pockets and had each item duly entered into a huge ledger; cigarettes, tobacco and matches were confiscated.

'Right! Now stand on that sheet and take your clothes off . . . come along, lad, move yourself! Right! Now turn around, stand with your legs apart and touch your toes. Come on, don't be shy, lad! We've seen it all before. Now put that sheet around you and go through that door into the bath-house . . . One on, Mr Mottle!'

'Thank you, Mr Merryweather!'

Freddie and George were the last to be attended to, but finally, bathed and uniformed, they were back on the wooden forms with the others, waiting to be examined by the medical officer. Following a brief encounter with the quack – Any serious illnesses? Any insanity in the family? Ever had VD? – they were given a mug of watery tea, a cob of bread, a pat of margarine and a spoonful of watered-down jam. After this luxurious repast they were kitted out with prison-made toilet utensils, sheets and blankets, cloth slippers, a dessertspoon and a tin knife. An hour or so later, a tall, thin screw with the peak of his cap turned down, guardsman-style, came from B wing to get the two 'boys in brown'.

'Okay, you two. Pick up your gear and follow me. Two off, Mr Merryweather!'

'Thank you, Mr Hardcastle!'

As they made their way through the depressing building, Freddie kept muttering little asides to George, making the big lad laugh.

'Stop that yakking, Birch!' Hardcastle said in a firm voice, checking from his board that he had got the boy's name right. Freddie ignored the big screw, who turned round and glowered at his diminutive charge.

'Birch,' he said. 'We seem to be having a problem of communication. Would you understand it better if I spoke in Swahili?' Freddie kept his mouth shut.

As with all borstal boys, before Freddie and George had the chance to learn a trade it would be necessary for them to undergo several months of preparations in B wing of HMP Wormwood Scrubs. Periodically, a selection committee would sit to decide which borstal institution was suitable for each individual. The tough guys were packed off to Portland. Rochester, in Kent, was for escapees and Feltham, in Middlesex, for the nutters and the simple-minded. Good conduct and 'team spirit' could result in being sent to an 'open' borstal, where heavy farm work was waiting. Mr Bleak, the housemaster, made it sound like fun in the sun. George decided that either Portland or Rochester was awaiting the pleasure of his company.

Vincent 'Goofy' Carrington, a hefty lad from Lancashire with teeth 'hanging out to dry', was the Daddy of B wing. A tough kid, he had taken the title from Vic Johnson soon after his arrival. Goofy, a dirty street-fighter, had head-butted his way to his position of authority and those who had witnessed the battle between Goofy and Vic were more than willing to carry out the new Daddy's orders.

Goofy lost no time in introducing himself to the newcomers, letting them know in no uncertain terms that he was running the show. The defeated Vic was now the number one man in Goofy's fawning entourage of half-a-dozen would-be-thugs. The group were the 'food orderlies', responsible for collecting the food from the cookhouse and distributing it among the rest of the inmates. The job provided certain perks in the form of any extra food that might be left over; Goofy served the little pats of margarine with a tin knife, shamelessly 'chivying' off part of each portion he served. George and Freddie were not long in seeing that it was going to be necessary to make a few changes.

The boys were first put to work in the woodshed, where 'Chalky' White was the screw in charge. Twice daily Chalky lined up his motley detachment of twenty-odd workers and marched them to and from the woodshed which was tucked away in a far corner of the prison. 'Left ... left ... left, right, left! Get hold of the step, Stephens!'

Two lads operated the circular saw, cutting old railway sleepers into six-inch logs. The rest of the gang, armed with axes, worked at benches, chopping the logs into little sticks and tying the sticks into small bundles. The Daddy's job was to go from bench to bench with one of his acolytes, collecting the bundles and chalking up the production on a slate.

The showdown came a few days later when Freddie said something to the big Lancashire lad that he didn't like. 'Oi, you little bastard! You'd better shut that big mouth of yours before I give it a slap for you!' warned Carrington.

'Fucking try!' provoked Freddie, brandishing his axe. 'If you're looking for a new parting you'll get some of this across your nut!'

This was enough to get Goofy's dander up. 'You little bastard!' he spat out, wagging a finger in Freddie's face, 'I'm going to fookin' 'ave you!'

The next morning a fuming Goofy was waiting for Freddie in the recess on the top landing. Most of the punch-ups and knifings took place in the recesses when the screws were out of sight. 'That fookin' Cockney is going to feel my knee up his bollocks!' he promised his followers. But George was one of the first to enter the recess and was quick to sum up the situation.

'Listen, Goofy, forget it, Freddie's my mate ...'

The Daddy's eyes bulged from their sockets. 'What did you call me, Rawlings? Goofy?! That's a name I fookin' 'ate!'

'Really?' said George balling his fists, 'Goofy! Goofy! Goofy! You're a goofy bastard!'

As the Lancashire lad went to grab George by the lapels of his jacket to drag him close for the traditional head butt, George released a battery of devastating punches to Goofy's face and body. Groaning, the Daddy went down, bloody, broken and beaten. B wing had a new Daddy and his name was George Enoch Rawlings.

George, with Freddie as his number two, ruled the roost with a great deal more compassion than Goofy had. Carrington was shipped out to Portland shortly after the incident and then on to Feltham once the authorities were sure he had a screw loose somewhere.

By mid-April it was George and Freddie's turn to go up before the selection board, a board of three consisting of the assistant governor, the housemaster and the prison padre.

The dot on the card was that George would be heading for Portland, and so it turned out to be. 'According to that poofy padre, God will be coming with me for good measure,' George told Freddie shortly before his friend went up before the board.

'Well, I'll see if I can make it a threesome,' Freddie quipped.

'Don't feel obliged on my account, old son,' George said. Unfortunately, or rather fortunately for Freddie, the board did not see him as a hard case, despite his devil-may-care demeanour.

'We have decided after reviewing your record and your recent behaviour that you will serve the rest of your sentence at the open borstal of Usk in Monmouthshire. You are a fortunate young man, make the most of this opportunity,' the assistant governor told him. Where had Freddie heard this song before? He thanked the panel for their consideration and kindness and made his way to the door.

'And Birch . . . !' the padre added. 'God go with you, my son!'

'Thank you, Reverend,' Freddie replied, as he stopped in the doorway, 'but I think you'll find you've already got him down for Portland!'

A slightly disappointed Freddie went to hunt George out. 'Done me up with Usk, haven't they?' he told his big friend.

'But that's great, Freddie! It's a doddle to have it away from Usk. You can go over the wall any time you choose. Don't worry about me, take the chance, I'll be fine in Portland.'

George was right about Usk. By midsummer Freddie was back on his patch in London and up to his old tricks. If he had gained anything from the experience, it was his blossoming friendship with George Rawlings. He looked forward to seeing the big lad when he got out. Freddie's life did not go entirely according to plan, however; by September Old Bill had tracked him down and he found himself back in borstal, this time in Rochester, which specialized in looking after escapees.

West London, August 1953

'It is not at all romantic, you know? Not like the boys from Fleet Street would have you believe. The work of a journalist means long hours, short wages and an inordinate amount of hanging around. But when you see your story in print, you'll find that is reward enough.'

The speaker was John Hartley – editor, publisher and occasional teaboy of a small weekly newspaper that served an area of west London. He had started the business just after the war, filling a void that had come about because local papers were something of a luxury in wartime – a luxury, the country had discovered, that it could easily do without.

To those who listened, Hartley would tell tales of wartime reporting. The truth, like so much you read in Hartley's paper, was somewhat different. Barely out of university at the beginning of the war, a slight limp had exempted him from active service. Instead, the army discovered that Hartley had run the students' magazine at university and had a basic idea of printing and a good eye for design. Hartley sat out most of the war in the comfort of an army print shop in Norwich and never got to *see* any action, let alone report on it.

Hartley's father had died in the war – of natural causes; not on the beaches of Normandy, as Hartley liked to tell people – and as a result his son was left with sufficient funds so that, when victory came, he was in a position to pick up some printing presses on the cheap and install himself as publisher and editor of his own weekly newspaper, the *West London Chronicle*.

The target of Hartley's little speech was David Jenkins, who at seventeen had decided that university was not for him but that possibly a career in journalism was. If Jenkins was honest, it was not the noble profession that appealed so much as the opportunity to stay in London and delve deeper into the murky side of the capital's criminal community. Journalism would open the doors for him, he thought.

'Your mother tells me you have ... how did she phrase it ... a "morbid" interest in crime? Is that true?' Hartley did not add that he himself had a more than passing interest in David's mum. She was the real reason he had decided to give the young man an opportunity as his glorified cub reporter cum office boy. In fairness to David, and to Hartley, the boy's headmaster, Peter Coates, had written a glowing reference and from the short piece David had written off the top of his head about the John Christie case, it was clear the boy could string his words together, even if his spelling left something to be desired. It was highly unlikely on the *West London Chronicle*, however, that he would ever get the chance to write about anything as exciting as the goings-on in Rillington Place, even if that notorious address did fall within the paper's catchment area. And hopefully the subs, who could spell if nothing else, would catch his typos.

'I would hardly call crime a forte of my newspaper' – Hartley emphasized the word 'my' – 'but our readers do like to know who has done what to whom within our little community. Make no mistake, David, we are here to serve the community first, and only after that report the wider news. People get their news from the national dailies and that is something we must never forget. Births, deaths, marriages and tea parties are the cornerstones of our empire. I am certain you will do your mother proud at the *Chronicle*. I will tell her as much when I have dinner with her on Thursday.'

London, July 1955

She had fascinated Jenkins from the start. Denise was a cut above the others that he had seen being bundled through the system at the local magistrates' court, a place of which even he was beginning to tire.

David had been with the *West London Chronicle* for the better part of two years now and had very little to show for his toil. It was a learning experience, his mother continued to assure him, but he knew she was simply echoing the thoughts of Hartley, who saw in him a cheap solution to most of the paper's donkey work and an excuse for direct access to his mother.

The life of a 'journalist' had not opened up the doors that David had dreamed of. On a very limited scale it had allowed him to study his local London crime scene at closer quarters than had previously been possible and he had even made his first real 'criminal' contacts. Cops and robbers continued to fascinate David, who was now old enough to be certain that, while journalism never brought out any real emotions in him, a life of crime would.

Denise Stroud was the catalyst that changed his life.

It was her looks that had first caught his attention. He had seen many pretty girls before, but something about Denise stirred a passion within him that he could never quite explain. She was a Goldie Hawn look-alike, years before Goldie Hawn herself rose to prominence.

The first time he saw her was during a purely routine visit to a police station on the *Chronicle*'s patch. He had called by to see if there was anything that might be of interest to the paper. A missing cat; a stolen bicycle; even a talk by the police to the local branch of the Women's Diocesan Association. Denise, who was barely sixteen at the time and looked even younger, had been brought to the station by the scruff of the neck by a shopkeeper who accused her of shoplifting. Unlike most of the kids he had seen in a similar predicament she was very self-assured

20

and willing to argue the point with the desk sergeant. It was all a terrible mistake, she explained, a simple misunderstanding on the part of the shop owner. To prove it, she showed those who were interested that she had more than enough money in her purse to buy the goods they were accusing her of stealing. She got off with a warning, but only after the shopkeeper had been told confidentially that it was going to be more trouble than it was worth for him to take the case any further. He should be satisfied, the desk sergeant told him, that the girl had been given a fright; at the same time, it was not at all certain that a court might not take the manipulative girl's side of the argument in court and do the shopkeeper for wrongful arrest.

After seeing Denise in the station, David made a few discreet inquiries, after which he went out of his way to cross paths with her whenever possible. At first he took to observing her on the bus as she went to school.

Her appearance at the local magistrates' court some months later came as something of a surprise to David. He was catching up on some reading and surreptitiously killing time with a sandwich, only half listening to the comings and goings in court, when he heard Denise's name. Predictably enough the charges involved shoplifting. The Denise who stood in front of the magistrates was not the Denise he knew from the police station and the bus. She had deliberately dressed down to look younger than her years and was immaculately turned out in her smart maroon school uniform, which he knew in other circumstances would have been customized in her typically rebellious fashion. Denise was no dedicated follower of fashion. She set her own styles and trends for others to follow, if they so wished.

Denise's lawyer, on behalf of her mother, who wept silently at the back of the court, pleaded with the bench. It was nothing more than a silly dare from her schoolfriends, he explained. It would never happen again, he had the girl's mother and father's word for that. David could not help but admire Denise's own performance. He was certain she was as guilty as sin and from the way her big blue eyes peered at him across the court through her thick fringe, he was sure that she could read his mind. Yet it did not matter what David thought. It was up to the magistrates. But for the first time in David's life it was personal, not just a name and number in the clerk of the court's ledger. He desperately wanted Denise to be let off and feared for the judgement as much as he would have had he himself been up on the charges. He bit his bottom lip and waited.

After much deliberation among the three magistrates, Denise received a stiff verbal warning and was told by the head magistrate in no uncertain terms that if she was ever brought before him or any other court again, she would discover what it was like to spend some time away from the comfort of her parents' home. She blushed and kept her eyes averted from the magistrate's staring gaze. She played the part of the contrite little schoolgirl perfectly and everyone was happy. Justice had been seen to be done.

David realized it was probably now or never if he was going to break the ice with Denise. If he did not talk to her today, he would have to face her on the bus and then she might be surrounded by her girlfriends and ignore him. He slipped out of the back of the courtroom and found Denise waiting patiently as her mother thanked the family lawyer. She fiddled nervously with the hem of her tunic.

David manoeuvred his way across her path after calculating that he could always make a run for the safety of the gents if it all went wrong. Just as he drew level with her he dropped his notebook. As he had planned in his dreams the girl bent down and retrieved it for him. 'I'm glad you got off,' he mumbled under his breath as she handed it back to him. It was difficult to know who looked more embarrassed, him or her.

'Thank you,' she said softly. 'Are you waiting to appear or do you work here? I saw you at the back of the court.'

'Not exactly. I report on what goes on in the courts for a paper.' Their eyes met for the first time.

'Christ!' her voice went up several octaves. 'I hope you're not going to write about me.' The 'innocent girl lost' look had gone from her eyes.

David quickly reassured her that her story was in safe hands. 'You were found not guilty, that's not really a story, you know? Now if you had done it, then that would have been different. It would have given me something to write about.' Their eyes betrayed them. They both knew the truth. David was thrilled finally to get to talk to Denise. Not only did she send tingles down his spine, she had actually committed a crime, something he himself had only managed in his dreams. But today was a day for dreams to come true.

'Don't I see you on my bus in the morning?' she asked. Denise did not want to make her interest in David too obvious. He was older and might see no further than the silly little schoolgirl that stood before him. David had no time to reply, Denise's mother was on the warpath.

'It's straight home for you, young lady, and think yourself very lucky. If this ever happens again I will let them take you away.' She emphasized the 'will'. 'It would do you good. Your father will want to talk to you, young madam, when he gets home. You've still got a few lessons to learn.' With that, an embarrassed Denise was bundled away. How could her mother be so cruel, and in front of a boy!

The ice was broken and it was only a matter of days before David and Denise ran into each other on the bus. They set up a first meeting – neither liked to call it a date – but soon they became an inseparable couple, a pairing made easier by Denise's mum, who was certain that a young journalist would be a good influence on her wayward daughter.

It was not long before David and Denise found themselves plotting imaginary heists in which they were never caught. A modern-day Bonnie and Clyde. Denise had as vivid an imagination as David when it came to crime and he finally understood that for her shoplifting was not a financial necessity, but an emotional one. She was the first person he could talk to openly about his belief in the perfect crime and the respect he had for criminals, as opposed to the forces of law and order whom he saw as a bunch of old stuffed shirts.

Crime came first. Sex came second. It was hard to know which gave them greater satisfaction. They attacked both with the same torrid passion.

It was David who persuaded Denise that shoplifting, unless carefully thought out, was a mug's game. Their first 'job' went like a dream. He chose as their target a department store in Ealing in which one department blended into the next. It was easy to pick up goods and wander from one section to another without the bored staff saying anything. It netted them more in one afternoon than David had earned all month from the paper. He did not admit as much to Denise, but it was, despite all his talk, his first true criminal act. Just as he had expected, he thrilled to the experience as much as he had the first time he had made love to her. An event which, happily for him and his fumbling performance, had also been a first for her.

David's salary, although small, had given him the independence to move away from his mother's home and set himself up in a small one-bedroom flat in the back streets of west London. It became their hideaway. Pride of place went to his collection of crime books and magazines. A similar collection of girlie magazines were kept away from Denise's prying eyes. Crime and sex dominated their schedule. Neither could get enough.

The couple's first really 'big' job was against the *West London Chronicle* itself. As Hartley, the owner and editor, got lazier and lazier, so he pushed more and more of the paper's donkey work on to David. This included a visit to Barclays Bank every Friday morning to pick up the weekly payroll. Whoever went carried the money back in a bag that Hartley had specially prepared in his own garage so that it could be handcuffed to the carrier's wrist. It was more for show than anything else, as Hartley, always one to do things on the cheap, had chosen poor-quality garden chain which could easily be snipped through with a pair of standard pliers or a good pair of scissors. They had discovered this at the newspaper's Christmas party after one of the young subs had been found virtually naked chained to the bathroom sink, much to the embarrassment of her boyfriend, who had had to call for help.

David and Denise calculated that all that was needed to snatch the money from the *Chronicle*'s payroll was to make it look like a robbery. So they planned it as such. Nothing was left to chance. They studied the average time it took to get from the bank to the newspaper on a Friday; the route; the people you might meet along the way. They planned the job that never was. They worked out how many people would need to be involved, and estimated at least three. What they would be driving and how they would be dressed. The police, if interested, would expect a newspaper reporter, even a fairly junior one like David, to make a good witness. David bet Denise that police interest in the case would last less than a week. There would be bigger fish for them to fry on the manor, he promised.

The job introduced David and Denise to the world of 'false alarms'. On the day they had originally planned for the hit, Hartley himself had gone to the bank on other business and took the opportunity to pick up the payroll. The second week it rained and Hartley, in a rare magnanimous gesture, told David to take a cab. It put the job back a couple of weeks, but eventually the big day came.

Denise used a secluded area behind a park-keeper's tool-shed to clip the bag from David's wrist. She substituted it with a similar-looking bag that she had nicked from the local Woolworth's and hidden in her shopping bag. She had persuaded David that at least one item should genuinely be stolen so that it could never be traced to them. Denise secured the handle of the bag to the remaining part of the chain with an elastic band. Any nosy witnesses who saw David after he left the park would swear he had had the bag with him, while if anyone had seen him go behind the shed he could claim that he had been taking care of a call of nature.

As Denise went home with the day's spoils, David walked on to the spot where he, if he was organizing the hold-up, would strike. It was a secluded cut-through. Leaving the chain dangling from his wrist, he disposed of the second bag in a large rubbish-tip, secure in the knowledge that the police would have neither the time nor the manpower to check the area. He emerged from the alley looking suitably shaken and making all the right noises.

They called Hartley from the police station. Two men in balaclavas had grabbed Jenkins, he was told. They had the wire-cutters ready and a car standing by at the end of the alley. Wage grabs were not uncommon in the area, the police told him, and it was almost certainly the work of a professional gang. There was nothing that David could have done in the circumstance, they assured him. David could hardly wait to tell Denise.

The wage snatch finally gave David the chance to write his first front-page crime story – from 'first-hand experience', too – while Hartley concocted a strongly worded editorial to run alongside the story, asking, in tones of outraged indignation, if anyone was now safe to walk the streets of London. Nobody suspected David, let alone Denise, and the case, like so many others in London, remained unsolved and was quickly forgotten. David and Denise celebrated with a slap-up meal and a session in the sack which beat all previous records.

Four months later, almost to the day, David left the *West London Chronicle* and Denise spent her last day at school. Six more months and they were married.

David told his mother that there was little future in journalism for someone of his limited verbal talents; instead he had taken a course to be a locksmith and was going to set up a little business on his own with money that he had borrowed from Barclays Bank. This was partly true, only neither the bank nor the *West London Chronicle* was aware that they had agreed to the loan! Denise, for her part, having told her mother and father that they could shove school and their lifestyle where the sun didn't shine, joined a local estate agent's and divided her time between their office and showing people around the company's various properties. Never had the basis for a life of crime seemed so easy. All they had to do was bide their time and be patient.

Denise had the keys, David made the copies. When the right target was in place they simply walked through the front door and took what they wanted, occasionally taking the trouble to make it look as if a smash-and-grab raid had taken place. Alternatively, they waited until the people had decorators in, knowing that they or their acquaintances would be blamed. David renewed and widened the criminal contacts he had made during his time on the paper. He needed people he could trust who would take care of the items he and Denise lifted without asking too many questions. They were beginning to build a reputation and a degree of respect among their west London colleagues.

London, February 1957

Freddie sloshed through the melting snow. He still wasn't sure which was worse, borstal or work. Just twenty-two, he had decided that he had better do an honest day's work or two, at least for the time being. He had been monitored by the police and his probation officer since his release and, with his mother still slaving away at the biscuit factory, any signs of wealth would be taken as a signal that he had returned to his old ways. Freddie did not take to the idea of continuing to live a life of poverty. Not with his talents.

It had been Freddie's probation officer who organized the job with British Rail for him. Freddie had hoped for something with a few comforts where he could put his feet up, read the papers, have a lunchtime drink and a laugh with the boys and generally skive off. It was not to be; his destiny lay in the shunting yards. That winter, one of the coldest on record, he spent most of his time being wet, chilled and miserable as he coupled and uncoupled the trains and generally looked after the carriages.

Since leaving borstal Freddie had come under the wing of George's Aunt Rose. She had met him a couple of times when visiting George and liked him. It had not taken her long to spot that Freddie had more up top than her nephew. Freddie's brain and George's brawn might make for the basis of a successful team, she thought.

'Don't you knock this railway lark, young man,' she had scolded Freddie when he had threatened to quit. 'Open your eyes and look around. Listen and learn.'

'Learn what?'

'Learn the ropes. How they work; how the equipment operates; how the people think. It will stand you in good stead.'

'But I don't want to work for the poxy railways, it's slave fuckin' labour.'

'Freddie . . . Freddie . . . Freddie, you haven't been listening, have you, luv? I'm talking about our line of work. Fuck the railways! Do you know how many people in London would give their right arm to have a chance to work down them yards? You're free to walk around and look in all those carriages, carriages which transport a whole variety of gear every day. You're a young man in a new job, you can ask questions about procedures and methods without anyone thinking anything is wrong. Some might call you an arse-licker, but so what, you can live with that. Bite the bullet, Freddie. Invest in your future.'

London, October 1957

Freddie managed to bite the bullet for almost a year before throwing in the towel at the railways. The money had remained what he considered to be an insult to his talents and he soon found he pocketed more in a weekend of petty and not-so-petty pilfering than he did in a whole month of working for BR. He did, however, have to thank the railways for his biggest early pay-day after he tipped off some of Rose's mates as to exactly where the petrol stocks could be found in one of the London shunting yards. Petrol had become a sought-after commodity with the shortages caused by the Suez Crisis in 1956 and there was a profitable black market to be exploited if you could get your hands on the liquid gold. George's dad, Ernie, had told Freddie stories about the black market in London during the Second World War and how he had done very nicely out of it, thank you very much. In the aftermath of the Suez Crisis Freddie could see why.

All he had to do for his share of the take was to make sure the side gate of the yard was not properly bolted. A matter he took care of by sawing an inch and a half off each of the bolts so that leaning against the gate was sufficient to pop the lock.

London, November 1957

George was released towards the end of the year. The experience of borstal had, if anything, hardened him further. He had taken some vicious beatings while he had been inside, all of them from the so-called wardens who didn't like the big boy's attitude. He had the scars to prove it. The most noticeable was just above his right eye.

Freddie had taken advantage of his windfall from the petrol scam to set himself up in a small flat. Aunt Rose had asked if George could share with him when he came out and Freddie had been only too happy to oblige. He owed the big man a favour or two. Rose explained to Freddie that it would only be temporary; her mother's days were numbered, she said, and when the old lady passed on Rose would inherit a small house in Maida Vale which she intended to give to George. The flat, therefore, could be seen as temporary accommodation until they found their feet and were able to move into the bigger house, where Freddie would not have to pay rent for having his own room.

Meanwhile George was itching to get back to work.

'Put me on the firm, Freddie. I'll take care of all the heavy shit. I know you need someone to look out for you.'

'Won't be necessary, old son,' Freddie assured him. 'What I have in mind won't need any violence, just your brute strength and animal good looks. You might even get a cup of tea out of it!'

'Bollocks.'

Freddie had been keeping a job up his sleeve just for George's release. It was Gordon Hill, a railway station in Enfield, just north of London. Freddie had learnt during his time with the railways that Gordon Hill would often not carry the weekend takings down to King's Cross until the Monday morning, the money from Friday, Saturday and Sunday being left locked up in an old safe in the stationmaster's office. It could add up to a considerable sum if the two big north London

30

football teams, Arsenal and Tottenham Hotspur, had been playing at home on the Saturday.

The boys chose their weekend carefully – a London derby for the Gunners, and Spurs at home to Manchester United – and hoped for the best. It was around two on Monday morning when they got to the station, which conveniently had an alley running down the back. George lifted Freddie on to his shoulders, from where he could prise open a side window. Freddie slipped through the opening and made his way round to the stationmaster's office, carefully closing the window behind him. He was surprised how easy it all was. No alarms, no guards – even the locked doors had glass windows and fairly rudimentary locks which gave way when sufficient force was applied.

The stationmaster's safe, an old Chubb dating from the year dot, was not even hidden, but located in an alcove in the bookcase. It was an easy model to crack, but Freddie would need to move it away from the wall if he was going to jemmy the back off it. He slid his way back around the offices to the window, making sure he kept low so that his silhouette could not be seen from the road. As he peeked over the window-sill he froze – all he could see was the top of a bobby's helmet and the sound of running water. As Freddie held his breath the policeman's hat moved on. It seemed like hours, but it was only minutes before George was standing below him in the alleyway.

'What the fuck's going on?' Freddie whispered.

'It's all right,' the big man replied. 'Just a rozzer on the beat. He came down here for a slash, the dirty sod.'

'Come on, George, I need you in here.'

Despite his size, George proved to be remarkably agile. With the width of the alley he could get a run up of only a couple of feet, but it was more than enough. Once he got a grip on the window-sill he was able to haul his massive bulk up and through the window. Freddie knew better than to give him a hand – George's weight would have pulled him straight back out through the opening. They slid on their stomachs back around to the office. Freddie peered out of the window on to the lifeless track below. A few houses overlooked the track, but as no lights were showing Freddie decided to take the risk and stand up. He could have blown the safe – he knew how after being taught all the tricks, such as stuffing the gelignite into a condom with water before placing it in the lock, while in Rochester – but on this occasion he decided that the station was just a little too public for that kind of performance. If the explosion went wrong and broke a few windows it might be difficult, if not impossible, to have it away. If they went down again, so soon after their last spell inside, they would be looking at five or seven apiece, minimum. Tonight Freddie would rely on George's brute strength and hope that there would be no other nosy coppers having a pee when they started ripping the safe apart.

It took George a few grunts and groans, but he managed to slide the safe into the middle of the office, where Freddie could get to work on the weaknesses he knew this elderly model of Chubb to have. Under Freddie's instruction, George set to with a hacksaw, cutting off the top corner of the safe so that Freddie could get his cane in behind the back plate. There was a sharp crack, which seemed deafening to the two men, as the rivets popped out of their moorings. It did not take George long to have the back off and, after he had removed the asbestos, the sheet-metal lining put up as much resistance as a can of beans. The take was just over £900. Not what you would call a big tickle, but a nice little earner all the same.

By the time they had stashed their haul and equipment in a small carry-all, it was getting on for five in the morning. In little over an hour it would be starting to get light. Freddie and George slipped out of the station the way they had come in and were thankful that there was nobody around. They crossed to Chase Side and kept walking until they found a bus that would take them down to King's Cross, where they would pick up the tube once it was open. There were already a few early risers out and about, so the two men striding along did not attract much attention.

The adrenaline was still flowing when they finally sat down at a café close to King's Cross for a cup of tea and a bacon sandwich. Freddie patted his top jacket pocket, which held part of their night's earnings. 'Nice cup of tea, eh, George?' The big man smiled. They were a team.

London, October 1962

D avid and Denise were becoming a legendary couple in west London, although like many legends most people were beginning to doubt their very existence. They were considered to be untouchable – the police hadn't got so much as a sniff to link them with any of the many unsolved crimes that dotted the London map. David was getting better and better with locks. There were few, if any, that could defeat him, in fact only one to date and that was an American import which he had subsequently studied and was now happy he could crack.

Denise was also getting better and better when it came to inside information and was not adverse to using her good looks to get her way. She promised it would never go beyond a kiss and a cuddle and David accepted that. Accepted it as part of their business – his little Mata Hari, he used to call her. He also had no complaints about their sex life and was blissfully aware how horny Denise got when they were on a job.

One of Denise's most productive sources was a young insurance broker called Thomas Fullsome. Thomas happily supplied Denise with the details of the insured contents of houses and offices, which she told him she then passed on to a friend, for a small financial consideration which Thomas and Denise split between them. Thomas' ultimate aim, however, did not appear to be his share of the money, but rather to get his leg over Denise, so whenever possible she met him for lunch, when she felt she had a little more control over her amorous date. She told David she was worried that Thomas was visibly living beyond his salary; it could only be a matter of time before the police started putting two and two together and tied the broker to a series of robberies from his firm's clients. Fullsome had argued that as his employers shopped their clients' business around many different insurance companies, it would be years before anybody noticed a pattern. By then, he said, he would be long gone. The key for now, he explained, was not to hit the same client, family or area of London twice.

Denise felt it was time to drop their most lucrative informant, but Thomas was dangling a really big carrot in front of her. 'He says it's the biggest yet,' she told David. 'The owners have got the decorators in and the alarms are all out. Thomas had to go and check on the house and report back to the insurance company whether the coverage should still be valid if the couple didn't put their valuables in the bank. He told the owners they could keep the stuff at home as long as it was well hidden. Thomas knows where.'

'And what does our little Don Juan want for the address and info?' David inquired.

'Me, I think. He wants a date and he wants more than a kiss and cuddle this time.'

'So let's give him more! But don't you start getting turned on by all of this. I know you.'

'To be quite honest, I'm beginning to enjoy it. He's got such nice manicured hands!'

London, Wednesday 17 October 1962

Denise picked at her food. She was more nervous than hungry. The young insurance broker also played with his food. He had other things on his mind, namely Denise. Denise found his conversation sickeningly romantic. As if he really cared for her and didn't just want to get into her pants as quickly as possible. Why can't men be honest, she thought, as she toyed with her fish.

It didn't take very much to persuade Thomas to come home with her. She told him her husband was away travelling. In fact they used David's mother's house. David had sent his mum off to see his gran for the week. She was in a home in Bognor Regis which had accommodation for visitors.

David dressed the house so that their young prey would not suspect anything was out of the ordinary. Denise got Thomas home just after ten and by the way his hands were all over her as soon as she shut the front door, she knew there might be no time for any pleasantries like a cup of coffee or a nightcap. She had to get the information before she dropped her knickers, though.

'Come on, a brandy will help you relax,' she purred in his ear as she stroked the crotch of his trousers. 'I would say it would put you in the mood, but you already seem to be well on the way to that.' A quick squeeze of his balls – to bring him in line – and she let him go.

Denise surprised herself at how easily and quickly she milked the information out of Thomas while keeping him amorously occupied, yet never having to deliver sexually. The house, or rather mansion, was close to Epping Forest. The owners were going to be away for ten days in the Canary Islands, where they hoped to catch some late-summer sun before winter set in well and truly in Britain and the rest of northern Europe. It meant a whole weekend when the house would be completely deserted, as there would be no decorators around and – by coincidence – no staff, due to a series of overlapping prior commitments. The valuables had

35

been placed in a strong-box that was now sitting in a hole in the garage floor under the couple's shining Rolls-Royce Silver Shadow. All anyone would have to do to get to the box would be to roll the car out and grab the gems and other valuables. Not all of them, Thomas had advised, because if they were lucky there was every chance that the owners might not notice that anything was missing for several months, as most of the stuff in the box was rarely used.

It was Denise who eventually steered the conversation back to sexual matters, as if she could not care less about Thomas's information. She pulled him off the couch and led him by his tie towards the staircase. As they made their way up the stairs Thomas slipped his hands under Denise's short pleated skirt, which she wiggled provocatively in front of his face. By the feel he could tell she had on silk panties and a suspender belt. He liked that and kept his hand on the bare flesh between the tops of her stockings and her knickers.

In the bedroom he was all over her again and before long they were stripping ready for action. Denise looked lovelier and sexier than ever in just her matching set of bra, panties and stockings which she had specially chosen for the occasion. They had been a Valentine's gift from David and always seemed to get him aroused.

Thomas was just slipping out of his trousers when they heard a key in the latch.

'My God, what's that?' he whispered in frozen panic. 'There's somebody downstairs.'

'Oh, Christ! It must be my husband. He may have cut short his trip to Manchester.' Denise pushed Thomas aside and rushed out through the door. He toppled over with his trousers still around his ankles. He heard raised voices and the sound of a slap. It sounded as if he was hitting her around the face. Denise had warned Thomas that her husband was a travelling salesman and a very jealous man – the reason, she had explained, why she had rarely been able to see him at night. Thomas managed to get his trousers up and over his rapidly diminishing erection before the door swung open and an enraged David appeared. Any ideas of being the gallant hero quickly vanished.

'So you're the filthy slime-ball who's been bedding my wife while I'm away travelling. I should kill you.' David went across the bedroom to the large dresser and rummaged in the top drawer. 'Where's my gun? I'm going to kill the two of you!' he exclaimed. Thomas took the opportunity

LONDON

to bolt out of the bedroom and down the stairs. He ran straight out the front door and kept running, barely stopping to acknowledge Denise, who sat sobbing at the foot of the stairs. David made a pretence of going after him, but only as far as the corner. He didn't want to attract any attention, or disturb the neighbours for that matter.

When David got inside Denise had moved into the front room, but was still on the floor and still crying, only from laughter. 'Oh, the poor fellow. He'll probably never get it up again. Scarred for life, that's what he'll be.'

'Deserves to be. Trying to shag other people's wives. Filthy bastard should be horsewhipped,' David declared.

'But he would probably enjoy it, he looks the type,' she said.

'By the look of you, you would and all, you kinky bitch.'

'And you're not, I suppose,' she said, dragging her husband on to the floor to join her.

'Well, just a little, Mrs Jenkins, so I think I'm going to have to put matters right and fuck your brains out.' They made hot and passionate love there and then on his mother's sheepskin rug in front of the fire.

'Keep going,' she whispered in his ear, 'I've still got a few grey cells left.'

London, Friday 19 October 1962

Denise left it until Friday morning before calling Thomas at work. She said her husband was out of his mind with jealousy and would kill him if he ever saw them together again. Considering everything she thought it would be best if they split. 'Best for both of us,' she confessed. She did, however, agree to meet him just one more time during his lunch break so that she could hand back his briefcase, which he had left on the lounge floor in the course of his unexpected departure. As Denise had thought, it contained all the information they needed about Epping Forest and more.

She met Thomas outside Moorgate tube station. She wore a scarf and dark glasses through which Thomas could see a badly bruised eye.

'If the swine hits you, why do you stay with him?' he asked.

'Habit, I suppose,' she replied. 'Force of habit. I'm afraid of him, sure, but I'm more afraid of whether I could survive without him.' With that she gave him a light peck on the cheek and was gone.

Before grabbing the tube home she took advantage of the ladies' room in the pub opposite the station entrance to wipe off the heavy make-up around her eye. An Oscar-winning performance, if she said so herself.

David and Denise never did hit the Epping Forest address. 'It stinks of rotten fish,' David had said. 'Sorry, love. I just don't like the sound of it any more.' But all Denise's work was not in vain: instead they chose a sumptuous mews house in Chelsea from Thomas's list and netted two and a half grand. Enough to keep them comfortable and out of trouble for a couple of months. Later they heard that the decorators had decided to turn over the house in Epping and had found a private security company employed by the insurers waiting for them. 'Vindictive little bastard, your manicured friend.' David commented when he read about the incident in the paper. Again – by good judgement or good fortune – David and Denise had kept their noses clean.

London, March 1963

Freddie had worked with Charlie Wilson before and enjoyed his company. Charlie was a true professional and was rumoured to have been involved in some of the biggest jobs to have gone down in London in recent years. Charlie had asked Freddie to meet for a drink at the Plough on Clapham Common. It was a little inconvenient for Freddie, but from Charlie's tone he felt it would be of interest for him to go, especially as gossip said Charlie was on a roll at present.

Charlie was standing at a bar when he arrived.

'Hello Freddie, what'll it be?' he asked.

'Pint of mild and bitter would slip down very nicely,' he replied.

The two men picked up their drinks and headed for a quiet corner. There were a number of other chaps around the pub whom Freddie recognized from his day-to-day activities. The Plough was the local for many in his profession.

'How have you been keeping?' Charlie asked.

'Mustn't complain. Makin' a quid – even got a little set aside for a rainy day.'

'Good to hear it, Freddie. Listen, I'll tell you straight up why I called you over. I want to see if you're interested in going into a nice piece of business with me. I think you could be of great help to us if you're interested in making one.'

'What is it?'

'I can't tell you much, but it's a big one. Bruce Reynolds is putting it together and I know he wants you and George involved. Is he out and about?'

'Didn't you know? George was released from the Ville about a month ago. I'm surprised you haven't seen him. He's done a year for me. He made a good call, got done for obstruction, but they couldn't pin the robbery on us as I was away with the goods.'

'Are you on, then?'

'Might be. I need a few more details, though, like when, where and how much.'

'As I said, I can't give you much info for now, but the minimum whack will be a forty pay-off.'

'Forty grand! Well, fuck me!'

'I told you it was big. The job's scheduled for early August, but we're going to need to go into training before that. Bruce only wants the best, that's why he chose you and George.'

'Okay, Chas, if you're in, I'm in and so is George. Same again?' Freddie got another round of drinks and they toasted the future.

'One last thing, Freddie.' Charlie interrupted. 'If you or George get nicked in the meantime, that's your problem. No pay-days for no shows. I suggest you don't plan anything after the middle of May. If you think you are going to come up short, talk to me and I'll see what I can do. But you might think of breaking into your little rainy-day nest-egg. You won't regret it. It'll be the best investment you ever made.'

London, April 1963

David Jenkins was someone else who had the utmost respect for Bruce Reynolds. He knew him as a man who had earned his title as the Prince of Thieves. He was one of the best, a man of class and panache. They had met briefly on a number of occasions and David was sure that Bruce knew of his and Denise's reputation and possibly admired them for it. It was a complete surprise, however, when he and Denise ran into Bruce and his wife in the Feathers in Merstham, Surrey.

'It's amazing,' Bruce said. 'I was on the very point of looking you up. Can we sit down and have a chat? ... Now listen, Dave, I know you're a loner, but I've got a really big piece of business coming up and I need people like yourself to pull it off.'

'I'll tell you what, Bruce,' David replied, 'it would have to be one hell of a plan for me to stick my neck out and work with a firm I don't know. I'm doing okay as I am.'

'Dave, if I tell you it's a big one, it's a big one. This job could set you and Denise up for life. I can guarantee a minimum forty grand for your whack.'

'Shit!' David gave a little whistle and glanced over at Denise, who was sipping her drink next to Bruce's wife. 'How many people are involved?'

'Fifteen.'

'Fifteen! Jesus Christ! And everyone gets forty grand?'

'Everyone gets the same whack.'

'Fifteen ... that's 600 grand!'

'It's a big job,' Bruce admitted, 'and I need the manpower. Nobody is along for the ride. Each and everyone chosen has a job to do. There will be no freeloaders.'

'And the risks?'

'You know as well as I do that there is a risk to everything we do.

41

Isn't that why we do it? But as far as I can see this has fewer risks than most. So do you want to make one? I would certainly like to have you along.'

'Let me sleep on it, Bruce. Give me forty-eight hours and I'll give you a bell.'

It was not an easy decision for David and Denise, but after much soul-searching and in the light of what had happened at Epping, David called Bruce less than twenty-four hours later to say he would make one. Forty thousand pounds would be more than enough to set him and Denise up for a considerable length of time without having to take any more unnecessary risks.

'I know you don't need to be told,' Denise said to David as he came off the phone to Bruce, 'but once the action is over we should have our own plan in place to lie low. This job sounds as if it is going to ruffle a few feathers, so let's make sure we're not caught in or around the chicken coup when the alarm goes up.'

Pretoria, South Africa, May 1963

The pleasantries were few and far between. This was strictly business and whether either party approved of the other was beside the point.

'If I understand correctly, if we get the shipment to you, you will hold a credit on our behalf and supply what information and items we require at an agreed price until our credit runs dry and regardless of any other UN sanctions. If that is agreed, then I think we have the basis of a deal.'

'I am glad to hear it. I will get somebody in our embassy to deliver the instructions to you personally on how the first payment should be made. When it comes to placing your requests you must only deal with this office through the agreed number in London. You are not to use your embassy contact for this under any circumstances.' The voice on the phone was British, but beyond that said little and betrayed nothing. How lucky, the South African thought, to be able to blend into the background. Nobody who spoke English as a mother tongue ever had any doubts where he was from and as a calling card being South African was starting to have its drawbacks.

'The first batch of diamonds will be with you in London by August.'

'We'll be looking forward to receiving them.'

'By the way, do you have any preference for colour?'

'Pink would be nice, I am told. Less bulky, you see.'

The line went dead.

London, May 1963

Freddie met privately with Charlie Wilson in his house in south London. 'Trains. I'm told you know a little bit about them from the past. That true?' Charlie asked.

'Certainly is. Spent the best, or rather worst, part of a year in a bloody shunting yard. What you need to know? What are we going to hit? A station? A depot?'

'No, it's a train. A moving train – the travelling post office from Scotland to London which will be chock full of money. I told you, Freddie, this is a big one!'

'How are you going to stop the bugger without anybody noticing?'

'You don't need to worry about that. That part of the plan is already taken care of. It will be at night, so we should have at least half an hour to strip the train before anyone thinks of raising the alarm. What we need to know is can you uncouple a train?'

'Do bears shit in the wood? Is the Pope a Catholic? Course I know how to uncouple a bloody train. I can couple it up again, if you want. And blindfolded!'

'Won't be necessary. How about driving it?'

'Ah! That's another kettle of fish altogether. I could give it a go, but I wouldn't bet my life on it. Too many variables. I would have to know what type of train was involved to answer that. If it's one of these big new diesel jobs, forget it, you need a professional driver.'

'But uncoupling's no problem?'

'No problem. Stake my reputation on that.'

'And George is fit and well? We're going to need his muscle, you know that.'

'Never been fitter or more eager. He won't let you and Bruce down when it comes to it.'

LONDON

David was also having a private meeting, but with Bruce Reynolds. 'What's it to be, then?' he asked.

'It's a train,' Bruce replied. 'Now I know I can trust you, Dave, so I'll give you a little of the background. Difficult as it is to believe, the Bank of England still shunts money about the country on trains, often on the travelling post offices that move around at night. No extra precautions are taken for the cash, beyond normal post-office security for keeping an eye on the mail. They feel that once the train leaves the station and is moving, there is no danger until it reaches its destination. I plan to stop one of these trains and relieve it of its load.'

'Do you know which train?'

'Not only do I know which train, but I also know how I intend to stop it and where. The plans are pretty much in place. I don't have the exact date yet, but it will be around the August Bank Holiday, when movements of cash will be at their greatest.'

'And what to you expect from me?'

'I want your expertise with locks in case it's necessary. The rest of the lads are also all experts in their fields. Two of them know how to stop the train; they have even put it into practice and shown me that it works. Then we have a man whose main task it will be to uncouple the train, he's good and has worked the railyards. Our main transport guy is one of the best, a racing driver, but I wouldn't mind you also giving it a go behind the wheel. I know you're quite handy. This will be steady as you go driving, nothing fancy. We are going to drive right up to the site in the middle of the night, take the money from the train and then disappear back into the night from whence we came. We even have a safe house being set up not more than forty miles from the site of the job. It's not going to be like doing a bank job or a payroll or even house-breaking. We are going to be in the country, miles from anywhere. At most we will have a few post-office sorters to deal with, but that's it. Christ! The notes aren't even listed or marked, that only happens when they get to London.'

West London, Saturday 15 June 1963

The phone was on its fifth ring before Denise reached it. She hated the way David let it ring when he was watching television. It was one of his more annoying habits, especially today of all days when she had to iron his shirts rather than take advantage of one of London's rare sunny summer days.

'Would that be Mrs Jenkins?' The voice was unfamiliar but it had a distinctly Irish flavour.

'It is.'

'I'm sorry to disturb you on such a beautiful Saturday afternoon, but I was wondering if I could have a word with your husband if he is at home? I'm a friend of Bruce's from Northern Ireland.'

Knowing how David hated to be disturbed while watching *Grandstand* Denise did not commit herself to her husband's presence, but offered to go and see if he she could find him 'in the garden'. Her answer amused the Irish caller. He would not have rung if he had not known for certain that David was at home. He also knew that the garden was a small concrete square, the door to which was less than ten feet from where she was talking. From his position at the pay-phone he could even observe the front door should David have the desire to make a sudden exit. He put some extra coins in the machine while nobody was on the line and waited.

An Irish accent of no given name who said he was a friend of Bruce was enough to drag David from the comfort of his armchair. Not many people knew of his connection with Bruce and, considering what was about to go down, the fewer the better. It had to be one of the gang, he thought, as he crossed into the hall. Possibly Gordon, he was from Ireland.

'Is that Mr Jenkins? Mr David Jenkins?'

'It is,' David replied coolly. He wanted time to get an angle on who

46

was on the other end of the phone. He prided himself on being able to sniff out trouble, especially coppers.

'You don't know me, Mr Jenkins. My name is Green. Patrick Green.'

David's hand had become quite clammy on the receiver. The call was not part of his preparatory planning for the job. Nothing out of the ordinary ever was. His mind raced ahead of the conversation. Was the tone threatening? Friendly? Well-informed?

'Mr Jenkins, this, as you will appreciate, is neither the time nor the place for a full round of explanations, but if you need any confirmation, I can assure you I'm very close to Bruce and his business. I need to meet with you to talk about something which I think could be of interest to you.'

'One minute, Mr Green, or whatever you say your name is,' David said, catching his breath. 'I think you are talking to the wrong man, I already gave at the office. Good afternoon, Mr Green.'

'David, if I may call you that? Don't hang up until you hear me out. The matter I wish to discuss is directly linked to our current commitment to Bruce.' He emphasized the 'our'. 'Look at it as an added bonus, if you like. Come and talk to me and then decide. If you say no I won't be hurt. Surprised, yes. Hurt, no.'

'When and where?' David was curt as he tried to regain the upper hand.

'No time like the present, Mr Jenkins. If it is convenient for you, how about early this evening?'

'That should be okay. Where?'

'I was thinking of the Oxford and Cambridge at Hammersmith Bridge.'

'I know it. What time?'

'About 6.30 p.m. Use the door nearest the bridge, sit up at the bar and buy yourself a drink. I know what you look like. When I am satisfied I will bump you as I am buying a packet of Players. Follow me out and come down to the towpath. We can chat as we walk along. If you're good, I might even buy you a pint at the Boatman.'

Bruce had mentioned the mysterious Ulsterman to him. If this was him, he was a very cool character. David quite liked that. He also liked the urgency.

Hammersmith,
Saturday 15 June 1963

David chose the bus rather than the tube and was in Hammersmith in plenty of time. The bus dropped him almost at the door of the pub, saving him the five-minute walk from the station. He had frequented the Oxford and Cambridge before, so was no stranger to the layout. He knew the early-evening news would be on the television set above the bar – this would help pass the time and give him somewhere to focus. He might even catch some of the sports stories he had missed earlier. He ordered a pint of lager and waited. He tried not to show too much interest in the other customers and avoided looking towards the door as the pub started to fill with the regulars, many of whom knew one another, many of whom were Irish.

'Twenty Players and a box of matches.' The voice came from behind. It was distinctive and now quite familiar, and it was not out of place. Most Londoners would have said the speaker was from southern Ireland, but once you had your ear attuned you could tell he was from the north. A dig in the kidneys was confirmation, if confirmation was needed, that this was David's man. There was a muffled apology and the man was gone. David looked at his watch, drank up and followed the departing figure through the door.

As it was June it was still daylight and as David adjusted his eyes to the light he saw the Ulsterman was already halfway to Hammersmith Bridge and the towpath. He followed. As he descended to the towpath he checked behind to see if he was being trailed. He found his quarry bent over the river wall watching the Thames flow by.

'I never tire of the Thames. Do you, Mr Jenkins?' Green did not wait for a reply, but turned upstream. David had often heard people talk about this near-legendary figure, but had never come across anyone who had met him face to face. He felt honoured, yet for the first time in a long time found himself scared by a single human being. He tried to absorb everything he could about the 'Ulsterman'. He was younger than David had expected. Late thirties, at most early forties. Fairly nondescript, nothing that would attract the attention of a passer-by. Even the sunglasses he wore to hide his eyes were not out of place on this summer evening.

'I know you know precious little about me, Mr Jenkins, other than my reputation, but I know a fair bit about you and your track record. I like what I see. I like your attention to detail and the way in which you operate. I have to consider, however, that if I know these facts and can even supply you with the dates, times and sites of some of your more rewarding escapades, such as the recent one in Kensington High Street, your career may not have been as watertight as you would like to think. I know everything there is to know about your plans for August. That, *per se*, should not cause you any alarm for now, because I am the person responsible for steering this little bit of business Bruce's way. I do not dirty my hands with the details, that is what he is for and what he does so very well. I am responsible, if you like, for the time, the place and the content of what you are looking for. It is the content, or an addendum to that content, that I wish to talk to you about.'

David sensed that the Irishman was setting him up to double-cross Bruce. Double-crossing was something he would not and could not condone. It might even be a trap, some kind of test of his loyalty, and he, David Jenkins, a man known for his word, was not going to fall for it. 'I appreciate your reputation, Mr Green, but I won't waste your time, I want no part of it.'

'Your sentiments are admirable, David, but hear me out. I can guarantee to you that I am not, as you are no doubt thinking, asking you to double-cross Bruce or anyone else.' Green was again leaning on the river wall looking over into the Thames. It was the halfway point between the two pubs. They would not be disturbed other than by the odd passer-by.

'The deal I have with Bruce is purely and simply for the content of the mail-bags you will find in the High Value Package Coach which, as you are by now aware, will be full of money on the night in question. More, I can tell you, than even Bruce has ever dreamed about. If you all do your job right, the take on the night is likely to be closer to a hundred K each than the forty Bruce has mentioned. You will be more than satisfied with your share, that I can promise, as I will be for my investment of time and information. Yet, since setting the deal up with Bruce, I have been informed that there will be something else on that train that I have an interest in. It is an envelope, the contents of which are of interest only to me and its owners. I want that envelope and I want you to get it for me. It will be left on the train if nobody knows what to look for. You and I are not cheating anyone, we are just taking advantage of an extra piece of information, and believe me, there is nothing more valuable today than good information. For your assistance in getting me the envelope I am willing to pay you a flat fee of £10,000, win or lose, and in advance. An amount which I am certain a man of your talents can put to good use in the planning of his getaway, because if you are as smart as I believe you to be, you will disappear the moment this little caper is over and keep your head down. Anyone who doesn't will almost certainly have their collar felt and end up in some dank flowery dell for more years than I would care to imagine.'

'How come you're not coming along for the ride if you're so involved?'

'I never "go along for the ride", as you put it. That's when you get caught. I design the rides and what I am offering you this afternoon is an all-expenses-paid ride within a ride. Whether you want to take it is up to you. But it is you that I want. To a degree it is your attitude to crime that guarantees my safety as much as yours.'

'Ten thousand? And in advance, you say?'

'Correct. And this money is squeaky clean. You could take it down the local nick to pay your fines and not even break a sweat. You can have it in a bank account in this country or abroad – even in cash if you prefer. If you take the job, the money will be in your hands by the end of next week. If you don't manage to get the envelope, the money is still yours and that means that when the day comes you will be the only one on the job with a guaranteed pay-day even if the train goes flying by. If that's not a good deal, I don't know what is.'

'Why do you trust me?'

'Because I know all I need to know about you. If you tried to cross me, which is not your style, you know it would take just one well-placed phone call to have you picked up for a number of past transgressions. As you may know, I have done just that in the past and no doubt will have to do it again in the future. Sadly there are far too many stupid people in our line of work. I want this to be a straightforward business agreement between two professional men. Ten thousand pounds for the delivery of one simple envelope. Christ! Even the Royal Mail might fancy those odds.'

'If I say yes, what's the SP?'

'I don't know how much Bruce has told you yet about what your role will be on the night, but it is virtually certain that his plans have you involved with the opening of the cage where the mail-bags are to be found. That is one of your specialities, after all. You will work the cage with one other. I'm not sure who that will be, but probably Charlie. You two will be passing the bags out to the others. My envelope will also be inside the cage, in a pigeon-hole off to the left. It should be the only one. How you get it out of the cage and back to the farm is up to you. That is what I am paying you for. As I will be telling Bruce which train to hit, I can guarantee that the envelope will be on board. If it's not, and I have had to give Bruce the go-ahead anyway, you still get to keep the money for doing absolutely nothing.'

'It sounds like we could have a deal, then.'

'If we do, it's a deal you should speak to nobody about. Not Bruce, not Charlie, not even your wife. If you have to explain your sudden windfall, tell her the money is an advance from the robbery. The only two people in the world who are to know about the envelope are you and me. I will call you soon to check how you want the money paid and give you your final instructions. You won't have to see me after the robbery because I am giving Bruce two identical kit-bags into which will go my share from the robbery. Bruce will be delivering these to me as soon as he gets the chance. That's his problem and not yours. All you need to do is slip the envelope in amongst the middle of the money in one of my kit-bags. With your proven skills, that should not be too difficult. This way, we never have to meet again, and can disappear out of sight and we can forget we ever knew each other.'

For the first time that evening the two men were standing face to face. Green extended his right hand and they shook hands. 'Right, let's go and get that pint. But before we do, here is a grand in advance to show that I am deadly serious. The other nine will be with you by the end of next week.' Green handed David a thick envelope filled with fivers, which he slipped into the inside pocket of his jacket. The two men strolled along to the Boatman in the dying light of day. There was still enough light for Green to justify the use of his dark glasses, but David was looking forward to getting a good close look at those eyes in the pub. Eyes, he always told Denise, could tell you so much.

The pub was more crowded than the Oxford and Cambridge, but still bearable considering it was a Saturday night. 'So what will it be?' the Irishman asked.

'A pint of lager would be great. I'll just go for a pee and be right back.'

David was right back, but there was no sign of the Ulsterman. A barmaid called him over. 'Your friend said he had a train to catch and you would understand. He left you a pint and a packet of twenty Players and said he would call you soon.' David smiled to himself. The Ulsterman was living up to his reputation for cloak and dagger.

Just over a mile from the pub Patrick Green pulled his red mini into the service station at the Hogarth Roundabout and told the man to fill it up. The phone-box was empty. He entered and dialled. He was pleased with his day's work. Another Irish voice answered.

'He accepted the job after a bit of light persuasion,' Green told the other party. 'He's good and he's careful, just like you said he would be. He also went for the idea that I'm the Ulsterman. At this moment he believes he is one of the few people in the world to have met you face to face and lived to tell the tale. The cover will hold.'

David got home just after eight. By the noises coming from the kitchen he knew that he was no longer Denise's favourite husband. He had promised to take her to the cinema and now it would be too late. He was thinking of ways to break the ice, but his face gave him away. Denise knew him too well. He had good news and stories to tell. They retired to the living room. Unlike many criminal couples, David and Denise saw themselves as a team. David trusted her with his life and vice versa.

'From tonight's meeting it looks as if we are going to have a little bonus in advance of August's job. Enough to help us disappear even before I go away. We have about a month to prepare for everything we planned, only now we have the money to pay for it without having to take any unnecessary risks.' He threw the envelope with the thousand pounds on to Denise's lap. She gave a delighted little squeal as the notes spilled out. What started as a congratulatory embrace turned into a deep kiss and before long they were heading upstairs.

HAMMERSMITH

'You'll enjoy this more than the cinema,' he promised, slapping her on the backside, which swayed sensually before him in a tight pair of shorts.

'You're as bad as that insurance bloke,' she teased. 'He was a leg and ass man, just like you.' Denise also knew that neither David nor she would have very many complaints come morning when, as it was Sunday, they could stay in bed and start all over again. It was going to be an exhausting twelve hours. She hoped she and her old man were up to it.

Chelsea, Thursday 27 June 1963

'Can I have a bit of hush, please,' Bruce Reynolds cried out, trying to bring the meeting to order. 'Will you lot shut the fuck up! ... Thank you. Now we've got a fair bit to get through today, so let's not all try and talk at once.'

It was only the second time that the entire gang had been brought together, and a frightening bunch they would have appeared to any passer-by. They were squashed into the smoke-filled front room of Roy James's Chelsea flat and covered every nook and cranny. 'Before we get started, can one of you open a window before we all die of lung cancer?' Charlie Wilson responded to Roy's request and opened the top two windows giving out on to the wet road below.

'Right, let's get started.' Bruce picked up an envelope on which he had scribbled the salient points to be discussed that afternoon. 'Firstly, everything is sweet! We're right on track for the Bank Holiday money, that's the takings from Friday, Saturday, Sunday and Monday from most of Scotland. D-day is probably around 7 or 8 August. Since our last meet, when Ron suggested bringing in the old man, I have met him and I reckon he's sound. That's the last piece of the jigsaw in place. Now it's nice to see you all getting along, but you don't have to become lifelong buddies. Some of you are mates of long standing, but the less you know about one another the better, so try and keep out of each other's faces. Jimmy, you had something to say, didn't you?'

'Gloves!' Jimmy White replied. 'Remember to bring with you one or two pairs of gloves and your balaclavas. We'll supply the overalls and the army uniforms. You will also be responsible for getting away from the farm under your own steam in the weeks following the job. You can't take any vehicles to the farm, so you'll need to co-ordinate your own transport when the time comes.'

'By now you all know what will be expected of you on the night,' Bruce continued. 'That night is less than six weeks away, so be careful.

CHELSEA

Keep your noses clean. Keep out of trouble, but let's not be silly. The law knows the sun don't shine out of your arses, so keep up appearances. Work your patch and your contacts. Be seen where you normally hang out. Basically act normally. If we all go missing, Old Bill will know we're up to no good. The real trouble, though, starts once we finish the job and, God willing, when you'll all be staring at at least forty grand. I can't hold your hands, you're all big enough and ugly enough to look after yourselves, but plan ahead. Have an idea as to what you will do after the robbery. Where you will hide your money. Many of you will certainly be pulled in for questioning on a job of this size. Old Bill will be under pressure to solve it and quickly, so don't give them any excuse to nick you. They may even be looking to fit people up, so stay on your toes. Set up an alibi and try and keep your life as normal as possible after the event. And for Christ's sake, keep a low profile, don't go flashing the money around in the weeks after the robbery. No flash cars, no furs for the wife. This can be your pension, boys – use it sensibly.

'Finally, I would like to say that you are all here because you're the best. Nobody needs worry about being grassed out. Everyone here is a pro. No one in this room is going to open his mouth or do deals if he gets his collar felt, so don't believe Old Bill if he says somebody has grassed you out. They will be clutching at straws, so keep your head down, mouth shut and with a bit of luck, 1963 will be a year to remember. I don't have to tell you that this is the tickle of a lifetime, so make the most of it.'

'Okay,' Jimmy interrupted. 'We will all get together one more time before the day. We'll let you know when and where. Until then you work within your groups and rehearse what will be expected of you on the day.'

David found that he had to consult with Roy about transport and Charlie, just as the Ulsterman had surmised, about the opening and clearing of the valuables cage on the train. Roy, for his part, had to talk with Freddie about the uncoupling, while George stayed close to Buster, who was co-ordinating the storming of the train. Freddie, knowing so much about the carriages, found he was in great demand as he explained layouts, door-bolt actions and procedures.

The men left the flat in ones and twos at five and ten minute intervals over a period of an hour. If they went as a group, even the local bobby on the beat might get suspicious and that was something they did not need so close to the big day. David left alone and took the bus home. He had felt slightly uneasy at the meeting knowing he had a hidden agenda. He wondered how many of the others did.

Freddie and George were as pleased as punch with the meeting and headed into the West End for a night on the town. They still had a bit of spare cash from some jewellery they had fenced after a recent raid. 'Just keeping my hand in,' George had said at the time.

London, Tuesday 6 August 1963

Freddie and George just about had time to grab a quick cup of tea and a piece of buttered toast for breakfast before going their separate ways. Freddie had to go and pick up the truck and round up other members of the gang, while Bruce had asked George to meet him by Victoria Station and go out to the farm in one of the Land-Rovers. Freddie reckoned that Bruce liked to have George around as a surrogate bodyguard in case anything went wrong.

George took the bus down to Victoria and found Bruce waiting for him at a café in Wilton Road, close to the station. He was with his brother-in-law, John, as well as Jimmy, the man he had entrusted with the job of being his quartermaster.

The first to greet him was Bruce. 'Pull up a chair, George, and grab yourself a sarney. We're still waiting for Ron and the old man and then we'll be off.'

It wasn't long before Ron arrived with Peter, the elderly train driver. After another round of tea and cheese sandwiches they were on their way to Buckinghamshire. The weather was good and the group were in fine spirits.

Across London, Freddie was making the final checks to the lorry with Roy. Roy may have been the better driver, but there was little that Freddie could be taught about the mechanics of an Austin five-tonner. He could strip one and put it back together with his eyes closed, he liked to boast. Roy gave him a route map which included the three pick-up points agreed with the other members of the gang. Roy was going to take the second Land-Rover and pick up Charlie.

It was mid-morning by the time Jimmy drove the first Land-Rover into Leatherslade Farm, a small-holding located off the B4011, close to the villages of Brill and Oakley in Buckinghamshire. The first 'settlers' explored the two-storey farmhouse and the various outbuildings. Despite the rounds of sandwiches at Victoria, the search and the unpacking of the food made the group ravenously hungry, so George and Ron offered to prepare lunch. Old Peter, for his part, found a deck chair and relaxed in the sun, puffing away at his pipe and blending in with the pastoral surroundings.

The tranquillity of the day was broken by the arrival of a man who came strolling in across the fields. He called to Peter, but like greased lightning Bruce was out and into the back area of the farm to take control of a potentially awkward situation. George abandoned the stove and remained in position behind the kitchen door, ready to pounce if Bruce needed his help.

'Hello, there,' the man called out, 'would you be the new owners of Leatherslade?'

'Afraid not,' Bruce replied. 'We're just decorators giving the place a face-lift. Owner's not due in for several weeks yet.'

'Who is the owner, then?'

'A Mr Fielding from Aylesbury. I'll be speaking to his office some time next week. Can I give him a message?'

'That would be most kind. Could you tell him that a neighbouring farmer, Mr Johnson, will be in touch when he moves in? I have been renting a couple of the lower meadows off the owners of Leatherslade Farm for the last three years and would like to see if Mr Fielding would be interested in continuing the arrangement.'

'Can't say I know what his plans are for the farm, but I'll pass on the message.' With a wave the man disappeared as he had come, through the fields.

The truck driven by Freddie turned up later in the afternoon. Arriving with him were Tommy, Jim, Bob, Buster and David, as well as Roger's bike. 'Sorry we're a bit behind schedule, Bruce,' Freddie explained, 'we had a few extra stops we hadn't quite planned on. We had to pull in at the gaff on the way down to pick up some pipkins. You know how Bobby likes his drink!'

'Call yourself a driver, Freddie? My old gran could have made better time than you,' Bruce joked. 'Never mind. Roy's still not here, so make yourselves at home, pick a place to bed down and unload the gear, but for Christ's sake keep your heads down. We've already had one surprise visitor and I can only explain away so many decorators to the neighbours.'

Roy and Charlie arrived soon afterwards in the second Land-Rover, bringing yet more supplies. Soon the gang had the farm looking quite homely, or as homely as it could with fourteen grown men crashing about the place.

Boredom could have been a problem, but this had been foreseen by John, who had thoughtfully brought along cards and games to while away the time. Freddie started a game of poker, while the business-minded five in the group set up the Monopoly. The Monopoly five were Ron, Charlie, Roy, George and David. While the poker got quite serious, the Monopoly was turning into a riot with Charlie the runaway winner and George being wiped out early on. 'All brawn and no brain,' Ron needled his big colleague until he was the second to be wiped from the board after some underhand dealings between Charlie and David. David had picked up the 'Get Out of Jail Free' card. He slipped the Chance card in to his top pocket. 'I'm keeping this one, Ron,' he said, patting it. 'Never know when it might come in handy!'

Bruce, Jimmy and Buster kept away from the games and huddled in the kitchen area, checking and double-checking that everything was in place for the job. Jimmy walked over to get a light from Charlie. He took Charlie's hand to steady the flame. 'Gloves, Charlie! For fuck's sake where are your turtle doves?' As he looked around the room he saw that at least half the men had removed their gloves. 'What is it with you people?! Listen, lads, it is all going to end in tears if you're not careful. Wear your fucking gloves. It's only for a couple of days.'

'Couple of weeks more like,' George butted in, 'but you won't catch me or Freddie without our gloves. I once got nicked for leaving my dabs and I can tell you it's not going to happen again.'

It was just after darkness fell that Roger arrived at the farm carrying a large suitcase. He was a popular man and received a vociferous welcome. 'You got my bike then, Buster?' was his first concern.

'Yes, I've got your rusty old bike, but how you intend to carry forty grand on that rickety old thing beats me.'

'I'll worry about that, thank you, Buster. I've had that bike for near on twenty years and I'm not going to part with it now.'

The gang now numbered fifteen – only Gordon was missing. He was close by in Pangbourne, at the home of Brian Field, a solicitor's managing clerk who had played his part in organizing the farm, amongst other things. Gordon was waiting for a phone call from the Ulsterman to let him know that the robbery was on. He eventually turned up at the farm just before eleven, making a dramatic entrance. Everyone stopped what they were doing and looked up at the big man, who was standing in the doorway swigging from a bottle of Johnnie Walker.

'You can all relax,' he announced, 'there's nothing doing tonight. Job's off.'

The announcement was greeted by a series of groans.

'At least I can try and win some of my money back,' Freddie quipped as he dealt another hand.

The gang sat around chatting, playing cards and drinking warm beer. There were a few exceptions, David being the most obvious: he took the opportunity – as soon as it came – to get a little shut-eye.

Leatherslade Farm, a.m.,
Wednesday 7 August 1963

D awn broke with the promise of another warm and sunny day. The light coming through the windows roused most of the gang from their sleep. George and Ron were two of the first up and started organizing breakfast for the other early risers. George amused those gathered around the table as he tried to cook the breakfast without removing his gloves. Peeling the bacon slices apart proved to be the trickiest task. 'Give it here,' Ron said, 'I'll do it.' Ron had no such problems – he had already long discarded his gloves.

The day did not offer much, besides good weather. The house was hot and clammy and, because of the scare the previous day, everyone was confined to barracks. Even the game-playing became somewhat half-hearted.

Glasgow, Wednesday 7 August 1963

A s promised, Brian Freeman had no problems with Customs and Excise after the ship docked in Glasgow. He was only one of three passengers to disembark there. The other eighteen had left the ship in Liverpool, a port he had been told to avoid.

A taxi was waiting for him. He had been warned that the ship docked some distance from Glasgow proper, where a suite had been booked for him at the Central Hotel. He should wait there until contacted.

Freeman was glad to be on dry land. It had been a long journey from South Africa. It would probably have been fine on a proper cruise liner, but being one of only twenty-one passengers on a cargo ship had its drawbacks, not least that most of them had run out of conversation just four days out of Cape Town.

Officially, Freeman was a courier for the South African Government, keeping an eye on some precious antiques and a selection of fine South African wines that were destined for the South African Embassy in London. Unofficially, he was also a courier for the South African Government, only his cargo was normally slightly more precious and a lot more sensitive than his official cover. Often, not even he was sure what he was carrying. Sometimes he preferred not to ask, although he had made them promise that it would never blow up in his face. That this envelope had fitted snugly into his briefcase was blessing enough.

The suite was ready and waiting when he arrived at the hotel. Something that did not always happen when he turned up before midday, even when he was running a day late. He took advantage of his sumptuous bathroom to have his first really decent bath since leaving Cape Town and ordered lunch.

The call came just after 3 p.m. It was the same non-descript voice that his boss had talked to from South Africa. The key words fell into place and each was happy that he was dealing with the real Mr McCoy. Freeman was to descend to Central Station just after 5.30 p.m. and go to the high-value freight office. He was to ask to speak to a Mr Buchanan, who had already been alerted that there would be a high-value envelope to travel on tonight's mail train to London. Buchanan would personally put the envelope on the train and give him a receipt. The caller would be at Euston to receive the package on arrival. The package should be addressed to 'W. Hardwood, Soho Square, London W.1.' The address was purely decorative.

The delivery was more straightforward than most, Freeman was pleased to hear. After he had done what he had been asked to do, he would need to hang around in Glasgow for another day or two to clear the embassy's shipment through the docks and then get it on a train or a truck to London. He would accompany it on its journey south and after that he was as free as a bird until his flight back from London to South Africa at the end of the month. He hoped to be able to catch some cricket while he was in England. The West Indies were touring and a fascinating test series was in progress. For the South African, it would be a rare opportunity to see the fast-improving West Indies side in action.

Leatherslade Farm,
p.m., Wednesday 7 August 1963

As the day dragged on Bruce grew concerned that his athletes might peak too soon. Towards late afternoon he assembled everyone in the front room to go over the plan one last time. Subject to getting the green light, they would leave the farm just after midnight and travel in the guise of an army detail on night manoeuvres. Bruce went over the evening's order of play in detail, just as he already had at previous meetings. He would be dressed as the officer and carry 'official papers' to show in the unlikely event that they were stopped by Old Bill or anyone else. David would drive one of the Land-Rovers and Roy the other. Freddie had responsibility for the truck.

'It is of the utmost importance,' Bruce said, raising his voice, 'that you only do what you have been instructed to do unless asked or told otherwise. So when you uncouple the train, I want only Roy and Freddie under the train. Likewise, Buster will take the driver and be the first into the cab, to be followed by Big George, who will go in from the other side after helping Jimmy with the fireman. Both of you will be looking out for any other trouble. Once Peter has moved the train up to the bridge it will be Dave and Charlie's job to get the cage open and the bags moving. Ron, you know what you have to do? Once the old man's done his little bit you take him down to one of the Rovers and watch the cars and the road. Make sure he don't run off into the boondocks, either. Gentlemen, that's about it, then. Good luck and let's make it a night to remember.'

The adrenaline was flowing. Bruce had rallied the troops back to top form. 'I just hope we get the fuckin' green light tonight,' he whispered to Buster. 'I don't fancy this lot having to sit around for another day without the sparks starting to fly.' Spirits were high and an air of confidence pervaded the group.

LEATHERSLADE FARM

As the boys chatted, Gordon, at Bruce's suggestion, slipped off into the night on Roger's bike and cycled down to the phone-box in nearby Bill. The Ulsterman had said he would call at exactly 10.30 p.m. and again at 10.40 if there was no reply. Gordon reached the green with ten minutes to spare and removed the light bulb in the phone-box, plunging it into darkness. The phone rang and Gordon answered on the first ring in the prescribed manner. The Ulsterman gave him the green light.

Gordon slipped back into the farm as silently and discreetly as he had left. Bruce called the gang to order. 'Gordon's got something to say.'

Gordon took centre stage. 'Fellows. The business is on and the train is well on its way. It's going to be fat pay-off.' A big cheer went up.

'Get yourselves knitted out,' Bruce instructed. 'We'll be movin' out in just over an hour.'

Buckinghamshire,
a.m., Thursday 8 August 1963

B ruce's body gave a shudder. Not from the cold, as his army greens were more than enough protection against the light wind that blew across the track. It could have been a reaction to the early hour, yet he had never felt more awake as he continued to stare up the track towards the station at Leighton Buzzard. He had been staring in that same direction, hardly daring to blink, for the best part of ninety minutes. His only surprise was that considering his uncomfortable perch on the embankment he had not suffered cramp or the urge to relieve himself.

It was neither a sound nor a physical presence that broke his concentration, yet he could tell that the time had come. It was as if the track and everything along it was being sucked down into an oncoming vacuum. Half a mile to the north the night mail train from Glasgow was approaching Leighton Buzzard at speed. A little more than a mile to the south his private army lay in wait. He wondered what was going through their minds and hoped they would all do exactly what had been drilled into them over the months. He was pleased that a night's delay had given him the opportunity to go over everything just one more time with everyone together.

Thinking about what the gang would be worrying about brought Bruce his own worries. The unknown factors, the aspects that, however much they had planned and prepared, they could not control themselves. As they had all experienced during their lives of villainy, it often came down to how those you could not control reacted. Tonight would be no different. How would the driver and his mate react? Would the sorters in the high-value coach put up a fight? More importantly, what would be the reaction to the train stopping of the seventy or so post-office sorters in the other carriages? All it needed, he had warned the gang, was for one nosy bastard to stick his head out the door to ruin the entire job. Their sheer numbers would require a hasty retreat if there was not going to be a lot of blood spilt, and spilling blood was not part of the plan. The very thought made him shudder, only this time he knew why. As he continued to stare up the track, Bruce fondled his walkie-talkie.

The vacuum was sucking harder than ever. From one second to the next it was there, the metallic monster that was the night mail train from Scotland. After months of planning the moment had come. Bruce swung the walkie-talkie up in front of his mouth. 'It's here! It's coming your way,' he yelled into the mouthpiece, hoping the call had not been drowned out by the passing train. He did not wait for the entire train to go past before sliding down the embankment to his Land-Rover. According to his calculations he would be cutting it fine to pick up his brother-in-law and get back to Bridego Bridge to greet the train.

Down the track the walkie-talkies crackled into life and brought the gang's focus back to the job in hand. They had talked about coded signals and passwords, but who cared if someone was listening? Just avoid names, be they of people, places or things, Bruce had reminded them. The most hurried figures were John and Roger, with whom lay the responsibility for actually bringing the train to a stop. John quickly got to work on the distant signal and in a matter of seconds had an amber light shining up the track at the oncoming train, which was now within sight.

Roger, who had had an uncomfortable couple of hours on the signal gantry, slipped the cover and a large glove over the green light and clipped the battery on to the portable red light which shone up the track. A last-minute check and he was sliding down the iron ladder. He felt a sharp pain in his leg. Something sticking from the gantry had gashed it – and quite badly, if the blood he could feel oozing into his trouser leg was anything to go by. Roger knew that this was no time to feel sorry for himself. It was a question of seconds rather than minutes, so he threw himself down the embankment, landing on Jimmy, who was already as tense as a scalded cat.

'Typical of the fuckin' railways not to look after their gantries,' Roger moaned as he regained his composure and made his peace with Jimmy. From their privileged position the gang could see that John's distant signal had worked. The train was slowing. It came to a stop just in front of the gantry. Sixteen men held their collective breaths, for if this was not a routine stop either the driver or his mate would shortly emerge from the cab to use the track-side phone. The gang's silence was unecessary, because not much noise invaded the cab of the train above the noise of the diesel motor.

Although this was not a programmed stop, the red light came as no great surprise to driver, Jack Mills, or his fireman, Dave Whitby. It just meant that they would be late into Euston. That, in itself, would not be a first.

It fell to Whitby to find out what was going on. Mills turned the light on in the cab and the fireman stepped down on to the track. He straightened his cap and headed for the signal gantry, where he knew there would be a phone that would put him in contact with the signal-box. They could give him at least a rough idea of how long the delay might be and – what was more important – when he might get to see his bed. Whitby opened the box and picked up the phone.

'Just what you might expect! Dead as a fucking dodo,' Whitby said out loud, to nobody but himself. A deep breath and he was plodding back to the cab. The options were not looking bright. Either they could sit it out and wait for the signal to change or, what he feared most, Mills would make him walk up the track until he found a phone that worked. If the signal changed, Mills would simply bring the train up to him.

Whitby's thought pattern was interrupted by a shadowy figure approaching along the track. A work party – perhaps he would not have to walk after all. It was only as the shadow got closer that he realized the man was wearing a black balaclava. His mind hardly had time to register that August was not the month to require balaclava protection before he was being bundled unceremoniously down the bank and out of view of the cab. By the number of arms and legs flying around, Whitby sensed that he had been grabbed by at least two men, strong men at that. This was no time for heroics.

The two men were George and Jimmy. George could have handled the likes of Whitby on his own without breaking sweat, but Bruce had insisted on two men to make it as swift and foolproof as possible. George had told Bruce that he was possibly overestimating the dedication of railway staff to their employer when it came to a scrap. Whitby proved George's point: he lay quite still in the longish grass, allowing Jimmy to secure his hands with handcuffs. 'Use your loaf, son,' Jimmy told the frightened fireman. 'Stay still and quiet. There are some right bastards among this lot who would be only too happy to see to you if you caused any trouble.' As Jimmy had Whitby well under control, George slipped away to prepare for the assault on the cab.

Bruce would have been proud of his lads if he could have seen them. They were already well into their routine, a routine which had become second nature to them, and, if anything, they were slightly ahead of schedule. A team led by Freddie and Roy was already under the train, working to disconnect the engine and high-value package coach from the rest of the train, whose twelve carriages buzzed with the chatter of the post-office sorters. Thankfully they were quite accustomed to stops along the route from Glasgow to London, a journey of six hours even when everything went to plan.

In the cab, Mills was becoming increasingly irritated by the time it was taking his fireman to make a simple call. He stared up the track to the box, but could not see anybody. Something was wrong, he sensed it.

It was a slight movement behind the cab that first caught Mills's eye. He was certain it was not Whitby, but perhaps the stranger had seen him. The driver moved quickly to the door and found himself looking down at a masked figure. Instinctively Mills kicked out, missing the hooded man's head by inches. Equally instinctively the assailant's arm came up to protect his head and in one movement he was able to catch the driver's leg and pull him off balance. Mills fell back into his cab, striking his head firmly against the side. The driver crawled up on to all fours and lunged at the figure coming up the ladder, grabbing him around the throat in the process. A cosh cracked down from behind. It was George, who had eased his way into the cab from the other side.

'Stay down if you don't want to get hurt,' George warned the driver. From the blood seeping through the man's hair and the groans he realized his warning had come too late. George hardly had time to take in the scene before the rest of the gang were swarming silently around the train and through the cab. The show had to go on and he remembered that, once the cab had been secured, his place was back down on the track on the off chance that any of the post-office sorters put in an appearance. His job, if necessary, would be to act as the last line of defence with Tommy and Jimmy as the rest of the gang beat a hasty retreat.

Gordon and Charlie pulled themselves up into the cab. Charlie took charge of the wounded driver and, ever the gent, reassured him that the bleeding made the injury look much worse than it was. He held his handkerchief to the driver's head to staunch the flow. 'You'll be okay, Dad . . . No, I promise.' Gordon called out for the old man. Ron took Peter by the arm and led him across to the cab. As a veteran of the tracks, Peter had less difficulty swinging himself up the ladder and into the cab than many of the younger members of the gang. Ron followed him. Peter pulled up short as he saw the blood on Mills.

'My word!' he exclaimed – not for the first time that night – before being grabbed by Gordon and bundled into the driver's chair.

'When I give you the word, pull away,' Gordon shouted to Peter. 'About a mile down the track you'll see the white marker. I'll tell you when to stop.'

Behind the cab Roy and Freddie waited for the final okay to complete the uncoupling of the engine and high-value package coach. Signals went back and forth until Roy shouted out that the uncoupling was complete. Gordon gave Peter the order to get the train moving, but the old man just sat looking steadfastly at the controls. 'I'm waiting for my brake pressure to build,' he said by way of explanation:

'What's the problem?' barked Bob from the track. 'Let's get going.'

'I can't take the brake off until I've got sixteen inches of pressure,' Peter replied matter-of-factly.

'Get him out of here and get the driver!' Gordon exploded.

Peter began to protest, referring repeatedly to the brake pressure needed to move the train.

'Fuck the brake pressure,' snarled Gordon. 'Get the driver up here.'

Peter was pulled out of the seat and the driver took his place. Gordon waved his cosh under the nose of the injured man. 'Listen,' he said. 'Get this thing moving – but not too fast – and stop when I tell you.'

Time was all that had been necessary to restore the pressure and almost immediately the large diesel lurched into life and began to move slowly forward. Peter did not look happy.

'I could have driven it, Ron. Why didn't they let me?' he protested to his friend.

As the train moved forward, the remaining members of the gang jumped up on the train with the fireman. For those who could not fit in the back cab the only solution was to cling to anything they could find for the ride down to Bridego Bridge. Inside the high-value package coach the five sorters began to sense that something was amiss.

'Something's wrong,' Dewhurst, the man in charge of the coach, said. 'I feel it in my water.'

'Should I take a look outside?' his number two offered.

'No, stay where you are for the moment. Let's wait and see if we stop again.' The five sorters had heard the pressure escaping from the valve below them when the train was uncoupled. They had also heard voices and sensed that there were people clinging to the outside of the carriage. Only Dewhurst was aware of the true value of the train's shipment that night, a shipment which he had been told was on a strictly need-to-know basis. They had reassured him that there was no need for extra security, any worries of a robbery aboard a speeding train were simply an overreaction.

Roy, riding on the outside of the cab, saw the markers at Bridego Bridge first and shouted for Gordon to slow the train. He no longer cared who heard him – the other sorters were nearly a mile back up the track, even if they did choose to look outside. The driver brought the large locomotive to a halt just as he had been told and watched the gang spill out from the train and on to the track.

Bruce, a little out of breath from his Herculean labours, was standing by the track cutting an elegant figure in his army officer's uniform. Beside him was his brother-in-law, John, who still sported his blue boiler-suit. 'Well done, chaps!' Bruce said, mimicking the typical British officer he had often so admired in the great war films. 'Carry on.' Confidence was growing in the ranks that Bruce's promise of a forty grand pay-day might be true.

At the front of the train there was clearing up to do. Ron got hold of Peter and took him down to one of the waiting Land-Rovers to watch the sacking of the train from a safe distance. Charlie, on the other side of the train, handed the driver and fireman over to the care of other members of the gang and rushed back to find David, who was emerging from the back cab. George joined the other heavies in their assault on the coach. The idea was to crush any resistance through sheer intimidation. 'We're going to be their worst fuckin' nightmare,' George had promised back at the farm. Four men took up positions on each side of the coach and waited for the signal from Charlie. The sound of metal on metal broke the silence.

71

'They're putting the bolts on,' cried David. 'Get the bastards!' The men set to work using pick handles, coshes and even a crow bar to break the windows and doors. It did the trick; soon the bolts drew back and the door swung open.

George and Charlie wasted no time with pleasantries and quickly rounded up the sorters, growling and terrorizing as they went. They did not want a repeat of the incident with the driver and in no time the five sorters were lying neatly in a line on the floor of the carriage at the opposite end to the high-value cage that held the mail-bags. George's sheer presence worked wonders when it came to concentrating the mind. David, with Freddie close behind him, followed Charlie and the 'heavies' into the van. David showed exactly why he had come so highly recommended and in seconds the door to the cage swung open and he was ready with the first mail-bag.

'Come on . . .' His voice trailed off. He had nearly broken the golden rule and used a name. He of all people. Charlie joined him in the cage and a human chain was formed so that one by one the heavy mail-bags could find their way from David and Charlie along the line to Jim and Bobby, who were loading the truck at the bottom of the embankment.

Freddie took over from George in watching over the sorters, as the big man's brute strength and power were a distinct advantage when it came to shifting the mail-bags from David and Charlie to the waiting line.

'Fuck, there must be a hundred or more, what do you reckon?' a slightly out-of-breath Charlie asked. David did not answer. Although he had had precious little to do until now, he found himself sweating profusely, certainly more than normal. He was glad that the manual work disguised the sweat and he hoped that Charlie had not noticed that his gloves were soaked with perspiration before the unloading began. Normally, on a job, David was as cool as a cucumber. The moment he had sprung the door of the cage he had seen the envelope the Ulsterman had told him about. At least he assumed it was the envelope, as it sat alone in a pigeon-hole to the left within the cage, just as had been promised. He was sure that for that reason alone it must have attracted the attention of Charlie and the others, and he cursed the day he had accepted the Ulsterman's offer.

Freddie, as was his wont, continued to reassure the sorters that no harm would come to them if they behaved themselves. No one was willing to put him to the test, especially with George as back-up.

BUCKINGHAMSHIRE

Bruce, who was standing close to George down on the track, was more preoccupied with his watch than with anything else. While the Ulsterman had focused David's attention on the envelope, he had focused Bruce's on time-keeping. He knew exactly from where Bruce would first see the train and had told him that from that moment to the second they left the scene of the crime must be no longer than forty minutes. Any longer than that, the Ulsterman had assured Bruce, and people down the line towards London would start to wonder where the up postal train was and begin to ask questions. Likewise, after forty minutes, seventy post-office sorters might be getting a little restless and begin to call the driver to see what was up.

Only a few of the gang knew about the tight schedule. All the rest had been told was that when Bruce said it was time to go, it was time to go, with no questions or delays. David was one of those who knew about the time constraints, but only the Ulsterman knew that – it was he, not Bruce, who had warned David. So David was aware of the need to pace himself if he was to have a reasonable chance of grabbing the envelope without being spotted. It meant that not all the mail-bags could be off-loaded. If they were, Charlie would certainly see the envelope and tell him to grab it. After all, if it was in the cage it must be of some value.

'One minute,' Bruce shouted up from the track.

'Sixty seconds!' Gordon and Buster echoed. Charlie stepped up the pace, urging George and the human chain to keep the bags moving. At the other end of the carriage Freddie warned the sorters not to try anything for 'at least thirty minutes'. They would be watched.

'Now!' barked Bruce. Charlie threw a final bag down to the human chain and grabbed one last one to carry back to the truck himself. In the same instant David swung around and grabbed the bulky manila envelope. It was lighter than he had imagined, but harder. He wondered what it could contain that was so important, more important to the Ulsterman than an extra sack or two of money. He stuffed the envelope down the front of his overalls and turned to follow Charlie and Freddie out of the train and back down the embankment. His stare was met by one of the sorters who had watched him pull the envelope. A slight chill ran through him.

George was now the only member of the gang left by the coach, but his presence was enough to keep the sorters face down on the floor.

Further along the train the driver and his mate were handcuffed to the cab. Everyone else scurried down to the truck and the Land-Rovers, taking off their blue boiler-suits as they went.

'Army issue!' Bruce reminded his troops. As one of the drivers, David carried out his task swiftly, carefully folding the envelope within his overalls and stuffing them under the driver's seat. Freddie took up his position in the truck and in seconds had it ready to roll.

'Let's go,' Bruce hollered. It was the signal for George to come tumbling down the bank to where Bob was waiting to pull him aboard the truck. The convoy moved off at no great speed. Bruce was ecstatic. 'We did it Ron, we pulled it off.' Bruce was not normally one to show his emotions, but Ron was an old friend and even the others now felt like family. 'You were all great, you were fantastic.'

'Fuckin' hell, I bet Bruce is well pleased with us,' Freddie said to his companions in the truck. 'Sixty or seventy bags he promised. Christ! There must be more than a hundred back there and we still had to leave some behind.'

The rest of the drive back to Leatherslade Farm was euphoric but uneventful. Despite the adrenaline there were a lot of tired bodies that appreciated the rest the drive through the silent country lanes gave them. For some there were still many hours of work ahead before they could get any real sleep.

It was around 4.45 a.m. when the convoy finally pulled off the road into the lane leading up to the farm. For the first time since they had left the bridge the VHF radio that Ron had tuned to the police frequency showed signs of life. A train had been robbed close to Linslade, it announced. There was a general call for all units to go to the scene. An ironic cheer went up, but as a precaution Buster and Jimmy elected to watch the road for a time to check that they had not been followed.

Freddie backed the truck up to the door as the rest of the gang spilled out of the vehicles on to the dirt drive. Bruce told David and Roy to park the Land-Rovers out of sight on the off chance that the police might try an aerial sweep of the area once it was light. David let Roy go first and parked his Land-Rover alongside. Roy was eager to get inside and see the money, and David was thankful for the solitude. It was his first moment alone since he got to the farm, other than a visit to the khazi. It gave him a welcome opportunity to catch his breath. Ever the professional, David gave the Land-Rover the once over. In the back he found a pair of gloves. 'Stupid, careless bastards,' he muttered under his breath. Satisfied that there was nothing else incriminating left behind, David dragged his overalls and the thick envelope out from beneath the seat. The contents of the envelope were hard and uneven under his touch. It wasn't paper or bonds, then. It had to be jewels. He turned the pouch over and stared at the name of the addressee. 'W. Hardwood'. It meant nothing to him.

Two figures unexpectedly emerged from the bushes behind him, making him jump and drop the envelope. It was Buster and Jimmy. 'Fuck! You two scared the shit out of me!' Something of an under-statement, as he knew Buster had Bruce's ear. He wondered how long they had been standing there and if they had seen the envelope.

Luckily Buster's thoughts had been elsewhere. To him it seemed natural that David should be edgy and shaken by his sudden appearance. He would have been. 'Sorry, mate! Glad to report we're sweet. It looks as if we're all clear at the road. We should be okay for the time being. Lads inside then?'

'Yeah. They're unpacking the bags, then they are going put the truck in the shed. Could you see the Rovers from the lane?' David was breathing heavily.

'No. Not in this light, but we may want to check later when it's lighter. Never know who will be snooping around in the morning. You coming in, Dave?'

'No. I'd better check Roy's Land-Rover to see nothing's been left in it. I've just found a pair of gloves in this one. Stupid arseholes taking their gloves off. They're asking for trouble.'

'See you inside, then. Come on, Jim, let's go and have a look at our goodies.'

David waited until Buster and Jim were out of sight before sliding the envelope out from under the Land-Rover where it had fallen. He tried to shake it. He hoped that whatever it was, it had survived the rough handling. Slipping the envelope inside the jacket of his army uniform, he made his way carefully across the drive to the house. He could already hear raised voices and somebody singing 'The Good Life'. He thought he recognized the voice as Gordon's. Tony Bennett he was not.

There was enough confusion in the house to allow him to slip upstairs without being noticed. A couple of the gang were already up there, including Roy, who was stretched out on his bed. David slipped out of his army greens, taking the opportunity to hide the envelope in the bottom of his sleeping-bag. It was a more relaxed David Jenkins who made his way downstairs. He needed a drink.

Euston Station,
Thursday 8 August 1963

The train was over an hour late, which in itself was not unusual. What was unusual was that nobody seemed to know where it was or why it was late. The last confirmed sighting had been as it passed through Leighton Buzzard, but that was now nearly two hours ago.

All William Hardwood could do was wait. It was something he would have preferred to do in the comfort of his own bed, but such was life. He appeared to be the only member of the public with any interest in the train. The others were railway employees or the men from the Royal Mail who were waiting impatiently for their nightly cargo to arrive from Glasgow.

'Mr Hardwood?' The voice came from his left. It was a railway employee who asked him to accompany him to the station master's office.

'Pity they don't follow the armed services,' he thought. 'At least I would know his rank.'

He had no doubt as to the rank of the man who greeted him in the office. He was clearly the boss and what was more he was accompanied by a senior member of the railway police.

'Mr Hardwood, may I ask what you are waiting to receive from the night mail train from Glasgow?'

'You may ask, but I am not at liberty to say any more than it is an envelope, the contents of which are of interest to Her Majesty's Government.'

'Would I be right in saying that under specific instructions from one of your colleagues this envelope was placed in the cage of the HVP of the up postal train in Glasgow last night?'

'The what?'

KEEP ON RUNNING

'The HVP – High Value Package coach.'

William was getting a little tired of questions relating to an item which was meant to be being carried by the Royal Mail with a great deal of discretion. 'Are you going to tell me that you have misplaced the envelope? Or did it miss the train?'

'Worse, I am afraid. We have just been notified by Scotland Yard that the mail train from Glasgow was held up about an hour ago, close to Leighton Buzzard. From the early information we have, it appears to be the work of a professional gang who knew exactly what they were looking for. They uncoupled the engine along with the HVP coach and ransacked the cage. First estimates from the track suggest that they got away with over one hundred mail-bags which were full of money rather than mail. It also appears that your envelope is missing.'

William wondered if he looked as bad as he felt. The colour had drained from his face and he felt decidedly wobbly.

'If you would tell us what was in the envelope, it could help our investigations.'

William needed to think. The repercussions were way over his head. It was time to bail out. 'I need to use a phone. And I need to use it now!' His voice was low and controlled. He had to take command of the situation. He was shown into another office where he could talk privately. He knew his boss would not appreciate being woken at this early hour. Sir Roger also hated being contacted at home, but there was no alternative on this occasion. William apologized to his boss and outlined what he had been told by the stationmaster.

'Listen carefully, William,' Sir Roger began. 'I want you to head out to Leighton Buzzard, but call me at the office before you get there so I can give you the name of a police contact at the scene. I'll see who is friendly and known to us. You are to get away from Euston just as soon as you can, but before you do make it quite clear to these jokers that there was a mix-up and thankfully the envelope missed the train in Glasgow. The press will be crawling all over the station within the hour and we don't want them being told stories about missing government envelopes by some halfwit from the railways who will be looking for somebody to blame for this catastrophe.'

William tried to looked relieved as he emerged into the stationmaster's office. He thanked the stationmaster and his colleagues for their concern and consideration but explained that through his own stupidity he had got the wrong day. The stationmaster was far from clear what was going on, but if the man said he had not lost the envelope who was he to argue? Losing over one hundred mail-bags belonging to Her Majesty's mail service was quite bad enough for one night.

Leatherslade Farm,
Thursday 8 August 1963

Inside the farm it was pandemonium. Bodies and mail-bags were flying about all over the place as Bruce and his two accountants, Charlie and Roger, set about instilling some sort of order. Bruce sent some of the gang upstairs to keep a look out and just as importantly to keep them out of the way. 'Too many cooks,' Bruce mumbled to Freddie.

'Well, let's start sorting the wheat from the chaff, then,' Ron suggested.

'No need, Ronnie. Take a look at this.' Freddie whipped out a knife and ran it down the length of a tightly wrapped bundle of paper, exposing a wad of blue five-pound notes. 'It's wedge,' he said with a grin. 'It's all fuckin' wedge!'

George helped Ron and Freddie tip out the contents of the mail-bags to make life easier for the accountants. 'One hundred and twenty.' Ron yelled from the cellar, as if he were playing darts.

'One hundred and what?' Bruce shouted back.

'One hundred and twenty mail-bags. That's the total. Not a bad little haul.'

Charlie and Roger worked silently and diligently as the money piled up. The only conversation was checking figures or discussing the appearance of certain notes which they then discarded. A large grin spread over Roger's face. 'After you Chas ... you have the honour.' Charlie pulled out a fiver and added it to the pile, mouthing the magic words 'one million'. The two men burst out laughing. 'Call the lads,' Roger said. 'It's not very often you get a chance to look at one million pounds.'

'Our very own million, at that,' Charlie added proudly.

The gang gathered around the table. Even David managed a smile.

LEATHERSLADE FARM

Charlie took a break, getting to his feet and twisting along to Gerry and the Pacemakers' 'I Like It', which was blasting from the radio. Britain was awaking from its slumbers to learn on the radio about the Great Train Robbery. It had happened too late to hit the morning papers.

'First reports,' the radio announced, 'suggest that the gang have got away with over one hundred thousand pounds.'

'Bollocks!' Charlie yelled as he looked across at the still uncounted notes. The first million had hardly made a dent.

'Oi, David!' he called. 'Aren't you Scottish? I've got a hat here from one of your ancestors.' Charlie rummaged around in the unsorted notes and pulled out an envelope from which he produced a tartan Tam-o'-Shanter which he chucked over in David's direction.

'Thanks, Charlie. I'm actually Welsh, but it's close enough. We're all Celts in the end. I appreciate the gesture, though – and the bonnet,' David replied, clutching the Tam-o'-Shanter to his chest.

'Might bring you luck, that hat; perhaps a fortune. It was in the cage, after all! The only thing besides the money. Funny that.'

David blanched. He wondered if it was Charlie's way of telling him that he had seen the envelope.

Bridego Bridge,
Thursday 8 August 1963

It was just after 10.30 a.m. when William Hardwood got to Bridego Bridge. The police and their forensic experts were crawling all over the train and the surrounding area. The press were being held back at a distance and after a series of complaints were promised that if they co-operated, they would have a tour of the train and be allowed to take their pictures in time for the morning editions.

William had been told to ask for an Inspector Trebbin, one of a number of senior officers at the scene. Trebbin had worked with the department before and was well aware that not everything was as straightforward as it first appeared. Not that a train robbery was ever that simple, especially if it involved a lot of the government's own money.

It took William some time to persuade a member of the local constabulary to look for Trebbin. His card said he worked for the Foreign Office. Hardly a priority, the local bobby had thought.

The bobby was full of apologies on his return and, much to the chagrin of the press corps, ushered William through the ropes.

'What's so fuckin' special about him?' one yelled at the bobby as they made their way up the embankment.

All Trebbin could tell William was that the envelope was missing. He knew better than to ask what its contents might be. He thought that a government agency might show a little more concern, however, over the 122 missing mail-bags, but who was he to question the thinking that went on in the corridors of Whitehall?

Trebbin found a spot trackside where they could not be overheard. 'I've done as much as I can without shining a spotlight on the issue, but for now your envelope can be considered to be missing in action. I spoke with Dewhurst, who was in charge of the HVP coach. He is still very shaken, but confirms that he personally put a small envelope in the cage after a Mr Buchanan had given it to him just before the train departed from Glasgow Central. For your information, the gang left a number of the larger mail-bags behind, which, unless you tell me differently, suggests that a member of the gang grabbed it at the last minute on the off chance it held something of value. One of the sorters believes he saw one of the gang grab an envelope as they were leaving the train, but he is not proving to be a very reliable witness and keeps changing his mind as to exactly what it is he did see. The trouble is, I don't know what we are looking for – that is something you have to choose to tell me or not. All I need to know from you for now is, is it at all possible that this entire robbery was set up just to get hold of your envelope?'

With the knowledge that Inspector Trebbin was cleared by the department for sensitive information, William explained that the envelope contained a number of precious gems, diamonds, which were being delivered to a certain branch of the government, by another friendly government. Unless there was a very serious leak at an extremely high level within the government, he had to believe that it was just a coincidence that the envelope was on this particular train. Whoever took the envelope, he explained, was in for one hell of a big surprise when they opened it. 'I would be very grateful if you did not mention this matter to anyone else,' he concluded. 'I will be in touch if there is anything else we need to know, but I have a feeling that officially the envelope never existed and was certainly never on the train. The paperwork surrounding it being on the train will simply disappear. Dewhurst and his sorters will also have to be persuaded to forget about it.' That was his next task.

'Mr Hardwood. We'll get these bastards, you know. It may take time, but we will get them. We think they are holed up within a thirty-mile radius of this site. If they move, we'll have 'em.'

William was not reassured.

Leatherslade Farm,
Thursday 8 August 1963

I t was around midday when the police announced over the radio that army vehicles had been used in the robbery. It would now be impossible to use the Land-Rovers or the truck to leave the farm without attracting attention. Jimmy was the first to come up with a solution. He would paint the truck yellow, he had seen the paint in the shed. George went out to help him.

As Charlie and Roger continued to count, they were now well past the two-million mark. Freddie started to collect the wrappings together and stuff them in the small but efficient stove in the kitchen. Roy, who was outside helping to dig a hole to put the sacks in, was the first to come running in. 'For fuck's sake, Freddie, put the fire out. There's smoke pouring from the chimney. We only need Old Bill to go up in a helicopter and he'll spot us from miles away.' He grabbed a pan of water and threw it on the stove. The fire was out. They would have to bury the evidence.

'How much have we got?' David asked when he noticed the accountants had completed their work.

Charlie held up his pencil as a signal for silence as he did one last piece of arithmetic. 'The tally comes to around two and a half million quid, give or take a little. That's not counting the ten-bob notes or the Scottish or Irish shit.'

Freddie gave a little whistle. 'Must be one of the biggest of all time. This job is heading for the *Guinness Book of Records*.'

Bruce, who had grabbed his own piece of paper and a pen, was also doing his sums. 'Take forty grand off for the old man and divide the rest between the fifteen of us here, with an extra whack for Brian and another for my Irish friend ... that gives us ... about one hundred and fifty thousand quid each if my maths is right.'

84

'Not quite,' Roger interjected. 'There's at least one hundred thousand in notes that me and Charlie think should be destroyed. They're either too tatty and old or are marked in obvious ways that could be traced. We reckon the split to be around one hundred and forty-five thousand, or thereabouts.'

'At this stage of the game,' Freddie laughed, 'I'm not going to bug you over an extra five grand, and you can keep the ten-bob notes and the rest. A hundred and forty-five will do me just fine.'

'Okay then, lads,' Charlie chipped in. 'Bring me your bags when you're ready and we'll load them up. No rush, now, there's plenty for everyone.'

'Dave, could you help me sort out the extra whacks?' The request came from Bruce and David could not believe his luck. 'You'll see some kit-bags and a suitcase by my sleeping-bag. Very practical, a suitcase. Mind you, Brian was always like that!' David collected the bags and lined up alongside Roger for the pay-out. 'Those two new bags are for the Ulsterman,' Bruce pointed. 'For Christ's sake make sure he gets a full whack and you don't short-change him. He's got no sense of humour; he's the type who'll be poring over the papers to see what they give as the final tally. Put these on the bags when you're finished.' He threw a couple of padlocks over to David.

David was surprised at just how bulky the money turned out to be. Bulky enough to hide an envelope in without any worries. He took the bags upstairs. When he felt sure nobody was looking, he slipped the envelope into the middle of the second bag and applied the padlocks. He returned the keys to Bruce.

'You look a lot happier now you've got your money,' Charlie quipped as David sipped a cup of tea.

'Yeah, and I'll be happier still when I get home and hosed and get rid of these fuckin' gloves.'

Getting home was now the predominant worry. They could no longer sit around at the farm for a couple of days as they had originally planned. Bruce had decided that he and John would go into London the next morning and round up some transport. 'It's not worth taking the risk with the truck or the Land-Rovers,' he said. Roger also had his own plans. He wanted permission to cycle into Oxford that afternoon. He had some close friends living there and could pick up some extra transport which would allow him to get away from the farm with his whack. He would return in the morning. Bruce could not see any problems with Roger's plans and gave him the go-ahead.

Whitehall, London,
Thursday 8 August 1963

It was late afternoon by the time William got back to London. He was told to go straight in and see Sir Roger. Today had not been one of his boss's better days. Sir Roger hated being left hanging about waiting on other people's information before he could make a decision. He had preferred his years as a field operative when he did not have to waste so much time with paperwork and arse-licking his superiors. He had never wanted to be a glorified civil servant, but he had not been given a choice.

'News, William?' he asked as the man he considered to be his best London-based operative came through the door.

'Not much, Sir Roger, but I don't know what the police are playing about with announcing that only a couple of hundred thousand was grabbed. A conservative estimate I have from Glasgow puts the value on the train at a little over two and a half million pounds.'

'And our diamonds?'

'No sign. I think we have to assume the gang, or at least one of its members, grabbed the envelope. He may not even know yet what is in the package. I'll keep digging.'

'Do so.'

Leatherslade Farm,
Friday 9 August 1963

The latest news bulletin on the radio invited the public to get in touch with the police if they had seen anything suspicious in the days leading up to the robbery. A police inspector told BBC Radio that the search was being concentrated on a thirty-mile radius of the robbery site. 'We have come to that conclusion from something one of the robbers said on the train.'

'How far did you estimate we are from the track?' a slightly embarrassed Freddie asked Roy. He knew exactly who had made the remark. 'We're in that radius, aren't we?'

'I reckon we're about twenty-seven or twenty-eight miles from the bridge as the crow flies, but quite a bit further by road. It all depends if they are going to use their school compass to draw a circle, or what.'

'I just hope Bruce and John don't hang around in London, because I have a gut feeling it won't be too long till Old Bill pays the farms in this area a visit,' David said.

'Car!' The call was from a look-out on the second floor. A black car was approaching the farm at speed. Because of the light it was difficult to make out what it was. It stopped in a swirl of dust just by the front door. There was a collective holding of breath and coshes as the door of the black Wolseley opened, and a louder collective sigh of relief when Roger emerged.

'I thought that would make you jump,' Roger laughed. 'Like the motor? Amazing what you can buy with a bit of cash.' He leaned back into the car, picked up a pile of newspapers and headed for the farmhouse.

'You prick, I nearly shat myself!' Freddie chaffed. Charlie was in a less forgiving mood: 'If it had been a been a tiny bit darker, Roger, you might have had half a dozen coshes land across your crust. You silly bastard!'

'Lighten up, my old china! Do something useful for once in your useless life, Freddie, and grab these newspapers before they fall.'

The group retreated back inside the house, with Roger its centre of attention. 'Old Bill's flying about, but at least there are no road blocks yet.' Roger took a paper from the pile Freddie was holding and spread it on the kitchen table. 'Isn't it lovely, we've made the headlines!' As if that was a signal, everyone made a grab for the remaining papers and devoured them hungrily.

'Come on, lads, let's not make a mess, we all want to read them.' Freddie said as he tried to hold one back for himself.

'Talking of cleanliness being next to godliness, or whatever, don't you think we should get on with cleaning up the farm before we leave?' David suggested. 'Personally, I don't fancy giving Old Bill any more assistance than is absolutely necessary and even with all their incompetence the law of averages suggests that they must stumble on this house one day in the not too dim and distant future.'

'What if there was no farm for them to stumble across?' Freddie ventured from behind the safety of a copy of the *Daily Express* that he had managed to salvage.

'What you talkin' about?' Charlie probed.

'Well, it's just a thought, but what would happen if there was no farm for Old Bill to find? What if we burnt the fuckin' thing to the ground as we left? Even with all the current action in the neighbourhood, if we do the job properly, by the time they get a fire engine over here the farm, and all the contents, will be history.'

'By a happy coincidence,' Buster chuckled, 'I know a couple of guys who for the right price would come out here and burn the place down for us after we have gone. I'm not saying we shouldn't give the place the once-over for now, but I agree with Freddie that we will all sleep a lot better at night knowing there is no farm to be found.'

'I'll vote for that, but what sort of money are we talking about for these mates of yours?' David asked, warming to the discussion.

'Less than will make any difference to you lot. So, gentleman, shall we call in the cleaners? If it's agreed, Roy and I will start a collection. Five grand a piece will do the trick. We'll leave the old man out of this as his dabs probably aren't even on record. Any objections or forever hold your peace?' The deal was struck and Buster and Roy set about collecting the necessary cash while the rest continued to give the place a wipe down.

'Anyone want a Monopoly set?' Ron joked. There were no takers, so he threw it on the table.

Roger, who had already tasted freedom, was keen to repeat the sensation. 'Look, fellas, there is little point in me hanging on till Bruce gets back. The sooner we get away from here the better. I'm sure Bruce would agree if he was here. Why don't I take Jimmy and George into Oxford, then Jimmy can come back with the car and George can catch a train up to London? I already have another car lined up and Jimmy can be back by early afternoon.'

What Roger said made sense and what few doubters there were, were reminded that they had also doubted that Roger would return to the farm after his first trip to Oxford. Yet here he was. In a matter of minutes the boot of the car was bulging from the bags and baggage that represented Roger's take from the previous night's work.

'This is definitely the best option,' Freddie explained to George as they walked towards the car. 'Who knows when Bruce will get back? Christ, he may have even been picked up for all we know. If we get the chance to get out, let's fucking take it and be thankful. Roger and Jimmy will run you into Oxford and drop you at the station. You can take the train up to London and I'll meet you back at the house just as soon as I can get out of here with our cut. Tomorrow we can go to the travel agent and with a bit of luck we'll be able to change our reservations and be in America by early next week. The earlier the better as far as I'm concerned. Listen, George, those Yank birds are gonna love our accent, I'm told! They like a bit of English.'

'Come on, you wankers, I ain't got all day.' The caller was Roger and his comments were directed at George. There was little time for sentimental goodbyes and nobody would say the obvious. If they did meet again, then something had gone badly wrong. George squeezed his large frame into the back of the Wolseley and found he had to share the seat with another bulging kit-bag. Jimmy slid in behind the wheel while Roger took one last look around. 'Gentlemen,' he said, addressing those of the gang gathered by the car, 'as always it has been a pleasure, but if I never see your horrible, ugly mugs again it will not be a minute too soon.' With that, they were gone.

It did not take Jimmy long to get into Oxford. He dropped Roger at Edith Road and helped him inside with his bags. A few minutes later, just before midday, he pulled up in front of Oxford Station. George hauled himself out of the Wolseley and on to the station forecourt. Not a man of words, he was not sure what to say. It was Jimmy who made the move. 'Good luck, George! It's been good working with you. Perhaps, when we have spent it all, we can get together for another crack.' George smiled and shook Jimmy warmly by the hand.

'Still the gloves, George? A trooper till the end. But if I could be so bold, you don't half look a wanker wearing gloves on a beautiful day like this!' George released his grip and, laughing, turned towards the station, peeling the gloves from his hands as he went. He used them to wave back at Jimmy as he drove off. Within two hours George was safely back within the confines of his own house in west London. All he could do now was wait.

As George was walking through his front door, so Jimmy was driving back into Leatherslade Farm. The farm was still a hive of activity and gang members continued to clear up, a chore which was more to keep minds occupied than anything else, as the 'dustmen' had been alerted. Jimmy left the car by the front door and told the others to join him downstairs. 'Listen up,' he began, 'Not much sign of Old Bill in the neighbourhood, so I don't expect him to coming knocking at our door, at least not yet. They appear to have better things to do and other leads to follow. I managed to speak to Bruce and he will be back a little later on with enough transport to get us all out of here. Bags, baggage and all. To show you I'm giving you no bullshit, I'm going to hang on here until he gets back and then I'll drive in with you lot of reprobates.

'Dave!' Jimmy looked around until he was facing David. 'Bruce suggests you take the Wolseley and give Freddie a lift into London. As there will only be the two of you in the car he wants you to squeeze in our benefactor's whack. Bruce will get in touch later in the week to pick it up.'

David liked the idea of getting out, but was far from thrilled with the idea of having to look after the Ulsterman's share. That had never been part of his plan. 'What did Bruce say I should do with the Ulsterman's whack?' he inquired uneasily.

Jimmy apologized. 'Sorry, Dave, I didn't make myself very clear, did I? It's for George and Freddie to look after the money, not you.' David tried to look unconcerned. He had no intention of hanging around in London, though not even Bruce, let alone the Ulsterman, knew that. It was information that was most strictly on a need-to-know basis and so far the only people who needed to know were him and Denise. It was funny, he thought, in all the excitement he had not given much thought to his wife in the last couple of days. He wondered how she was coping. She would have read the newspapers, so would know that they had pulled it off. He also thought of the Ulsterman and the confidence he had had in the plan and in David's ability. He had, after all, put the money up front.

Charlie and Ron helped David and Freddie load the Wolseley. It was not easy with a mixture of bulging kit-bags and carry-alls, all of which had to be made to look inconspicuous to prying eyes.

'We're history, then,' Freddie said as Ron and Charlie struggled to close the boot. 'If you don't need us for anything else, we'll be on our way.'

'Fuck off, then, and leave us to do the washing up!' Charlie retorted. Of the seven men gathered around the car, only David and Freddie continued to wear their gloves – a fact that was not lost on Ron, who continued to rib them. 'See you around, boys,' he called after them.

'Not if we see you first, Ron,' Freddie replied. Freddie and David waved their gloved hands from the car as they drove up the lane leading to the main road, but neither man looked back. The robbery was over. They were on their own. No Bruce to help them, no mates to talk to. It was how David, for one, liked it.

It was left to Freddie to make the conversation on the drive to London. David preferred to keep himself to himself. He knew Freddie understood very little about him and that's how he wanted to keep it. He knew more than he needed or wanted to know about Freddie and George, and realized that it was already far too much for their own good.

'So what are you going to do?' Freddie inquired.

'I'm going to drop you off and then go home.'

Freddie had hoped for a more general answer about the future, but let it go. 'You live near Shepherds Bush, don't you?'

'That's right. A little to the north.'

'So we don't live that far apart? We should get together for a drink next week and compare notes.'

'Why not?' David said dryly. Both men were lying. Both had other plans.

'Look, if you would like to hang on to the Ulsterman's dough, I don't mind. It might even be better for Bruce . . .'

'No!' David cut him short. 'Bruce has made the plans and we should stick to them. He's done all right so far and he wants you to look after the whack. That's the way it has to be, unless he says different.' The two men remained in stony silence as the Wolseley wound its way through the back streets of west London.

'Take the next left,' Freddie directed. 'The house is about 500 yards up on the right with a red door. You can pull up just past the green camper van.'

Other than a group of children playing at the far end of the road there was not a soul to be seen, which was just as well as David had to double park, blocking the road to all but one lane of traffic. Freddie went in and called George to help with the bags.

'You got here okay, then?' Freddie inquired of his big friend.

'Yeah, no sweat. So which of these are to come in?'

Freddie pointed to the bags in the boot while David eased a kit-bag off the back seat of the Wolseley.

'Do you want to come in or will you be getting off?' Freddie asked David, somewhat sarcastically.

'I'll be moving on, if you've got everything. I need to take care of my baggage by nightfall. Some other time then.' Before Freddie even had a chance to reply, David was in the car and away.

'Has he gone, then?' George inquired as he returned to the street. 'I was coming out to say goodbye.'

'Fuckin' good riddance, if you ask me. A real cold fish, that one. Professional but cold. Fuck him, let's celebrate.' The two men turned back inside.

West London, Friday 9 August 1963

D avid was his own man again and it felt good. Everything was how he had planned it. He was alone, away from the farm and with his money. He drove on through the streets of London until he was back on his own patch. His new car, a second-hand Zephyr bought prior to the robbery, was parked in a private lot behind White City Stadium, not more than a stone's throw from the Scrubs.

David drove the Wolseley alongside his shiny Zephyr and when he felt the moment was right transferred the bags across. The boot held all his bags and baggage, except for an overnight bag which he threw in the back. He drove the Wolseley the short distance to Sawley Road and found a suitable place to park. With luck, he thought, the car might get nicked. If not, it would be weeks before anyone complained about it. He walked back and threw the keys into a small park on the way. Keys gone, it was his first chance in nearly four days to rid himself of the gloves. He found a bin and dropped them in. It felt good. A little further along the road he came to a phone-box. An operator answered on the second ring. He asked to be put through to Mrs Wood.

'Is that the wealthy and extremely tasty Mrs Wood?' By the little scream at the end of the line he knew that Denise had recognized his voice. He tried to keep it short and sweet although he had much to tell her. 'I'll be with you tomorrow, I promise. So warn the hotel. I'm leaving London now and if I don't run into any problems I should be there for lunch, so put the champers on ice . . . Yeah, I'm away early . . . I'll tell you about it when I see you . . . Love you, D.'

The hour was later than he would have chosen to leave London, but the day's events had rather scuppered his plans. He was several days ahead of his original schedule, however, as Bruce had warned him that the stay at the farm could be as long as a week or more. It would not matter. He was going to enjoy a week in a nice hotel while he and his wife house-hunted in and around Chester. David slipped on to the A4 around dusk and headed west. The direct route to Chester would have taken him up through Watford to Aylesbury and on to Oxford. That was a part of the country he had no desire to see, especially with over £140,000 in used bank notes in the boot. Instead he headed due west: to Swindon and up through Cirencester to Gloucester. It was then a run almost directly north to Chester and his reunion with Denise. They would spend a second honeymoon in Chester, their first as Mr and Mrs Wood. Mr and Mrs Jenkins no longer existed. At least until the dust settled.

London, Saturday 10 August 1963

T hese were truly nameless, faceless men. They would forget their own names if they had to. Their lives were based on lies. They lied to their wives, they lied to their children, they lied to the world, which saw them as drab little civil servants. They even lied to their lords and masters, the government of the day, if they thought it was right to do so. They were above the law of the land because as far as they were concerned, the country slept more soundly at night thanks to their work. They were diplomats and as such their specialty was diplomacy, which had once been defined by one of their predecessors as the patriotic art of lying for one's country.

William Hardwood's boss, a leading figure among faceless men, cleared his throat. 'Gentlemen, I regret to report that there is no word, as yet, as to the whereabouts of the envelope. We can only hope that it will either be recovered during the on-going search or be found along with the people who perpetrated this heinous crime. Mark my words we will find these people, and soon.'

'Forgive me, Sir Roger.' The interruption came from another nameless figure who, like the rest, was dressed for a day at the golf club, their only cover for a meeting on a Saturday morning, a day that would have been sacred to the real civil servants. 'But have we yet ascertained if the envelope was the target of the robbery?'

'A reasonable question and not a possibility that we can completely rule out at this early stage. What is clear is that we have a major leak at high levels; not just because of the disappearance of the envelope, but because the gang knew exactly which train to stop to maximize their take. No other train these past fifteen days has carried such a vast sum of money. Can this really be a coincidence?'

'Have you mentioned the problem to our friends in South Africa?'

'Until now, I have been incommunicado, but I will talk to them no later than Tuesday. By then, we will have to decide how we wish to play the game. Sadly, I believe we have no alternative but to swallow our pride and the loss, and credit them as if we had received the stones. If we put pressure on them to assume the loss, they might just find ways to leak the deal to the press and prefer to do business with our American, French, Dutch or German colleagues in future. That is something I would rather avoid at all cost, even if that cost is the diamonds. It's control and trust we want, not money. It is embarrassing enough that a gang of thugs can hold up a train carrying Her Majesty's mail and walk away with over 120 mail-bags, without having the press start asking questions about underhand dealings between Britain and South Africa. Not only would the goverment be put in a very embarrassing position, but so would Her Majesty's Opposition who, for the sake of appearances, would have to be outraged by an action that they themselves would condone if in power. As far as we are concerned, the diamonds simply do not exist and never did.'

'And what about the Minister, does he know?'

'I have decided, for the time being, to keep this matter strictly within house. Although our actions have the Minister's blessing, I am quite certain that he knows nothing about the diamonds or how they were being transported. That is why we must keep a lid on this occurrence. After Profumo and Philby, this government and this department cannot afford another scandal, and skulduggery with the South Africans would give the press and opposition a field day. As you have no doubt noted from the press coverage of the robbery, the government and the authorities have already been made to look pretty stupid and the gang are beginning to become something of folk heroes, latter-day Robin Hoods if you will.'

'Could the South Africans have been behind the robbery?' The interruption was from another faceless individual, one of the few to take notes.

'It is highly unlikely,' William interjected to take a little of the heat and give his boss a breather, 'and not an angle that the police will be looking at, but it is certainly something this department will be investigating because we will look at every possibility, however remote. Our counterparts in South Africa would have to be far more organized and better connected than we believe they are to pull off such a stunt. They had no warning as to how the envelope was to be transferred from Glasgow to London. It would have to have been one hell of a lucky guess to hit the right train on the right day and have a team trained and in place to do so.'

'So who did know the diamonds, or for that matter the money, would be on the train?'

'I'm promised a full list will be on my desk by Monday,' Sir Roger assured his colleagues. 'If the thieves did know about the diamonds, the list, which I am assured will contain fewer than thirty names, will only be the start. I am afraid that we will have to dig deep until we find any light at the end of this tunnel and as the list is so restricted, we may not even like what we find when we get there. It could be a runaway train heading in our direction!'

'And if it is a simple accident that these brigands stumbled across the diamonds?'

'If it is an accident – which currently seems the most likely scenario – then whoever got hold of the gems may just have pulled off the perfect crime. These stones are not registered and despite being extremely rare will be almost impossible to trace, unless we want to go very public with their disappearance and give a description of each and every one to the jewellery trade. If the criminals know what they are doing and realize that there is no mention of the diamonds in the press, they could burn the money from the robbery and live off the proceeds from the diamonds. We can only hope they don't.'

Maida Vale, London,
Saturday 10 August 1963

Freddie and George woke late. Their heads told them that they had perhaps overdone their celebrations. They had virtually drunk their flat dry after a lengthy session at the local. About the only thing left was the vinegar and even George had drawn the line there.

Both men dressed and, after a strong black coffee and a Coke, felt they were fit enough to face the world. Freddie thrust his hand into one of the bags and pulled out a wad of notes which he stuffed into the side pocket of his leather jerkin. As time was pressing, they hailed the first cab they saw and set off for Queensway. Traffic was light and in little over ten minutes they were outside the travel agent's. They had made it with about half an hour to spare before the shop put up the shutters for the weekend. The staff in the agency were pleased to see them. Clients who wanted to visit America were still something of a rarity.

George let Freddie do the talking. He explained that they were now going to be able to travel sooner than had been expected, so they could take an earlier flight to New York than they had originally requested. Freddie emphasized that this must be a Pan Am flight, not BOAC. He did not know why, he just felt more secure with Pan Am, as if he would be out of Britain's jurisdiction that much faster with an American carrier. The travel agent suggested they wait for the Tuesday afternoon flight as they would need Monday to put their visas in order. Freddie was happy that he had foreseen the visa problem and had arranged enough paperwork to satisfy the normally pernickety US consulate. As far as it was concerned, George and Freddie were simply a couple of likely lads off to tour America for a month. Their tickets, the only thing the consulate still needed to see, were returns. They even had referees who would swear that the boys were due back to take up a well-paid job on a

London building site on Monday 23 September. It was to be the first jet and first transatlantic flight for both men, although neither was a stranger to travel in continental Europe, a place they had visited for business of one nature or another on numerous occasions.

The travel agent was more than delighted to accept payment in cash and, after checking with Pan Am, told the two men that the flight on Tuesday was confirmed and that the tickets would be ready first thing Monday morning. She suggested they make a hotel reservation before flying out. George and Freddie settled for the Statler, opposite Penn Station, a hotel made famous by Glenn Miller, who had used the hotel's phone number, Pennsylvania 6–5000, for one of his songs. It appealed to Freddie's sense of the ridiculous.

Chester, Saturday 10 August 1963

I t had not taken David long to find the Grosvenor Hotel. It was
as much a landmark in Chester as the cathedral or the Eastgate
clock. The staff were on hand to greet him and carry his kit-bags
up to the suite where Mrs 'Wood' was waiting for her husband. He
and Denise embraced. It was a sweet moment, the result of years of
careful planning. It looked as if it had come off. The big tickle, the
tickle which would allow them to go legitimate or, at the very least,
take fewer risks.

'You son of a bitch. You did it, then?' Denise squeezed her husband,
hardly daring to believe that it had gone exactly as Bruce had planned.
She had secretly worried that this might be the job where it all went
wrong. Too many people had been involved for her and David's liking,
yet in the end David had persuaded her that that was the price to be
paid for such high returns. She squeezed him again to prove to herself
that he really was there with her in Chester. She could not bear to think
of him being locked up in the nick. From the stories she had heard, she
did not think he would enjoy or possibly even survive it.

'I like the hair,' he said, playing with her new coiffure.

'Do you? Do you think it makes me look different enough?'

'Yeah, and even sexier.' He gave her bottom a little squeeze through
the material of her dress. 'Your own mother wouldn't recognize you.
But what am I going to do?'

'Well, we could shave it off, but I don't think I fancy a bald husband.
At least not yet!'

'What about a beard?'

'No way! Maybe a moustache. Then again, I could dye your hair.
How about a nice blue rinse?!'

'Now you're takin' the piss!' After some more small talk David
suggested that they get some room service in and check through the
money. It took them the best part of two hours to go through the first

bag. David and Denise were meticulous. Any note that looked slightly strange or marked was separated from the rest to be destroyed, while series of notes were split into different bundles so as not to attract attention. Denise also made a point of separating the piles into fivers and ones.

'I thought Bruce told you that the money was being sent from Scotland to London to be burnt?' Denise asked, as she sat cross-legged on the floor, neatly stacking the piles of crisp new notes in front of her. 'Some of this stuff looks and smells as good as new.' She was not wrong – some of the bundles still had the bank ties on them and looked as fresh and pristine as the day they were printed.

'What we got so far?' David asked.

'A little over £80,000. What do you reckon the final tally will be?'

'If the accountants got their sums right, we'll be looking at around 140 grand. I started out with 147, but I kicked in five grand for the cleaners. Charladies don't come cheap in Bucks, but all in all not bad for a night's work, eh! Makes old Paddy's ten grand look a bit sick.'

'Did you find the envelope okay?' It was the first time they had mentioned the Ulsterman since David's arrival. David explained the whole story to his wife. How the envelope had been tagged and placed exactly as the Ulsterman had promised; how he had had to pace himself with the bags despite Charlie wanting to go faster; how he had thought he had been sussed out by Buster; and the problems of finding the right moment to put the envelope in the middle of the Ulsterman's kit-bag. 'But on the whole it was a piece of piss,' he laughed. 'Bruce should be getting the bags to him next week. I hope he thinks it was worth it. Come on, let's get the other bag done and then we can really relax.' David started sliding his hands up beneath his wife's dress and between her smooth thighs. 'I was rather hoping you might be in the mood for an early night because "I'm in the mood for love"!'

'Oh! So you think it's my turn for a little tickle then?' she teased, slapping her husband's hands away. 'You'll have to wait until I've counted every single little note.' She rubbed her nose against her husband's. He pushed her back playfully. 'Okay, let's get on with it then.'

David grabbed the second kit-bag and hauled it on to the bed while Denise stacked the rest of the money in the suitcases she had brought with her. One was for fivers, the other for ones. Suitcases, David had told her, were more secure than kit-bags and didn't attract as much attention in hotels.

The phone rang. It was reception. They wanted to know if David needed a reservation for dinner. He looked over at Denise and she confirmed they did.

'Throw us the key, then,' Denise said as she stood by the locked kit-bag. David fiddled in his pocket and chucked the keys across the room to his wife. She tried one key, then another. Most didn't even fit the lock and those that did wouldn't turn.

'Dave, I think I'm going to have to call on your talents. I can't get the lock to budge.' David crossed the room and took the keys.

'What's this, the helpless female act?' he teased. The moment he had the padlock in his hand he knew what was wrong. 'Bollocks!'

'What's happened?'

'They've taken the wrong fuckin' bag from the car, that's what's wrong. This fuckin' thing belongs to our Irish friend.' Both sat down and stared hard and long at the kit-bag which held centre stage on the king-sized bed. It was almost identical to David's except for the zip and fastening.

'Easy mistake to make, but what now?' Denise asked her husband softly.

'I don't know, but there's no going back, that much is for sure. If the bag's just full of money we should be all right, as there won't be too much difference between this bag and my bag, at least not that's going to worry any of us at this stage of the game. All we've got to hope is that this isn't the bag with the envelope. Got a nail file or a hair grip?'

Denise went to the bathroom and came back with both items, thoughtfully supplied by the hotel in its bathroom kit. She handed them to her husband, who had the padlock open in second. Something that never failed to impress her because, patient as she was, she could never master the right touch with locks. Free of the padlock, David started pulling blocks of money out of the kitbag and on to the bed. There it was. No needle in a haystack, just a large manila envelope surrounded by the fruits of the Great Train Robbery. 'Fuck!' David exclaimed for the umpteenth time since he had discovered the switch.

They needed to think, so David and Denise worked in silence as they bundled up the rest of the money. Their final total was close to £150,000, so the Ulsterman was going to be short-changed whatever the outcome. It was after four by the time they finally had all the money locked safely away in the closet. The envelope sat face up on a low glass coffee table, addressed simply to Mr W. Hardwood, Soho Square, London W.1.

Denise called room service and asked them to bring some tea up. They drank it in silence, but for once it was not because David was engrossed in the final results coming through on *Grandstand*. They checked the early evening news. The robbery was still the lead item. Police were talking about arrests to be made soon, but David's experience told him they were bluffing. They were working in the dark and he knew it. Secretly he had hoped to hear that the farm had been found after it had been burnt to the ground. Perhaps Buster's friends had been so good that the fire had not raised any suspicions and had only made a local news bulletin. The end of the news reminded David that he had to make a call to his new 'financial adviser'. He dialled a London number.

After apologizing for disturbing the recipient of the call at the weekend, David got down to the business of finding a safe home for his money.

'I am sure we can help, Mr Wood. As you appreciate we are not cheap, but we believe that we offer the best and most secure service. We have had no complaints so far.'

It had taken David nearly six months of courting to set up the 'bankers'. He had met them several times in London. They were not concerned where his money came from or how he got it. But they would take a healthy slice off the top for giving it a good clean. All through the courtship, David had assumed his new identity of Mr Wood. He had told them he was expecting a windfall in August which he wished to keep well away from the eyes of the Inland Revenue. He was concerned that, given the media coverage, the 'bankers' might link Mr Wood and his money to the Great Train Robbery.

'What do you estimate the final total of your deposit with us will be?' the voice from London asked in a clearly bored manner.

'I expect it to be approximately £140, 000 all of which I would like to bank with you.'

'Oh well!' the voice at the other end of the phone was suddenly very much alive. 'That, of course, should not be a problem. I assume we are talking pounds sterling? Our fee for that sum, as we discussed, will be

12.5 per cent for the first £100, 000 and 10 per cent after that. I take it as read that this is agreeable?' David was far from happy at handing over nearly twenty grand of his ill-gotten gains for banking services, but Denise had reassured him that it was a lot less than the tax he would have had to pay on earning such an amount legally.

'Would a meeting on Wednesday be to your satisfaction? If it is, I suggest you take the ferry over to the island on Monday morning. Take your car. It will be easier for you to transport the money that way and attract less attention. When you get to Douglas, drive down to Castletown. Close to Castletown you will see signs to the Golf Links Hotel. Call and make a reservation and plan to stay a week there. It will look as if you are touring in the island. My colleagues, led by Mr Richard Wright, whom you met in London, will meet you at the hotel for lunch on Wednesday. Oh, under what name will you be registering on the island, Mr Wood?'

'My own!' The question raised a smile on David's lips. Everything was going as well, if not better than planned. The only cloud on the horizon was the envelope which his wife had continued to play with throughout the phone call. After David had hung up, it was Denise who made the first move.

'David, let's just go over this one more time. As far as the world is concerned Mr and Mrs Jenkins no longer exist. We have simply disappeared from the map. Nobody knows we are here, not even our families. The bankers have no reason to link the Woods and Jenkinses, so what are we worried about? Let's open the envelope. Come on, you're dying to know what's in it. I am, I admit it . . . Look, if the worst comes to the worst, and the Ulsterman does track us down by some bizarre fluke we can give him his ten grand back and the envelope. What do you think?'

Denise made sense, a lot of sense, and David knew it. If they had covered their tracks as well as he liked to believe, they were away scot-free, at least as long as they didn't break any of their own rules and stuck to their original plan. Any attempt to contact anyone they knew, including Bruce or any of the other members of the gang, might put their liberty at risk. As if reading his mind, Denise added, 'It's not your fault that the Ulsterman never gave you a contact number. He should have trusted you more. So, Mr Jenkins, the only question remaining seems to be do you take the money or open the box?' She waved the envelope enticingly below his nose. David took a long, deep breath. 'Okay, D. Open her up, let's see what we've got.'

The couple sat side by side on the settee in front of the glass-topped coffee table. David reached across and pulled a knife from the tea trolley; he handed it to his wife, who inserted it through the side of the envelope. The contents were well protected in a further series of envelopes. They were surprised to find no paper, no letter, nothing that would give anyone a clue about to whom the package belonged. Finally Denise came to a leather pouch which was laced tightly shut. Her trembling hands pulled the laces apart and the contents spilled out on to the table. The gems, some fifty of them, rattled about on the glass top, some bouncing off on to the carpet. Denise gasped in awe and wonderment.

'Bugger me with a barge pole!' David exclaimed. 'No wonder that mean little Irish shit wanted to get his hands on these. There must be a small fortune here.'

'How much? How much?' Denise inquired as she ran her fingers through the sparkling gems – they clearly excited her far more than the cash had.

'I haven't a clue, pet, but if these are real then each one must be worth a small fortune. Don't think we'll need to worry about a pension plan. Fuck our little Irish friend. Diamonds, if that's what these little beauties are, aren't just a girl's best friend.'

The only thing that puzzled David and Denise, besides the stones' slightly strange pink colour, was why the diamonds had not been mentioned on the news. 'If they had been, that would have stirred a few people up. There would have been sixteen of you pointing the finger at one another and not a happy camper in sight,' Denise chuckled.

'Yeah, but only Charlie and I were in the cage,' David added on a serious note.

'True, my dear, but only you, our Irish friend and whoever put the jewels on the train knows that's where the diamonds were. Right?' At times he loved his wife's logic.

Chester, Sunday 11 August 1963

David explained to the front desk that he and his wife would be leaving early in the morning to go touring in the area but would be back in a week to continue house-hunting. He asked the hotel to look after some of their extra baggage while they were away and to keep a similar suite for them for their return.

Next morning the suitcases they needed were brought down and loaded into the car. The Jenkinses left around seven and had plenty of time to drive across to Liverpool and catch the morning ferry to the Isle of Man. Being early, they looked forward to a pleasant drive and if the weather held, a relatively calm crossing.

Maida Vale, Monday 12 August 1963

Thanks partly to their hangovers, it had taken Freddie and George the best part of Saturday afternoon and evening to check through their money. During the early planning Bruce had warned all of them of the need to go through their whack and destroy any notes that were in any way suspicious. Sunday the boys spent preparing to travel.

Freddie was still anxiously waiting to hear from Bruce as to what they should be doing with the Ulsterman's whack which sat inside the door to the attic in two almost identical kit-bags. He had no doubts as to what was going to happen to his and George's share. That was going over to George's Aunt Rose, Big Ernie's sister, who would be looking after it for them. Rose had many more contacts than the boys, she always had had. She knew the right people to clean, transfer and invest the money or anything else they might nick. Two full shares were a lot of money. More than she or any other member of the family could ever have dreamed of. She was proud of her nephew, he had done good and come a long way since nicking the lead off the church roof. Rose was pleased and relieved, however, that he would have Freddie to look after him on his travels. It was Rose who had persuaded them to leave the country until things quietened down after the robbery, although not even she had foreseen the amount of media coverage the robbery would attract.

Freddie and George called Rose from a phone-box across the road from the American Embassy. They had their visas and would be able to fly out to New York the following day. Rose was waiting for them in the house on their return. Her idea was that George's younger brother, Albert, would look after the house while they travelled so that if anyone came calling, there would be somebody on hand to make the explanations or even pretend to be George, if necessary. Rose had been working hard since the boys had called her. She had already set up the

New York connection to transfer the money and warned the boys again that they must not travel with too much money, as immigration officials were wont to ask embarrassing questions of those that did. 'Just enough for a US holiday,' she said. With George and Albert's help she loaded Ernie's van with the bags of money. 'What do you want me to do with those two?' she asked, pointing to the Ulsterman's kit-bags, which had also been brought down from the attic.

Freddie had no clear idea. 'I think you had better hang on to them for the time being, luv. They can't stay here, that's for sure. It's the dough of someone who worked on setting up the job. Bruce should have been in touch and relieved us of them by now, but nothing. Not a dicky bird.'

'Who is this bloke?' Rose asked.

'We dunno, the only thing we heard was Bruce referring to him as the Ulsterman. Beyond that, we know nothin',' George said.

'Not the fuckin' Ulsterman?!' Rose had heard of him and his reputation, which made her feel far less comfortable about baby-sitting his whack. 'Well, at least if he or Bruce come calling, Albi can tell them I've got the bags.'

Isle of Man, Tuesday 13 August 1963

The 'Woods' checked into the Golf Links Hotel around four on Monday afternoon. It was a pleasant and friendly place which seemed a million miles away from the worries the couple had faced in the run-up to the robbery. If the doctor had ordered, this would surely have been it.

By Tuesday morning they had confirmed with the hotel that they would be staying the week. They could not think of a nicer location to keep their heads down. David promised his wife that in time he might even consider taking up golf. A sport, he said, that befitted his new financial status in life. 'Oh my, ain't we posh!' Denise teased in a Cockney accent. 'I would have thought the old nags were more your style.'

With time to spare, David and Denise drove back up to Douglas to look at the island's capital. The visit was not just with sightseeing in mind. They were sure a town the size of Douglas, with a population of around 18,000, would have a good jeweller where they might get a valuation on one of the stones, which would then give them a rough idea of what their bonus catch was worth. Denise had selected a stone that was neither too large nor too small. It looked about average for their collection, all of which were a strange shade of pink. A shade she had not seen before in a diamond, and over the years she and David had handled their fair share of gems. 'What if it's junk jewellery?' she asked David.

'I don't think our Irish friend would have gone to so much trouble for a few bits of cut glass.'

Before looking for a jeweller, David slipped into a barber shop and, under Denise's supervision, made a few discreet changes to his appearance. At a neighbouring optician they purchased a pair of heavy horn-rimmed frames with plain glass. They explained themselves by saying they did amateur dramatics at home and David needed them for

110

a role he was playing. The glasses were the final touch and sufficiently broke the line of his face so that only his very best of friends, of which there were few, would recognize him.

'You'll have to be careful,' Denise whispered as they walked through Douglas. 'They might take you for Bruce! But you know, they are the business, they even make you look half intelligent.'

'You takin' the piss . . .'

It was not difficult to find a good jeweller in Douglas. At first the expert they had chosen seemed far from thrilled to be asked for a simple valuation, but as they spun out their story his manner changed rapidly. Mr Wood, he was told, had just returned from a business trip to South Africa where he had picked up a diamond for his wife for their wedding anniversary. They wanted a valuation for insurance purposes while they were visiting the island to consult their financial advisers. They were also looking for suggestions as to a suitable ring setting for the diamond. The jeweller spread his cloth on the glass-topped counter and invited Mrs Wood to place her diamond on it. Just from the man's initial reaction, David knew they had hit the jackpot.

'My . . . my . . . my . . .' the jeweller muttered under his breath. 'A very fine specimen indeed. Even on the island we don't see very many of this size, quality and colour. Very fine. The conventional brilliant cut of fifty-eight facets, which is good, but this exquisite pink colour makes it very rare, very rare indeed. Both the cut and the colour allow for a wide selection of settings, many of which will stand the test of time.'

'Exactly what is the significance of the colour?' Denise inquired. 'I thought diamonds were basically white?'

'Far from it, Mrs Wood. As I'm sure they told your husband in South Africa, diamonds can come in a variety of colours. After white, yellow, green and brown are relatively common, while the blues, reds, and pinks, such as your stone, and even greys, are unbelievably rare, even in Africa. Her Majesty the Queen has a number of extremely fine examples of pink diamonds, the most famous of which is probably the Williamson, given to her by the owner of the Williamson mine in Tanzania on the occasion of her wedding.'

David had already decided that of all the diamonds in their collection – a collection which was currently hidden in a giant jar of Ponds' cold cream located in the depths of Denise's suitcase – the one lying in front of them on the jeweller's cloth would be his wife's own. It had a special significance for them both. They chose a simple but classy setting, which the jeweller promised would be ready by Thursday along with a full valuation of the stone.

David was pleased he had taken the Ulsterman's £10,000. It allowed him the freedom to do as he wished without the temptation to dip into the unwashed money from the train. He had never intended to rip the Irishman off. Fate, that's what he put it down to. Perhaps Mr Green had met his match. He no longer feared the man he had met on the Hammersmith towpath. Money had made him strong and was making him stronger.

'Funny going into a jeweller and not lifting anything, isn't it?' Denise remarked matter-of-factly as they walked back to the car.

New York City,
Tuesday 13 August 1963

The flight to New York had been less of a hassle than either Freddie or George had imagined. Although there had been a noticeable police presence at London Airport, neither they nor their baggage had attracted any special attention. At New York's Idlewild Airport the only problem had been the queues to clear immigration. The two men treated themselves to a cab ride into Manhattan and found themselves checked into the Statler in plenty of time for an early dinner.

If the flight to New York aboard Pan Am's new Boeing 707 had been an eye-opener, it had been nothing compared to the impact the New York skyline, with its aptly named skyscrapers, made on them. The same could be said of the hemlines of the New York women.

'What goes up must come down, Freddie,' George joked as he stared out the cab window at a particularly shapely young lady in what at the time was an almost obscenely short skirt.

'The only thing that will be coming down when I get hold of the likes of her will be her knickers,' Freddie retorted. This was a town to party in and both men felt ready for it.

Isle of Man,
Wednesday 14 August 1963

The papers said all that needed to be said. 'One Big Clue', screamed one headline. Leatherslade Farm had been found seemingly unburnt.

'That crowd couldn't organize a piss-up in a brewery, I said so all along,' David called across to his wife in the bathroom. Despite the farm being found he still felt relatively comfortable. He had never taken his gloves off and even if they did discover that he had been involved they would have to find him first. He was beginning to like the feel of the island with its easy access to both the British and the Irish mainlands. 'Perhaps we should consider setting up shop here,' he shouted through to Denise.

'I'm sure there are worse places to spend our money,' she replied with a smile as she emerged into the room looking more glamorous and classy than ever and showing off one of the new outfits she had bought in Douglas the previous day. David's main concern was that his new bankers would not associate his sudden 'windfall' with the train robbery. If they did he was certain that their commission rate would rise. Then there would be the question of trust.

The phone in the room rang just before one. The bankers had arrived. They found a quiet table overlooking the golf course and got down to business over lunch. The bankers would relieve him of his money and within the week the balance would be credited to accounts at a number of banks on the island and other international tax havens.

'It's just as if you had a British bank account, but safer,' one of the two bankers explained. 'You can use the cheques as freely on the mainland as you can here on the island. If you wish to make large cash withdrawals, however, say in excess of £1000, I suggest you contact us first and we will handle it for you. It attracts less attention. As you have been told our fee is 12.5 per cent of your first £100,000 investment and 10 per cent on the rest. We also charge a further 7.5 per cent commission on any profits we make for you through our investment funds, assuming you want us to handle that side of the business. Believe me, Mr and Mrs Wood, if you let us play the markets with only a small fraction of your capital, we can make it multiply, and very rapidly. Commodities, shares – there are a wealth of options which this volume of money can buy into and without raising an eyebrow or attracting any unwelcome attention.'

'Diamonds!' Denise suggested with half a smile.

'A fine investment, Mrs Wood, at the right price and over the long term. But think about stocks and shares. With the correct information it is like being able to bet on a race when you already know who the winner will be. The right information in the right hands is today's hard currency. Information, more than cash, is power, although it is the initial cash that buys that information. The market, Mr and Mrs Wood, is totally impartial – unless you have information. But as Thomas Fuller once wrote, "Send a fool to the market and a fool he'll return."'

Business done, the four got down to enjoying their lunch. Not surprisingly, the conversation eventually turned to the Great Train Robbery. David was amazed how easily he and Denise kept their cool and were able to discuss the event as detached outsiders. Everyone around the table had their own theory as to who was behind the robbery and where they were now. All had great admiration for the gang.

'If they've found the hide-out, though, you can be sure that arrests will be made before close of business today. Unless, of course, they were really good and careful,' Richard Wright suggested. David managed a weak smile before taking the men out to the car park where the bags were transferred. Everything was done on trust. The bankers did not insist on counting the money. They would do that later in the privacy and safety of their own office. They were happy to accept Wood's word for the moment that it was £145,000, of which £17,000 would stick to them in the wash. They would return on Friday with the account details and the first temporary cheque books. They all agreed that it had been a most fruitful lunch.

That night on the news, David and Denise heard what they feared most. The first arrests had indeed been made. Roger had been taken in Bournemouth along with one William Boal.

'Who the fuck is William Boal?' David exclaimed as he watched the news. 'There weren't any William Boal on the job. They're making it up as they go along.' Considering their worries, both David and Denise slept surprisingly soundly.

Isle of Man,
Thursday 15 August 1963

The next morning the Jenkinses headed back into Douglas to pick up the ring. This time they received a right royal welcome and discovered that one of the jeweller's London partners had flown over especially to the island to meet them and see the diamond, a stone which they had valued at 'around £50,000' – enough to buy at least ten of the three-bedroomed semi-detached houses in which they had resided prior to the robbery.

David and Denise had carefully checked over the other forty-eight gemstones and come to the conclusion that all were of a similar size and shade of pink. If the jeweller had done his sums right they were sitting on gems that were worth more than the entire haul of the train robbery in money terms. Roughly £2.5 million.

'A most magnificent stone, Mr Wood,' the London jeweller gushed. 'It really is remarkably rare to see such a fine pink specimen. You obviously have an eye for the very best.'

David pinched Denise's thigh and smiled. Rare was good, but not so rare as to attract too much notice. A lucrative haul the Jenkinses certainly had, but one that would need to be carefully nurtured if they did not want to draw attention to themselves.

'So you reckon that when I find myself back in Jo'burg I should pick up another half-dozen or so?' David joked.

'Joking aside, Mr Wood,' the London jeweller said, peering over his half-moon glasses, 'depending on what you have to pay and how you manage to get the diamonds back into this country, there are far worse investments to be made. I, for example, could certainly take two or three of this size and colour off your hands, for clients both here on the island and back in London, and no questions asked.'

Chester, Thursday 22 August 1963

I f David had had any doubts before the delivery of the morning
papers, he had no more. Staring out at him from the front page
of the morning papers were the names, descriptions and photos of
five wanted men – Bruce, Buster, Charlie, Roy and Jimmy. The shit
had well and truly hit the fan.

David and Denise had returned to Chester on Monday 19 August,
since when they had been weighing up the pros and cons of settling
in Chester, Liverpool or the Isle of Man. From conversations with
the 'bankers' and the jewellers, the Isle of Man, with its easy escape
routes, was beginning to look an increasingly attractive option. David
also liked the idea of joining forces with the bankers on their own turf
to exploit the information they were receiving from their London office.
At the Friday meeting they had outlined in more detail how the scheme
would work and the possible rewards. No one had ever been caught,
they assured him, in fact it was still not clear if an individual operating
on inside information was even breaking the law.

Denise had no doubts. The island was the place for her, at least until
the dust settled, something she now realized, given the enormity of the
crime and the press interest, might take several years. Strangely, neither
discussed the Ulsterman. It was as if the incident was a closed book.
The diamonds were theirs. It was that simple. David had a sneaking
feeling that his new business colleagues and the island's jewellers might
even find a lucrative market for his diamond collection. The Jenkinses
were getting used to the idea of being a couple of plenty, and they were
enjoying it.

David told the assistant manager of the Grosvenor that because of
the location of his new office, he and his wife had chosen a house
in the Manchester area. They had received the keys and would be
moving in on the following Monday. Sunday would be their last night
at the hotel. In truth, they would cross back over to the Isle of Man

118

from Liverpool on Monday morning, by which time the bankers would have arranged temporary accommodation for them until they found a house that befitted their new financial status. They had decided to live in Douglas at first, as being Londoners they still wanted to feel the hustle and bustle of city life, even if it would be at Douglas's more limited and sedate pace.

London, Friday 23 August 1963

'I believe it is now only a question of time until we have most of the men in question behind bars,' Sir Roger announced to his faceless colleagues. 'The Yard informs me that they picked up one Charles Wilson yesterday morning, hours before his picture was featured in the morning papers. Other arrests are expected to follow in the next few days; in fact the police told me less than an hour ago that a number of other suspects are being questioned at this very moment and they will be deciding later today if they are ready to press charges or not.'

'And the diamonds?'

'Vanished, I'm afraid, like some of the members of the gang. The difficulty is we still don't know exactly how many people we are looking for, or who. It could be anything from fourteen to twenty or more, and that's not counting the ones that were not at the track. For us, the most plausible scenario is that only one or two members of the gang, at most, got hold of the diamonds and the rest don't even know of their existence. We also still cannot rule out the possibility that one of the five post-office sorters has the envelope. We have them all under surveillance, so we will soon know if any of them do.'

'What about our South African friends?'

'I have spoken to them and took the liberty of saying that we had received the package safely. Obviously they had heard about the robbery and were concerned that the envelope might have been on the train. I decided a little white lie was in order, but took the opportunity to request a full description of each of the fifty diamonds. Something they have on record which should be with us by Tuesday. Their account has been credited with the agreed amount?'

'Can we know the value?'

'Approximately three million pounds, I regret to report.'

Liverpool, Friday 23 August 1963

No news was good news for some, but not for the Ulsterman, who was looking for the answers to a series of unanswered questions. Initially he had bided his time. It was the safest thing to do. But the call from Bruce never came and it was now over two weeks since the robbery. As he sat and waited he read in the press and heard on the radio about the discovery of the farm, where the gang were meant to have stayed for at least a week; the arrest of Roger; and more recently the arrest of Charlie. He had even heard through his network of informers that the police had other members of the gang in for questioning, and quite separately had stumbled across a bag full of money in the woods close to Dorking. He only hoped the money and the bag weren't his.

The fact that the diamonds had not been mentioned in the press puzzled the Ulsterman. He wondered if Jenkins had managed to get his hands on them or had had to leave them on the train after all. Much was at stake, so he sent his shadow, Patrick Green, around to Jenkins' house in west London to find out the answers to at least some of his questions. He wanted justice, but most of all he wanted his diamonds.

The Ulsterman was sitting in a Liverpool hotel room – not eighteen miles from where David and Denise were enjoying a slap-up meal in the main restaurant of the Grosvenor. He waited for the call. He hoped it would come soon because he had to get down to the hotel ballroom for yet another mind-numbing function, but one which might bring him information. Information and contacts were his stock-in-trade, so he would attend.

The phone rang. 'The news is not good.' The voice was Green's. 'I have been calling Jenkins' number for the last two days without any luck. Today, I went round and the door was opened by a woman who says she has never met the Jenkinses and only knows of them from the mail that arrives at the house. She moved in last week. From what I

121

can discover, the Jenkinses moved out of the house at the end of July and simply disappeared. The estate agent was not bothered as they were up to date with their rent and even paid a month extra to break their contract. They said they were moving abroad. They also left an extra fifty pounds with him to cover the bills for gas, electricity and so on and as he realized it was more than enough to cover the outstanding items, he wasn't about to complain or ask questions.'

'And their families?'

'If they are telling the truth, they are just as much in the dark as we are. I spoke to Jenkins' mother, who has not heard from him in over a month and seemed genuinely concerned and upset when I told her they had moved away from Shepherds Bush.'

The Ulsterman was silent at his end of the line. He knew by reputation that David was good, which was why he had chosen him in the first place. He could drop his name to his police contacts, but that might be unfair and why should he imagine that the police would have any more luck in tracking him down than the Ulsterman and his associates were having? David may have done everything expected of him and simply be covering his tracks, as he himself had suggested. The last thing the Ulsterman wanted was the blood of an innocent man on his hands. 'Stay on the case and see what you can find out, but don't do anything that might attract attention. Bruce's name and picture is all over the papers. We must keep our distance and wait for him to make contact. He will know when it's safe.'

London, Sunday 25 August 1963

B ruce called from a phone-box. In the circumstances he could not be too careful, even with the Ulsterman. The money, he assured his Irish friend, was in safe hands and could be picked up at any time from Birch and Rawlings. He gave the Ulsterman their address and admitted that he had been having trouble getting through to the boys. He would have gone round to the house himself, but he had to keep off the streets. He promised to call the Ulsterman at the end of the week, if he got the chance, to confirm that everything had gone okay.

The Ulsterman trusted Bruce. He admired his skills as a thief. He also liked him as a man. He was happy that Bruce knew nothing about the diamonds and was almost sorry that he had not cut him in on the deal. That was it, then – either the diamonds were with Birch and Rawlings, or he would have to go in search of Jenkins.

New York City,
Tuesday 27 August 1963

F reddie and George had been in New York for two weeks and they loved it. The city was everything they had been promised and more. The same could be said about the women.

New York seemed light years away from London, Leatherslade Farm and the rest. The Great Train Robbery was not even a major story in New York, the locals preferring the goings on of their young president, John Fitzgerald Kennedy, and his family.

It was another Kennedy, Desmond Kennedy, who was their contact in the Big Apple. Kennedy, who had been born across the water in New Jersey, where he still lived, had a small office close to the Empire State Building and a short walk from their hotel. He would supply the boys with enough cash to survive their day-to-day activities, as well as a few pointers as to where to find the best bars and clubs to pick up girls. He had moved Freddie and George out of the Statler after four days. He did not like the idea that they had made the reservations in London. It made them traceable. He chose instead a small, non-descript hostelry which he had used in the past as a safe house. He would have been unhappy to hear that one of his charges had gone straight back to the Statler and rebooked a room. Freddie had decided that if he was going to be entertaining New York skirt he wanted to do it with a bit of style. The hostelry would be plenty good enough for George and his dates.

Kennedy did not ask what the boys were running from or why. Not only was it none of his business, he also knew better than to ask. Considering the people he had looked after in the past, it helped him sleep a little better at night. He normally only discovered who his clients had been once they had been arrested and their pictures were splashed over the front pages of the British tabloids. Kennedy's job, as he saw it, was simple. He reacted to the requests that came out of London, nothing more, nothing less. The news from London suggested his boys were a very hot property with lots of money to burn. His contacts said they might be looking for some work or at the very least a few investment opportunities while in the US.

Human nature being what it is, Freddie and George kept an eye out for the British papers. Their American counterparts, they had discovered, were as alien as anything they had seen in a foreign language on the continent. They were all about sports the boys did not understand and people they had never heard of. It had been over the weekend that they first saw the British papers with the photos of Bruce, Charlie and Jimmy staring out at them. They read as many different reports as they could find; none suggested that the police knew exactly how many people were involved in the robbery or, more importantly, who. But if some of the key names, such as Bruce and Charlie, were known, it might only be a matter of time before the police put together the names of the rest of the gang members. Freddie and George, like David, were disappointed to discover that the farm had not been burnt to the ground, as had been promised and paid for. They felt betrayed and at the same time relieved that they had not removed their gloves while at the farm. Yet if somebody squealed or did a deal, it would all be in vain. Most of the lads they would have trusted with their lives. But what about the ones they hardly knew? Still, if Bruce had chosen them, they reassured one another, they must have been all right.

By the Monday, Freddie and George had decided that it might be better to move on than stay put in New York, where there was an outside chance they might be traced. They went to Kennedy, who promised them answers by Tuesday.

Kennedy's solution was for the boys to move west. He would organize a good car for them, a route and a list of contacts. He would also, for a price, supply fake documentation so that they needn't use their real names or passports as a means of identification. This would be vital if they wanted to disappear and still be able to receive the money which he would wire to them along the route. If they took their time as they crossed the US, he would try to come up with some more long-term solutions by the time they hit the west coast. Until then, they should take their time, enjoy America and disappear. He also reminded them that as of 1 October, when their entry visas ran out, they would be classified as illegal immigrants and a warrant would be put out for their arrest and subsequent deportation.

Maida Vale,
Wednesday 28 August 1963

'All right, all right, I heard you the first fuckin' time. No need to knock the door down!' Albert Rawlings wiped the sleep from his eyes and in just his underpants staggered down the stairs and towards the front door. Unlike the rest of the family, Albi had kept himself relatively clean with the law. He was tough, like his big brother George, but had preferred to put his strength to use on the building sites of London, where he made good money as a hod-carrier. He was well liked by his mates and happy that, unlike the rest of the family, he was not always looking over his shoulder to see who was coming up from behind.

Albi did not think twice, he just undid the latch and started to open the door. It was all that was needed. The sheer inward force threw even his immense frame up the hallway. Before he had had a chance to recover he was bundled over and into the lounge and a knee firmly placed on his chest. As his focus cleared he did not have to be Sherlock Holmes to recognize that he was staring up at the barrel of a gun.

'How've you been, Georgie boy?' The question came from a hooded Patrick Green. Green was not alone: besides the man pinning him to the floor, who was also hooded, Albi could hear at least two others going through the house.

'Now, Georgie, if you had been a good boy and answered the phone like you're supposed to, I would not have had to come around here at this 'orribly early hour to disturb your beauty sleep and God knows you need it. Now I hear that you and that little darkie friend of yours have something here that belongs to me. Well, at least you had better have, if you want to enjoy the rest of the day.'

'All clear, no sign of Birch or anyone else in the house,' one of Green's sidekicks reported.

127

'Get him on the sofa, but if he makes so much as a squeak give him a smack,' Green instructed. Albi did not scare easily, but these guys were heavy, even by his family's standards.

'Start talking, Georgie boy, talk . . .'

'You're making a big mistake, sir, I ain't George, I'm his brother, Albert. George is travelling.'

'Travelling where?'

'Dunno, but I think my Auntie Rose might know. I can give her a bell if you like.' Albi had been told that people might come calling for George and Freddie and if it was not Old Bill he should co-operate and call his aunt.

'So you ring out but you don't answer, is that it? Now if your brother left you baby-sittin' this house, how come he didn't leave you looking after a couple of bags for me?'

'You'll have to ask my auntie about that. I don't know nothin' about no bags and that's the truth.'

'Well, isn't that sweet? All right, let's get your auntie over, then. That'll be old Rose, won't it, Ernie Rawlings' sister?'

'Yeah, that's right. Rose is my aunt and Ernie's my dad.'

'All right, let's get her over then, but no funny stuff. I just hope you haven't been telling porkies, young man. Nothing like a few porky pies to get my back up.'

Rose was already awake when Albi called. She had always been an early riser. Having reassured her nephew to sit tight and not to worry, she grabbed her hat and coat and in less than fifteen minutes was over at George's house. She blew into the house like a ship under full sail.

'What the fuck's goin' on in here and who the fuck are you?' she said as she advanced on the man with the gun. Green had never witnessed anything like Rose in full flight and before he could do or say anything his henchman, Terry, had given the old girl a hard slap around the chops which sent her dentures and glasses flying across the room. Albert went to react, but heard the gun cock behind his left ear.

'All right, all right, calm down, Terry! Everyone calm down,' Green cried, putting up his arm to cool the situation. 'Nobody needs to get hurt and we don't need your insults either, missus. Get your teeth and glasses, before you frighten me and my boys to death. We're just here to pick up a couple of bags that belong to us, and believe me you're not one of them. Okay?'

'So you must be the Ulsterman,' Rose replied as she got to her feet, wiping the blood from the corner of her mouth. 'You should keep these animals of yours on a leash. I'll have that fucker you called Terry taken apart for slappin' me about.'

'Now would you be making threats again, lady?' Terry asked.

'I don't make threats, young man. I state the facts, so watch your step. You don't fuckin' frighten me. I was cracking heads on the streets of London when you were still in nappies in Belfast. Now whoever is in charge of this shower had better state his business and then get the fuck of out of my nephew's house if you know what's good for you.'

'As I said, Rose, that is your name, isn't it? . . . We came for the bags,' Green began, 'the bags your nephew George and that creepy little mate of his with the touch of the tar brush, Birch, so kindly brought here up for us.'

'Now you don't honestly expect with my family's reputation with Old Bill that we would be daft enough to leave the fuckin' bags hanging around in here, do ya?' Rose hissed. 'I'll have to have'em collected and delivered to you. Name a place and I'll get 'em to you.'

'It's an offer I find hard to refuse, Rose, but I'm here to collect now. So while we sit here entertaining Albert, you can go off and get the bags. If you need a lift, one of my lads will drive you, but we ain't leavin' and neither is this young man until I have my bags.' Green emphasized the point by giving Albert a slap around the top of the head.

It took Rose forty-five nerve-racking minutes with one of Green's minders to get the bags. When she got back there was no sign of Albert. Green had removed him for safe-keeping. 'Albert's safe and sound for the moment. I just wanted a little insurance in case you decided to get cute. Now bring the bags in and then you can sit down and have a nice cuppa, there should be one in the pot, while I check 'em out. This can all be done in a civilized manner, if you'll just guard your tongue,' Green said.

Green recognized only one of the bags before him in the hall. He had personally bought the two bags at the Co-op, so he knew that they should have been identical. These two weren't. A small difference between them, but a difference all the same. He went back to the lounge.

'Rose, we seem to have a little problem which you might be able to resolve for me. You see, one of those bags is not the bag I'm looking for. Any thoughts on the matter?' With that Terry grabbed her hair from behind and pulled her head back roughly. She screamed in pain.

'None, you miserable Irish bastard. Those are the bags that George and Freddie gave me. Those are the bags they brought here after the job. I swear on my old mother's head.'

'From what I hear your mother doesn't have much use for her head, but Albert's will do. Get the boy.' They bundled Albi into the lounge. They had kept him upstairs with a gun pressed to his head. Albi was ashen white. He had heard the conversation from the upstairs landing and he didn't like violence, despite his size. 'Who knows, you might just be telling the truth, Rose, but I suggest you go home and have a good look for that other bag . . .'

'I've seen George and Freddie's bags, for Christ's sake, and they're not even similar,' she interrupted.

'I would like you to take another look all the same,' the Irishman added calmly. 'Until then, Albert is coming for a little drive with us and if everything in the bags tallies then he should be on the building site by lunchtime. Now, how do I contact you, or don't you answer your phone either?'

'Keep Albi out of this,' she whispered to Green, trying to pull him closer to her. 'He ain't got nothin' to do with it. I'll write my number down and you can call me when you want, but those are the only bags we got. Perhaps they got switched at the farm. I don't know. Honest . . .'

'Honest! What do you know about being honest, Rose?' Green said, pushing the woman away from him. 'Sure, you don't even know what the word means. Perhaps you should ask George and Freddie what they did with the bag. Perhaps they took it with them on their little trip,' Green sneered. He was almost starting to feel sorry for the old bitch, who by now was showing signs of suffering from her ordeal. Yet he could not afford the luxury of displaying any weakness in front of his men, especially Terry, who he knew was itching to rise up within the ranks of their organization. He knew the boss was already on intimate terms with Terry and even accepted his calls. The boss would never tolerate any slip-ups through weakness. 'Never trust anyone, not even yourself' and 'Do unto others before they do unto you first', he used to tell Green, were his favourite mottoes.

'George and Freddie are travelling and it will be some time till I can get a message to them, but you've got my number and you know where to find me, so have a heart, let the boy go.'

'A heart, missus!? Forget heart. You might try prayer. It's up to you, Rose. I want my bag. Let's go, lads. That means you, too, Albi.'

'But how do I find you?' Rose implored.

'You don't. We find you. Got a problem with that? You see, Rose, you've got a reputation and I don't believe you got it by chance.' Green turned on his heel and was gone. Rose slumped in the chair and cried for the first time in as long as she could remember.

'Oh, boys! What have you gone and done this time?' she choked.

It did not take Green and his boys long to get back to a safe house in Chiswick. Albert had been blindfolded and made to lie across the floor in the back of the car where heavy feet held him down as a reminder not to be too clever. Not that there was anything he could do. He cursed his brother and the rest of his family for their crooked ways.

The bags were full of money. That was the very least Green had expected. But there was no sign of 'the' envelope. There was an envelope, but all it contained was a tartan Tam-o'-Shanter which seemed totally out of place amid all the cash. 'If Rose is takin' the piss with this,' he said waving the bonnet, 'I'll have her guts for boot laces.' Green took a deep breath and dialled the Ulsterman. 'We've got problems, I'm afraid. No package. It looks as if the bags have been switched at some stage, because even the money is going to come up short. Looks to be about 140K or thereabouts.'

'And what about the old crone?' the Ulsterman asked in controlled tones.

'If I was a betting man I would say the crafty old bitch is telling the truth. She really didn't seem to know what was going on. I'll keep the pressure on her for the rest of the day.'

'You should also take care, Pat, she's a vindictive old harpy and she may not take too kindly to the rough stuff. Some of her family, especially that brother of hers, Ernie, have a very nasty streak when cornered. We don't want to start a war with these people. So what are our options?'

'Two come to mind, sir. Either George and Freddie found the package and have done a bunk. We are trying to trace their whereabouts now. The second option is our friend Jenkins did a double-cross and has walked off with the jewels. Neither option is terribly reassuring.'

'Any other possibilities?'

'There are. The package could have missed the train . . .'

'You can rule that out. The real owners are very agitated and are starting to turn things over. They are certain the envelope went on to the train in Glasgow and was missing by the time the police got to the scene of the crime . . .'

'Then it might be that another member of the gang grabbed the package . . .'

'See if you can get anything else out of the old woman. Let her bleed a bit. But for Christ's sake, don't let her get a sniff of what we are looking for. Then see if you can get a lead on Jenkins: he seems most likely to be our man. At the moment he is the only one who can clarify this matter once and for all. A matter, I might say, which is starting to leave an extremely unpleasant taste in my mouth.'

Green told his men to go and drop Albert off. He wanted to be alone when he talked to Rose. He found her at the number she had given him. He started by apologizing for the rough treatment she had received earlier in the day and turned on the charm. 'You'll be pleased to know that we're inclined to believe your story, Rose,' he continued, 'so I am going to ask you to do me a little favour, a favour which I will be very disappointed if you can't fulfil. You see, those bags were very special to us, for a number of reasons which I won't bore you with right now. I want you to check with George why they were switched, where and when. I'm certain there is a quite innocent and harmless explanation for all of this.' Green's disarming manner surprised Rose. Whatever he was looking for was obviously extremely important to him. She promised to talk to the boys and asked Green to call her on Sunday morning.

'Where's Albi?' she inquired nervously.

'Don't you worry about Albert, Rose. He'll be back on the site as we talk. He's a good boy, Rose, you should be proud of him. Speak to you Sunday. Now don't disappoint me.'

London/New York,
Saturday 31 August 1963

It took Rose three full days to get the message through to New York that she needed to talk to Freddie. Kennedy set the call up in one of the offices he looked after in the Empire State Building. Saturday meant there was sufficient movement in the building not to arouse suspicion, but the only people in the office itself were a team of cleaners who worked for Kennedy. Kennedy asked George to stay back at the hotel. His sheer size turned heads, while his dress sense screamed 'Britain' in fashionable New York. Freddie was much better at blending in and adapting to his surroundings.

Rose cut Freddie's small talk short and went straight to the point. 'Tell me the truth, Freddie, did you and George take something that didn't belong to you? I've been visited by some Paddies who roughed me up looking for a package. They weren't messing about. They're pissed at someone.'

'Hold on, Rose, you've lost me.' Rose explained to Freddie what had happened earlier in the week. The visit of the Irishmen and the threats and violence. The questions about the bags and the package. 'Been roughed up?' Freddie interrupted. 'Who's been roughing you up, luv? George'll do his nut when I tell him. This sounds naughty, Rose, if there was something from that business that we didn't know about. I wonder what it is and who stepped out of line. I'm sure it's not Bruce.'

'Forget all that, Freddie. They want their package and they mean business,' Rose interrupted.

'Bingo, Rose!' For Freddie the penny had dropped. 'Remember I told you how George got home by train and David dropped me off at the house? In the car we had the bags for me and George, plus David's and the Paddy's. That could mean that Dave took the wrong bags by mistake, including the bag they're look-ing for.'

'How do we find this David? What manor's he off?'

'Don't know for sure. He was a bit of a dark horse. Kept to himself. Only Bruce would know where to find him, but don't go sticking your neck out any more, you've already done enough. And don't you worry, we'll even the score with these Irish slags when we get back. We'll be movin' on soon, so you look after yourself. We'll give you a call from down the road.'

When Freddie told George what had happened to his aunt he was fit to be tied. He was all for flying back to London on the next plane to even the score then and there. Freddie had to assure him that that was not what Rose wanted. They called Kennedy and told him to speed up the paperwork.

London, Sunday 1 September 1963

Green hated calling the Ulsterman at home, but had no option. His wife answered, which was a rarity in itself. The Ulsterman transferred the call to his study.

'Speak!'

'I've just come off the phone to Rose. She says that Birch was dropped off at the house with the bags by David. I assume we're talking about our David Jenkins, but she didn't have a last name. Apparently the car Jenkins was driving transported both Birch and Rawlings' whacks, plus David's and ours.'

'Ours?'

'I mean yours, of course, sir. It seems in the unloading the bags got switched and Jenkins drove off with the wrong bag. The problem is, he's disappeared and we don't know where to find him.'

'I suggest you start looking and don't rest until you do. Are you certain that the old girl is telling the truth?'

'As much as you can ever be with that woman. She's a crafty old bitch and kept wanting to know what was missing, but I told her she should forget that we had ever met, just as I was going to forget that her nephew and Birch ever had anything to do with the train robbery. I think she got the message.'

'If you find she is talking to people, you should send Terry round to shut her up. Did she say where her nephew was?'

'Not in so many words, but I don't think it was Europe. My money would be on Canada or the US.'

'Why?'

'Just a hunch.'

'Well, your hunches are normally good enough for me, so let's see if you can have another one and find Jenkins.'

'Good as done, sir.'

New York City,
Friday 6 September 1963

I t took Kennedy over a week to get all the papers in order, in which time there were more arrests in England, including that of Ronnie Biggs. Kennedy had offered the boys various options as far as their papers went. They wanted the best that money could buy, papers which showed they were US residents rather than tourists. The only sticking point was whether they should be forgeries or the real thing. The price tag was steep. £1,000 for each forgery or £2,000 for the real thing. Freddie and George decided to go with forgeries for the time being – they could always upgrade later if they decided to stay. Freddie was to become Mr Statler, in honour of their hotel, and George Mr Sullivan, after Ed Sullivan, whose shows they had been enjoying on television. These were names they were not likely to forget. By the end of the first week of September, Freddie Statler and George Sullivan were ready to motor.

Whitehall, Monday 9 September 1963

'It's been a month, William!'

'I'm well aware of that, Sir Roger, but everywhere we turn we run into a dead end. Scotland Yard have been doing quite well on the robbery, however. They've already booked five of the gang and I'm promised that at least five further arrests will follow in the next ten days or so. From the statements taken from those already charged, there is no mention of the diamonds, not that any of them is admitting even to taking part in the robbery at this stage. Trebbin's promised to keep me advised if anything emerges. He is also putting together a bulletin to go out, subject to our approval, which will set the alarm bells ringing if the diamonds start to turn up. Apparently being pink they will be extremely difficult to fence, but then again being so valuable a lot of jewellers aren't going to be interested in asking questions. The customer is always right, and all that.'

'So are senior civil servants, William, and government employees, for that matter,' Sir Roger replied caustically. 'I'm going to have to ask you to back off from questioning the people on our list who knew that the diamonds or the money were on the train. I've been getting a few complaints from high levels. I don't like it any more than you do, but some of these people have the Prime Minister's ear and might just want to let slip what we were up to. Personally I don't fancy ending my days pushing papers around a desk in Glasgow or somewhere like that, so be discreet if you can, William.'

'I'll try. Will that be all, sir?'

'For the moment, yes. Except, William, this is now your baby. I want the team working on the recovery of the diamonds cut to a minimum. It looks like a straight theft. Nothing menacing or threatening to the security of the nation in that. Sadly we need to get back to the work in hand – keep an eye on those "reds under the bed" and all that. And let's face it, the way the present government is going, those reds could be our next lords and masters. That would put the cat firmly amongst the pigeons in the corridors of power. I wonder who we will be asked to spy on next? The Americans, no doubt!'

Isle of Man, October 1963

D avid and Denise had been amazed at how easy it was to complete their move over to the island. Their main banking contact, Richard Wright, had helped oil the wheels and had set them up in a small and comfortable town house in the heart of Douglas, just behind the Gaiety Theatre. Almost everything they needed was within walking distance.

In the first week, David cashed in one of the smaller diamonds with the jeweller. It netted around £40,000, which he deposited with the Isle of Man Bank. He and Denise had decided that they needed to have at least one bank account outside the control of their bankers as an insurance policy and, as this was a legitimate transaction, it raised few eyebrows. The longer that passed before he touched the train robbery money, the better he felt.

From the island, David and Denise monitored the police campaign. They watched as one by one the gang members were rounded up and charged. David could not believe that so many of them had been so careless and, despite the warnings, had made no preparation as to what they would do after the robbery. It came as no surprise to the Jenkinses that nobody had collared Bruce, Buster, Jimmy or Roy. It was a blow, however, when Gordon was nicked on 3 October.

As David and Denise had cut themselves off completely from their past lives, they had no way of knowing if anyone was looking for them or if they were even on the police's list of missing suspects. Given their clear run to date, they could not see any earthly reason why they should be.

'You came at a good time,' Wright told them over coffee one morning. 'You arrived when the island was still in season, so nobody took any notice of a couple of new faces. They assumed you were just here for the holidays. Now the season is winding down you are already known faces and accepted into Douglas life. Although you will never be Manx, like me, and you'll be a come-over for many years to come, you did the move without raising too many eyebrows and I get the feeling that's what you wanted?' David and Denise nodded their approval.

Denise was already in seventh heaven. Not having money worries. Being able to eat out in posh restaurants and not think about the bill. Old Bill or otherwise. David for his part was getting into his new role as a financial wheeler-dealer. He instructed the bankers to take it easy at first. He had heard many horror stories in London and while he trusted his people implicitly, he wanted to make sure he could walk before he started to run. He appreciated Wright's patience. The banker called on them nearly every day to show David what the recommendations would be and then how they fared. By the end of October, David gave the word. It was full steam ahead on the investment front. 'A very sensible decision,' Wright had said. 'As Jane Austen once wrote: "A large income is the best recipe for happiness I ever heard of." If she's right, and I believe she is, I think you and your wife are going to be very, very happy with us on the island.'

David also signed a lease for six months on the house, for while they were not certain they wanted to buy a house in the centre of Douglas, they knew that until the spring it would be the safest place for them to hide out. They would keep a low profile as long as the Great Train Robbery remained a high-profile case.

Wyoming, November 1963

Freddie and George got a tremendous kick out of being in the Wild West. Throughout their childhoods they had spent time sneaking into their local flea-pits by the back door to watch the latest westerns coming out of America, yet never once, even in their wildest dreams, had they imagined being there in person. The 'flicks', at the time, had been one of the very few breaks from the drab and dreary existence that was post-war London.

As they cruised along the modern American highways, George studied the maps that Desmond Kennedy had given them in New York. He saw many a name which tickled the imagination, but nothing pleased him as much as spotting a town called Rawlins on a map of Wyoming. 'Nice one! They've named a fuckin' town after my family!' he exclaimed to Freddie, who was driving.

They had enjoyed their slow trek west for nearly two months. From New York they had driven down to Philadelphia and then across to Pittsburgh, Cleveland, Toledo and on to Chicago, where they had spent ten days in open-mouthed wonder. Kennedy had told them to stay in motels along the route, but when they wanted a break to take it in the big centres of population, where they would attract less attention. He was still worried about how George stuck out, even in a crowd.

Chicago had been an attraction in itself for the boys. The ultimate gangster town. From Chicago they continued their journey of discovery on through Illinois and Iowa and were now crossing from Nebraska into Wyoming.

'Come on, Freddie, we got to stop at Rawlins and send a few postcards. One to Auntie Rose and the old man at least. They'll get a real kick out of it,' George pressed.

'All right, but only if you sign them from Gertrude and Daisy.' Balancing the map on the steering wheel, Freddie let his eyes skim

141

along their route. 'And that's Rawlins, R-A-W-L-I-N-S, not Rawlings, R-A-W-L-I-N-G-S, you dickhead.'

'So they dropped the G, what of it? You're always dropping your Gs, ain't ya, and I don't have a go about that. Maybe the Septics are smarter than me and you. They got rid of a U in colour, didn't they and they spell centre like it sounds? Anyway, all you got was some bloody pot plant named after you.'

'Pot plant my arse! Birch is a fuckin' tree. A nice-lookin' tree at that. Like me!'

Freddie and George drove into Rawlins on Tuesday 19 November and set themselves up in one of the town's more comfortable motels, close to what looked to be the centre of all the action. They had grown to appreciate the simplicity of US motel life and – knowing what crooks could get up to – were always happy at being able to keep an eye on their car from the window of their room. The car had come to represent, more than anything else, their freedom.

A hundred and fifteen miles north-west of Laramie, Rawlins was a friendly town of a little under 10,000 inhabitants. The only damper to the boys' spirits was that Rawlins was home to the Wyoming State Penitentiary and the imposing Carbon County Courthouse. They were acutely aware that most of their fellow thieves from the job were now biding their time at Her Majesty's pleasure in Aylesbury Prison, awaiting the start of the trial which, rumour had it would finally get underway some time early in the new year.

Despite the grim reminders, Freddie and George decided to pass the weekend in the town before continuing west. Friday was a crisp and clear day and George got to buy his postcards. Freddie was happy to see a smile on George's face – George had not made the adjustment to the American way of life as easily as Freddie had hoped. George found America distinctly 'foreign' and a complete culture shock on top of that. He missed his home comforts and often went on about it, much to Freddie's annoyance. If it wasn't the bacon it was the brown sauce. If it wasn't the tea it was the beer. At times he felt that America could never win. He tried to persuade George it was an educational experience, but to no avail.

That Friday they headed for the same bar they had frequented every day since getting into town. They planned to get in a few jars before lunch and shoot a little pool. The bar was empty, except for a few of the more elderly locals, but as lunchtime drew near the crowd swelled and the boys had their work cut out to keep a place on the table. Freddie and George were a good pool team and knew it; they also knew how to bend the rules to maximum advantage. 'Well, we don't play like that in London' was a favourite excuse of George's if he felt the game was slipping away from them. It normally won them the point, as few men in Rawlins wished to get into a heated discussion with the big Londoner whom many had trouble even understanding.

The relative calm of the morning was shattered just before noon. A woman screamed and a glass fell to the floor. A report had just come through that somebody had tried to shoot President Kennedy in Dallas. Pandemonium ensued as everyone in the bar crowded around the small black and white television to catch the latest news. Freddie and George decided a tactical retreat of the Brits was in order and they headed back to the sanctuary of their motel room with two six-packs of beer. They felt more comfortable following the day's developments on their own television and in private. You did not have to be American to know that when somebody takes a pot-shot at the national leader, the law enforcement agencies start to get very edgy, especially with strangers. They would keep their heads down for a couple of days and stay off the roads. They did not need any trigger-happy state troopers taking a really close look at their documentation. Illegal aliens were probably not the flavour of the month right now, even less so after the arrest of Lee Harvey Oswald.

Freddie and George were stunned at the impact the death of the President had on the country. 'You'd think it was the bloody Queen,' George said. For the first time since arriving in the US, even Freddie felt like an intruder.

By Sunday morning the two men decided it was safe to venture out of their rooms and go back to the bar again. As usual, Freddie was taking his time over his morning ablutions, which left George, who was itching to get in the day's first drink, with just the television for company. He flicked through the channels to see if anything caught his attention.

'Hey, Freddie!' George yelled across the room in the direction of the bathroom door. 'They're about to transfer that arsehole who shot Kennedy!' From the muffled reply he assumed Freddie had gotten around to his teeth. 'Fuck! They've got more cowboy hats down there in Dallas than you see in an episode of *Bonanza*. What a bunch of prats . . .

Do you think they know what they look like? . . . You've got to wonder if these guys are serious or what? . . . Fuckin' arseholes!!!' George was on his feet pointing and shouting at the television set. 'They've shot the bastard . . . Freddie, they've shot the bastard . . . they've got the bloke who killed Kennedy!'

Freddie emerged from the bathroom, toothbrush still in hand. 'What's that? What you said?'

'Look for yourself,' George shouted, still pointing to the small television set. 'They've just blown away the arsehole who shot Kennedy. In a police station and in broad daylight! Can you believe this country, it's unreal! They still think they're living in the bloody Wild West!'

'At least it will save them the cost and trouble of a trial,' Freddie added sardonically before returning to his teeth.

Beverly Hills Hotel, Los Angeles, 23 December 1963

'Not a bad wee spot now, is it, lads? Have you had much chance to look around since getting into town?' The speaker was a young Scot who to Freddie and George looked as if he had stepped off another planet rather than Glasgow's Sauchiehall Street. Judging by their reactions, some of the guests at the hotel were of the same opinion.

William MacAndrews, Willy to his friends, a category which now seemed to include Freddie and George, had been in Los Angeles for over two years and was studying at UCLA. His hair was long and his choice of clothes colourful. His father, currently serving a ten-year term in Parkhurst, was a close friend of George's dad Ernie, who had set up the meeting.

'I heard from the old man that your auntie's been having a rough time from some bloody Paddies. Don't you worry, when my dad gets out there will be some sorry-looking Micks.'

'You can tell him to hold off,' George interrupted. 'That's one score I'm looking forward to settling myself when I get back to Blighty. I'll get my hands on that Irish bastard who slapped my auntie.'

Willy led Freddie and George through the hotel to their room. 'I did get it right that you guys wanted to stay together? Personally, with your dosh I would have got separate rooms, because you are going to flip when you see these Californian dolly birds. You ain't lived till you've rooted one of these beach babes. Ooo . . . man! They can't get enough of us horny Brit types. Believe me, I speak from experience.' Willy deposited the cases on the floor and strode out on to the verandah. 'Catch the rays, man. This is life.' He blew a kiss down to a passing Latino chambermaid, who waved back.

Over a few cold beers Freddie and George talked about their

145

three-month drive across the US. After Rawlins they had driven on to Ogden, then down to Salt Lake City, on through Utah and into Nevada. Both Las Vegas and the desert drive had been eye-openers for them. They would have liked to spend more time in Vegas, but they knew Willy and his boss were waiting for them. Willy explained to the boys that his business partners were extremely keen to meet with them. They felt, he said, that they would have much in common.

'How come you bother with the studies, then, if you're in business for yourself?' George asked.

'Once the boss explains our little operation, all will become clear, at least from a business point of view. But don't think that UCLA has anything in common with our British universities. No sir, UCLA is like Butlin's on speed, a full-time party and a passport to quality Californian crumpet! It also lets me stay on in the US, as I'm technically here on a student visa, but then that's probably beside the point, as you well know.'

Los Angeles, Christmas Day 1963

They had never felt less Christmassy in their entire lives. The sun beat down on their heads as Willy, who was dressed even more colourfully than when they had first met, weaved his bright pink drop-head in and out of the freeway traffic and the Beatles' 'I Want To Hold Your Hand', the British number one hit that Christmas, blasted from the radio.

They headed into the Hollywood hills for Christmas lunch at the house of Willy's senior partner and mentor, Louis Collier. Collier's house was tucked away off the main road and just from the fencing and guards Freddie and George realized they were dealing with a man who valued his privacy.

'Fuckin' palace, man!' said Freddie.

'But you should see his boat. The original floating gin palace. Knock your fuckin' eye out,' Willy replied as he pulled up in the gravel by the front door and leaped out without bothering to open the car door. George squeezed out of the back and followed him, if at a more leisurely pace. He sweated profusely, still unaccustomed even to California's winter climate.

The front door opened and two goons came out to greet them. Freddie was aware that at least three others were observing them at a distance from the garden, two of whom held vicious-looking Dobermanns on a leash. 'Fuckin' Dobermanns! I hate fuckin' Dobermanns,' he said, trying to keep calm. 'One of those bastards once took a piece out of my arse while I was trying to remove a safe from a scrapyard in Islington. I still got the scars to show for it!'

'You don't think I haven't seen it?' George replied as he eyeballed the approaching goons. Suddenly, to Freddie and George's surprise, Willy slipped an automatic from the waistband of his jeans and handed it over to the first of the goons, who quickly frisked him. It was obvious, by now, that Freddie and George should follow suit, so they lifted up

147

their arms for a pat down. 'So much for the season of goodwill. I told you they were all fuckin' nuts!' George whispered to Freddie.

'Sorry, guys,' Willy butted in. 'I forgot to tell you that Collier's dad is ex-company and it seems to have rubbed off on him.'

'Company?' George said, raising his scarred eyebrow.

'Company . . . you know, CIA and all that shit. That's where Louis made all his best contacts!'

A tanned, well-groomed American in beige slacks, an expensive shirt and loafers came through the front door and extended a hand to George, who was the nearest to him. 'Sorry for the unorthodox and somewhat unfestive welcome, but as you have probably seen during your short time in my country we can never be too careful. The President wasn't and look what happened to him. I trust my young Scots friend has been looking after you and showing you a good – or rather wicked – time in LA?'

Collier had not loosened his grip on George's hand and took advantage of this to steer the big man through the front door. Freddie and George caught their breath as their eyes adjusted to the light. They had never seen anywhere quite so sumptuous, not even during the days when they were burgling houses in Belgravia. For the first time since they had stopped the train, George and Freddie knew that they would have no problems at all in spending their take from the robbery. Collier led them out by the pool, where a small group of people were enjoying beer and champagne. The women, who did not seem to say much, oozed class, beauty and sex, while their men exuded health, wealth and happiness. The only one who looked out of place in the idyllic setting, other than George and Freddie, was Willy, with his flowing locks and colourful clothes.

'A touch of Christmas cheer for you gentlemen? A few bubbles to be going on with before we sit down to lunch?' Collier was an elegant host.

After a magnificent Christmas spread, with all the trimmings so that not even George had anything to complain about, the men retired to Collier's games room. 'I imagine you two are snooker men,' Willy said, 'but you'll soon get the hang of this Yankee game, might even take some money off them if you're lucky. They're not very good, you know? I blame their education system!' Willy invited Freddie and George to pick a cue. The balls cracked into the pockets and the champagne, brandy and beer flowed. Finally Collier turned the conversation around to business.

'All play and no work can make Louis a poor boy,' he joked as he chalked his cue.

'If I understand what Willy has told me, and I don't see any reason to beat around the bush here: you guys pulled off something very big in your own country and are currently cooling your heels until the heat is off. I also understand that whatever you pulled off netted you a nice tidy sum which you are looking to invest in other, shall we say, lucrative, non-legitimate, low-risk business activities. I'll make it clear from the start, I am not interested in what you were involved in or where the money came from, as long as it don't attract the flies or the fuzz. For all I know, you two could be part of that train heist, I really don't care.'

'Correct. Keep talking.' Freddie took aim to close out on the black.

'Would I also be correct in assuming that once the heat is off you will be looking to get back to England – say in the next six months or so?'

'Could be, although I can't say I would mind giving the old US of A a shot. I think it's great from what I've seen so far, although I think me old mate George is a bit homesick.'

'It's what you're used to, isn't it?' George added. 'We don't go around with shooters back home, for one thing. We're more physical back there. We like a bit of a punch-up. That's right, isn't it, Freddie?' Freddie did not look up and the black sailed into the top pocket. The Brits were ahead.

'And where is home to you, Freddie? I heard your father hailed from the Caribbean. Jamaica, wasn't it?'

'The land of plenty! Yeah, but I haven't seen the old fucker for over fifteen years and know Jamaica even less. I'm told by my mum that I still have a relative or two around the north side of the island. My old man might even be there, for all we know.'

'But you have heard about the island's vices, haven't you Freddie?'

'If you're talking about the weed, I certainly have. Quite partial to a smoke myself. Something I picked up from my Jamaican brothers when I was in the slammer.'

'The what?'

'I think it's what you call the can, the joint, the calaboose ... you know, prison,' Willy explained to the Americans.

'Oh, I understand. And you, George, are you a weed man?' Collier continued as he prowled gracefully around the table to get a better angle on the ball.

'Had a go, but it ain't my scene to be honest. Mr Collier.' The big man raised his beer glass. 'You can keep your dope. I prefer the old liquidy stuff myself.'

'But no serious objections? Moral or whatever?'

'None at all, so if you want a smoke go ahead. You might even play better. Two-nil to us. Am I right?'

Collier nodded, but it was clear he was no longer thinking about the game. 'Gentlemen,' he said, placing his cue in the rack, 'what I am going to propose to you is more than simply rolling a joint. I am now talking about the business of supply and demand and rolling up large profits for the investors for very little risk and in a very short time frame.' For the first time since they entered the games room no one was crouched over the table. Collier had every one's undivided attention.

'All of what you see around you today was built on the back of supply and demand. Most of it over the last eighteen months. Supply and demand of grass, speed, cocaine, call it what you will. We are talking drugs, narcotics . . . and the more illegal the better as far as the bottom line goes. It's a new and expanding market and one that is ripe to explode over the next five years, not just here in California but all across the US and into Europe. If you have the money, the sort of money I am led to believe you have, now's the time to jump on the gravy train, take control and get a large and profitable slice of the action.'

Collier explained to the boys about the growing hippy culture in California, which was sending the demand for LSD and marijuana spiralling upwards. With it went the prices and the profit margin.

'Willy is our token campus hippy,' Collier laughed, pointing to the Scot, who was starting to light up. 'He is my direct contact with our small army of foot soldiers, the people who take the risk in the supply chain for that last dollar. But the hippies are just a tip of the iceberg and as the demand for drugs spreads outside the restricted groups, and I am talking about groups like the hippies and the Hollywood élite, you can be certain that the law will come down on it and us like a ton of bricks. You would have thought these guys could have learnt from the past, but no, they are going to drive the drugs, even such innocuous substances as grass, underground, just like they did with booze in the Prohibition days, and that's how we like it.'

'We do? So how do me and George fit into your plans?' Freddie interrupted. 'I can't see either of us mixing with the hippies or the Hollywood élite. We didn't see too many of those in our London scene.'

'But you will, Freddie, believe me, you will. I ask you, who is supplying the drugs to London's artistic community? The musicians, the actors, the painters, where are they getting their weed and speed from? I'll tell you. From the Chinese and a bunch of small-time amateurs. Think big, boys and London's yours. I know more about your little country than you may think and what I hear tells me that I need to have a base of operations there, a partnership which can then expand into Europe. And let's not think that we won't find other lucrative markets in France, Spain, Italy, Germany, Scandinavia and even Holland, a country which is considerably more tolerant to man's various vices than most. I want British partners, like yourselves. I want partners willing to work the streets and put their money behind their beliefs and their mouths. So why do I need you? Simple. My cash and profits are committed for the next twenty-four months into expanding and consolidating the North American market. I can't afford to ignore Europe for two years. If I did, I would be in serious danger of arriving at the ballpark too late for the big game. But if you can finance a UK operation for now from your recent earnings, and take me on board as a third and equal partner, then I bring to the table the contacts and structure to get you up and running from day one. I'll let you in on all the important tricks of the trade and you, or rather we, won't get burned. We can't fail, it's that simple.'

The men were sprawled around the games room. Collier chose to lean against the wall while Freddie and George sat on the pool table eyeing their prospective partner. The only one who could not sit still was Willy, who continued to charge everyone's glasses, occasionally slipping outside to check that the ladies were happy and to fetch some more cold beer or bubbles.

'The facts, gentlemen,' Collier continued. 'Currently it is Mexico, rather than Jamaica, who is our biggest supplier of marijuana and will be for the foreseeable future. I am paying anywhere between $30 and $35 a kilo in Mexico. That's a little over two pounds in weight. Once I get it over the border and into the US that same kilo is worth – depending on the city – between $150 to $200 if I want to wholesale it as it is to the other big street dealers. However, when broken down into thirty-four ounces, it sells on the street to the final consumer for

$15 to $25 an ounce, that's between $510 to $850 a kilo. If you know of any other business offering that sort of return on investment, then you let me know and I'll be right beside you. The rewards, as I am sure you can see, are such that there is plenty of cream for everyone. If you are smart, you will keep several layers of cream between you and the ultimate consumer, as that is where the risk to your ass is, if any. A few foot soldiers may get hit and put away, but never the top dogs if everyone keeps their mouths shut and you pay fairly. First rule, never let the troops see you get greedy, even if you are.'

Freddie laughed and signalled for Willy to come across to him. He took the joint from Willy's hand and took a long drag. 'Mr Collier, we won't be greedy and we look forward to a long and prosperous relationship. When do we start?' He took another long drag and handed the glowing joint over to Collier, who accepted the peace offering and took his hit. Both men laughed, and so did the others. It was contagious.

'Mugs away,' said George and the men returned to their game of pool.

Douglas, Isle of Man, January 1964

These were halcyon days for David and Denise. They could not see how life could get any better. They were financially secure; there had not been any news to suggest that David was in any way a suspect in the Great Train Robbery investigations; there had been nothing in the press about the diamonds, which suggested they should not have been on the train in the first place; and best of all, they had been accepted within the island community.

They celebrated Christmas and New Year in style and made a number of friends in the upper echelons of island society. David who felt confident enough to drop his heavy glasses, now drove a smart dark blue Jaguar Mark 8 and the gossip in the community was that he was a very successful international trader. A front which Wright had been cultivating for him in the island's financial circles.

Beverly Hills Hotel, January 1964

Freddie and George were enjoying breakfast around the pool when they saw Willy weaving in and out of the other tables to join them. The hotel was used to exotic types, even if some of the more conservative guests were not.

'Manager tells me that you two have been naughty boys again. Sneaking young ladies of ill repute into your rooms. Next I'll hear you've been skinning up around the pool. How very non-U!'

Freddie and George had grown to enjoy the company of the wacky Scot and his wacky baccy. People in London had good things to say about him and his family, and it looked as if he had solved the problem of what they should do with their lives and their money.

'The boss told me to tell you that one of his houses is going to come free at the end of the week. He thinks that as you are going to be around for a while, you might like to move from the hotel and have a few home comforts. He even promises to stock the fridge with a few British delicacies for George. The house comes with its own maid, who I can tell you is a real sweetie. A lovely Mexican poppet of sixteen. Best blow-job in town, I hear, but be discreet, as the boss can be partial to her at times. On another matter, the boss wants to know if you still have your original passports and air tickets, or did you ditch them in New York?'

'Yeah, we have 'em. But what interest is that to Collier?' Freddie replied.

'Well, Mr Collier has contacts everywhere, as you might have guessed, and if he has your passports he will get them stamped to show that you left the country before your entry visas expired. He will also have your ticket stubs put in the right Pan Am file, so it will appear to anyone who cares to look that you were on the right return flight to London out of New York. You won't be much use to us in the future if you can't come back to America because you overstayed your welcome the first time around, will you?'

Collier, who liked to have all the bases covered, decided that Freddie and George should learn the nuts and bolts of the business in sunny California. If they were going to be cooling their heels for six months, they could at least put the time to good use. Collier had also assessed the working relationship between the boys, so while Freddie accompanied Willy to the university campuses and hippy communes, and went with Collier to the Hollywood dealers for the stars and studios, George spent time with the goon squad. They showed him everything from the latest state-of-the-art surveillance and security methods to the use of shooters and poisons. George had never been keen on guns, but Collier persuaded him to swing with the times. 'The day you discover you should be carrying a piece will be one day too late,' he told the big man.

The boys also spent long sessions with Collier's closest advisers and chemists, who went through exactly how they intended to set up the European operation; the number of people to go on the payroll; and how they would get the first shipments into the Britain. Initial supplies of marijuana would come from Mexico and Jamaica as well as Morocco, Collier said, with the harder, more specialized drugs being dealt with on an order-by-order basis until they had a clear idea of the demand for each type. One of his chemists would go over to Britain to monitor movement and set up a laboratory. The Moroccan supply line especially appealed to Freddie, as it meant he could bring the merchandise in through Europe to Britain, something he had had plenty of practice with in the past, although never with drugs.

Los Angeles/Las Vegas, March 1964

'I thought it was time you had a closer look at how one of our delivery runs work,' Collier told Freddie. 'I think you will find it interesting, especially as we will end up in Vegas for the night. We'll see if you have the same lucky touch on their tables as you seem to show on the pool table at my house.' Collier and Freddie were being driven to Los Angeles Airport, LAX, where a sizeable shipment of narcotics was due to arrive shortly from Mexico. Before checking in for the flight to Las Vegas, Collier kept a close eye on the arrivals board.

'Flight's in. Now the fun starts.'

'Exactly what is going to happen?' Freddie asked.

'One of my mules was on that plane that has just arrived from Mexico City. He has with him three large cases of what we will call sensitive merchandise. His bags are marked with a sticker that is exclusive to us. It is for a holiday resort that does not actually exist, but only we know that. He will not pick up his bags, but will walk through with a large carry-on bag so as not to create any suspicion with the immigration boys. The bags will remain unclaimed and left on one side. I have people working air-side who will now retag the bags and send them on to Vegas for me. As it's an internal flight the baggage won't be searched or even looked at. A second mule, a girl this time, will board the flight to Vegas with us. She will be given the new baggage tags before she joins the flight, so that she can safely claim the bags at the other end. Simple, but it works every time. The only thing is you must trust your mules and the people working for you in the airport implicitly. If they fuck up, you lose not only the shipment but also the route. You can try it in London, if you like, but only once you have the right people in place. And make sure nobody can trace who bought the airline tickets.'

'This scam won't be a problem in London. The airport's not known as *Thief*row for nothing. My only worry in London would be some other clever bastard nicking the bags before they left the airport.'

'Okay, let's go and try our luck in Vegas.'

Throughout the flight Freddie tried to spot the mule. He narrowed it down to three women travelling alone, all but one of whom struck up a conversation with her neighbour. It was her, he surmised, but he was wrong. The mule was an off-duty stewardess who was sitting in the jump seat at the back of the plane. Maggie, the stewardess, was an absolute cracker, Freddie discovered when she called by Collier's hotel suite later in the day. She had legs the like of which Freddie had only seen in the pages of women's lingerie ads. They went all the way up, and then some. She had a body to match.

When she arrived in Vegas Maggie had passed the bags on to a third mule, who was at that very moment driving the merchandise back to the safety of the group's LA distribution centre. Maggie was ready to party and so was Freddie. The three spent the evening together in the casino before Collier had to excuse himself to attend to other pressing business matters, which involved a new contract for the regular supply of large quantities of cocaine and marijuana to one of the main casino hotels.

'Enjoy yourself, Freddie,' he said with a departing wink. 'If you play your cards right, Maggie might even introduce you to the pleasures of the five-mile-high club and your feet won't even have to leave the ground. She's what I believe you call in England a quality piece of pussy. I'll see you in the morning!'

It was a tired and worn-looking Freddie who joined Collier in the lobby next morning. 'Christ! Can that woman go or can she go? I've never know anything like it,' he confessed. She didn't leave me alone for a second. My knob looks like the fuckin' Japanese flag!'

He was looking forward to getting back to LA so that he could get some rest before giving George a blow-by-blow account of his night with Maggie. He knew it would wind up his big friend, who was still only managing to pull the hookers. Good-looking Californian hookers, but hookers just the same.

When they got to Vegas Airport they discovered that their seats had already been allocated for them at the back of the plane. A familiar smiling face greeted them as they boarded. 'Good morning, Mr Collier,' she nodded. Freddie hardly recognized her in uniform. 'And good morning to you, Mr Birch,' Maggie continued. 'Nice to have you aboard. Will that be coffee, tea or me again?' she whispered in his ear. From the twinkle in her eye Freddie knew the flight would be short and sweet, if a little turbulent. The plane may not have reached five miles high, but he joined the club anyway in the cramped confines of the washroom. Collier just smiled and read his newspaper. He made a mental note to send for the Mexican maid, who could take care of his immediate needs just as soon as he got back to LA.

Douglas, 15 April 1964

In some ways both David and Denise were relieved. The trial was over and nothing that had come out in the whole three months had suggested their involvement in any way. The court proceedings had shown that the police did not know exactly how many people were involved in the robbery and those who had been caught had only been pinned down by the fingerprint evidence at the farm.

David often wondered what had happened to Bruce, Jimmy, Buster, Freddie and George, all of whom had vanished without trace. Had they stayed in Britain or gone abroad? One thing was for sure, he could never find out, because to ask questions was to draw attention to himself and that was the last thing he and Denise wanted. It had come as no surprise to him that, with the exception of John whose lawyers had convinced the jury that the fingerprint evidence was inconclusive as far as he was concerned, all the other members of the gang sent for trial had been found guilty. He felt for them, as their fate had been held in the balance while Ronnie underwent a second trial after a successful plea for a mistrial the first time around. (One of the police witnesses had inadvertently let slip a mention of Ron's previous record.) Ron's second trial lasted only five days and sentencing for all the accused was set for 15 April.

David stayed close to the radio the entire day. 'I bet they get twenty,' he told Denise. 'That fuckin' useless government will demand at least twenty. They'll want to wave it in Bruce's face.' Broadcast after broadcast brought nothing but frustration, until finally the news came through.

'Mr Justice Edmund Davies has sentenced the men who took part in the Great Train Robbery to thirty years' imprisonment,' the news reader announced. 'The judge, who described the convicted as "greedy men" and the robbery as a "sordid crime of violence", handed down thirty-year sentences to seven of the convicted

159

men and terms of between twenty and twenty-five years to another five . . .'

'Thirty years! He's fuckin' mad, that judge. It's insane, you don't send robbers down for thirty years. That's for spies and murderers, not train robbers. You'd think we killed somebody!'

David turned round to face Denise. A tear rolled down her cheek. 'Those poor, poor bastards,' she sniffed.

David held her close. 'It's all right, love. We're all right. Nobody knows we're here and they never will. Nobody's ever going to take me away from you, I promise. They nailed them on fingerprints and I never took my gloves off once. They could never tie me to the farm. Not now, not ever. They've never been able to get anything on me, you know that.' David coaxed a little smile from his wife. 'That's better! Anyway, it's not over yet. Once the trial is forgotten by the public and the press, they'll reduce the sentences to twenty years or less on appeal. You'll see. Come on, let's go for a walk. I think we need the air.'

The air still had a rough winter bite as it blew in off the Irish Sea and across the promenade. They walked to the end of Victoria Pier and let the wind blow away the cobwebs and whatever sad thoughts they had.

Los Angeles, April 1964

The sentences were long enough to attract the attention of even the American media. Thirty years, some editorials argued, was a death penalty in itself. News of the sentences made Freddie and George think twice about heading home, but Aunt Rose was adamant – the police had nothing on them even if they did know they were involved. Rose had invested part of the boys' money in paying informers, some buried deep within Scotland Yard. The police, she discovered, were looking for at least five other men directly involved in the assault on the train and possibly a further two or three backroom boys who had helped mastermind the operation and had not been at the farm. But for certain, Scotland Yard only had three real leads to follow and they were Bruce, Jimmy and Buster, against all of whom they had sufficient evidence, including prints, to send them down for thirty years with the rest.

'The thing is, George, Old Bill is trying to play down the fact that anyone got away,' Rose assured her nephew over the phone. 'Bit of the old public relations, if you ask me, but they want the public, the voters like you and me, to believe that law and order is alive and well and winning the day in Britain. They've got to go after Bruce, Jimmy and Buster because they splashed their photos all over the papers. Now if Freddie's there, can I have a quick word with him?' George put Freddie on the line.

'Freddie? It's Rose. Listen, I thought you might like to know that besides Old Bill, there appears to be one of those hush-hush government departments sniffing around, asking questions about the job. Seems there was something else on the train which went missing. Nobody knows what, unless of course some of the money belonged to them, but it might be the reason them Paddies came around and knocked me and Albi about.'

'Could be, but don't you worry yourself any more about those Paddies.

161

KEEP ON RUNNING

If Ernie doesn't take care of them, George will. You be good and keep your head down until we get back. We've got some exciting things in the pipeline thanks to you. Start thinking about getting a nice place for us to live in. Nothing too flash from the outside, mind. We still don't want to attract any unnecessary attention, do we?'

London/Isle of Man, July/August 1964

I t seemed appropriate that Freddie and George's return to British soil should see the Rolling Stones on top of the charts with 'It's All Over Now'. And over it truly was. The gang's appeals had been heard in London and with the exception of Brian Field, Roger Cordrey and Bill Boal, all had been dismissed. Charlie, Ron, Roy and the rest continued to look at thirty-year sentences.

As Freddie and George got back into the London way of life after nearly a year on the run, Bruce and Buster were rumoured to be heading in the other direction and going abroad. It was good to see family and friends again, but both men knew there was work to be done. Collier was anxious that they set up shop as soon as possible. He kept emphasizing that to the pioneers went the spoils.

Recruiting the ground troops was not a problem. Freddie and George still had a good reputation on the street and while there were whispers on the manor that they had been involved in the Great Train Robbery, hence their absence from the scene, nobody said as much. It just meant that their credit was golden.

The US jaunt had made a sizeable dent in the boys' savings, but as they had two full shares in the robbery to play with there was still plenty to get the business up and running. Freddie was amazed at the accuracy of Collier's predictions. There was a buzz on the streets. Certain sectors of London society were after drugs, and the more exotic the better. A laboratory was set up for Collier's chemist in West Drayton, close to Heathrow Airport, where there was a lot of suitable accommodation and good access to the rest of the country. Small warehousing and distribution centres were established in Liverpool, Birmingham, Manchester and Glasgow. The boys were in business and, as Collier had promised, they were up and running from day one: a fact that did not endear them to some of their less well-organized rivals.

On the Glorious Twelfth, 12 August, Charlie Wilson had it away from HM Prison Winson Green in Birmingham. It gave the boys another reason to celebrate. Further north, in the Irish Sea, Denise raised her glass. 'One away, Mr Jenkins!'

'Thank you, Mrs Jenkins! Good old Chas, I had a funny feeling he would be the first to go. Let's just hope he's the first of many.'

David and Denise had other reasons to celebrate; besides Charlie's escape and the first anniversary of their life of plenty, they had found their dream house. A sizeable country house located in its own grounds some three miles from Douglas. They had completed at the end of July and now the decorators were in. Denise finally understood what it meant to have money. Whatever she wanted was hers. No luxury was spared, no detail overlooked. David said they could afford it as their investments were doing better than even Wright had predicted. And then there were the diamonds for those little extras, including a new mini for Denise to run around in.

It was about this time that David got word from one of the few contacts he still retained in London that he could come and pick up the papers relating to Mr and Mrs Wood. It had been an expensive and time-consuming job, but all were originals. The documentation included passports, driving licences, social security cards, birth and baptismal certificates – the works, in fact. David didn't want even to ask how his contact had managed to pull it off, but he had, albeit at a hefty price. He told David that the next time, he would choose the name, rather than David. David turned down the invitation to pick up the documents personally in London; instead he arranged for the transfer of money and asked for the papers to be sent by registered mail to Mr D. Wood, care of the Grosvenor Hotel in Chester. He had decided that he and Denise deserved a weekend away on the mainland, and what better place than their old haunt? He called the hotel and made the necessary reservations, asking them to keep an eye out for a package that would be arriving for him from London in the coming week.

London, October 1964

A desire for revenge was burning within George. He needed to right a wrong, it was that simple. Whoever the Paddies were that had roughed up his favourite auntie and put the frighteners on his kid brother would have to pay for what they had done. As he told anyone who would listen, 'They were bang out of order. I'm going to see the colour of their claret before the year is out, those fuckin' Irish slags.'

As business grew, so did the number of informers in Freddie and George's pay, but for months they continued to draw a blank on George's request for information on the mystery Irishmen. They weren't normal crims, of that he was certain. The only explanation he could think of was that they were genuine Paddies, based over in Ireland. He spread the net further afield.

London, January 1965

David had decided not to be too adventurous with the first use of their new passports. He settled on a weekend away in Dublin. The ferry crossing from the island was one of the last of the season and Mrs Wood spent most of the journey heaving her guts up over the side of the boat. They would fly next time, her husband promised.

They both enjoyed Dublin, but David wanted something more exotic. He found it to celebrate the New Year – a package advertised in one of the Douglas travel agents. He bought the tickets and sneaked them into Denise's Christmas stocking. It was their first Christmas in their new house and he wanted it to be special. He could not help sparing a thought, however, for the gang members spending their second Christmas of thirty behind bars.

They made the short hop over to Manchester on 7 January by plane rather than ferry and took the train on down to London. It was their first visit to the capital since their disappearance over a year earlier. They felt it was unlikely that they would be recognized – as David told Denise, it was not as if they would be frequenting any of the haunts their old acquaintances used to hang out in. David also realized that it was the first time that he had been on a train since the robbery. As he peered out through the misty windows, much of the countryside looked just as it had that August night. The train hurtled through Leighton Buzzard and on past the actual site of the robbery. David gripped Denise's hand. He closed his eyes and fought back the demons. Moments later he opened his eyes and they were gone.

At Euston, David hailed a cab to the Savoy, where they had reservations until the Monday. They saw a side to London they had never seen before, dining in the Savoy Grill and the next day lunching at Simpson's in the Strand. The highlight of the visit David had kept a secret from Denise until the day. He had tickets for the Beatles'

166

Christmas Show at the Hammersmith Odeon. With all the screaming they did not hear much, but it was a memorable show all the same. The Beatles, who had topped the year-end charts with 'I Feel Fine', headed a bill which included Freddie and the Dreamers, a sentimental favourite of Denise's; the Yardbirds, whose young guitarist, Eric Clapton, had caught David's eye; Elkie Brooks, Jimmy Savile, Mike Haslam and the Mike Cotton Sound.

After the weekend in London they flew on to Paris. Being naturally nervous when things were out of his control, David held his breath at both Heathrow and Orly when their passports were checked. But the documents passed muster. David had booked himself and Denise into the George V – the best in Paris, he had been told. They did all the sights. In many ways it was the honeymoon they had never had. They even broached the subject of having a baby, but decided to wait another year or so. Neither wanted to say as much, but Denise did not fancy starting a family and then finding David had been locked away for thirty years. It never crossed her mind that she would be sent down as well.

In Paris they caught the show at the Crazy Horse Saloon. Denise said, 'It's not the Beatles!', but she realized that her husband wasn't quite as excited by the Beatles as she was. A week after leaving the island, they took a flight directly back from Paris to Manchester, where they changed planes for the hop across the Irish Sea. It had been an unforgettable seven days for them both.

London, February 1965

'What do you mean, they're not exactly Paddies?' George was talking to one of his many informers, one to whom he had given virtually a full-time brief to hunt down his auntie's attacker. A waste of time and effort, Freddie had said.

'Well, they're not from the south, that's what I mean. They're from the north. Belfast boys, I think. Don't know who the top dog is, that's still a mystery. But the one called Terry, the one who clobbered Rose, is back in London and appears to be doing nothing of any importance. He's got plenty of dough in his pockets, though, if the way he has been splashing it about the West End is anything to go by.'

'Got a home address?'

'He's been very careful and he moves around a bit, but he often goes back to a house in Chiswick which he shares with two other lads.'

'It's not the other lads that I want, it's this Terry and whoever his boss is. They were out of order and need to be taught a fuckin' lesson they won't forget because you don't hit a member of my family, especially my auntie, unless you've got some very serious insurance coverage.'

Spain, March 1965

The sun felt good on Freddie's back. It reminded him of California. This was the life, he decided, not the cold and the wet he had suffered throughout the British winter which still had the country in its grip. In Spain he had no reason to hide his money. He could be as flash as he liked and nobody asked any questions. He remembered Collier's house in the hills above Los Angeles and realized that in Málaga he could achieve his own dream. Land was cheap and so was labour. He could build a dream home without having constantly to look over his shoulder.

Freddie was not in Málaga for a holiday, however. Collier needed him to increase supplies from Morocco so that he could divert stocks from Mexico to the US market. Freddie's contact was Juan Carlos, a young Spaniard who had been given his name by his mother, a fervent anti-Franco monarchist. Prince Juan Carlos, the future king, was the leading pretender to the Spanish throne at the time.

Juan Carlos spoke perfect English and doubled as a travel guide during the summer season. His cover allowed him to move around the region quite freely without attracting attention to himself. It even allowed him the luxury of being on deserted beaches with foreigners after dark. 'The gringos like skinny dipping,' he once explained to a passing police patrol as the 'tourists' frolicked in the water. It was a close call, but Juan Carlos liked the excitement of the chase. To him it was all a game, but a game he played to win.

Freddie was suitably impressed with Juan Carlos – he had come highly recommended and it was clear from the very start that he could be trusted. 'I'll die for you, Freddie,' he said, and Freddie did not doubt him for a minute. He made a mental note to keep him financially well rewarded.

In some ways Juan Carlos reminded Freddie of Willy in California, but exactly why, he did not know. No doubt about it, though, it was

169

Juan, rather than the Brits, who had been the real star in the expanding Spanish operation. An operation which had brought few worries worth mentioning, except for the odd bribe or two to a corrupt official when a mule got careless. But nothing to cause Freddie or George any sleepless nights.

Juan Carlos was a regular on the ferry between Málaga and Melilla in Morocco. 'The tourists, you know?' he told the ferry operators, who even gave him tour-guide discounts. He preferred the shorter crossing of the Strait of Gibraltar between Tangier and Algeciras or, when necessary, Tangier and Gibraltar itself. The prices in Morocco, as Freddie knew from experience, were higher than in Mexico, almost triple, but the quality of the marijuana was better and so were his rewards on the streets of London compared with the take in Los Angeles. Much of Freddie's expanding market, especially in London, demanded quality, which had led him to open up a route to Afghanistan to supply the prized Afghan Black.

If Freddie paid the price, the Moroccans assured him, they had all the supplies of 'puff' he could possibly need. Freddie was already one of the big boys; they knew it and he knew they knew it. It made business so much easier. Most importantly, they knew his track record and that his word and credit were golden. They also liked Juan Carlos and respected Freddie for choosing a Spaniard as his right-hand man. They had had a difficult time with some of the Brits.

Juan and his team organized the donkey work of getting the shipments out of Morocco into Spain or on occasions, when the timing and destination were right, straight on to freighters bound for Britain.

After tidying up the loose ends in Morocco, Juan took Freddie to see the sleepy little fishing village of Marbella, which was strategically located almost halfway between Gibraltar and Málaga. He was sure Freddie would find it even more appealing than Málaga, and so it proved. Freddie made a down payment on a large piece of land and started planning his dream home. He looked forward to the day when Collier would be his house guest. 'And I'll make the bastard play snooker and darts,' he muttered to himself.

London, March 1965

K nowing how Freddie hated violence, George waited until his friend was down in Spain before going after Terry. It would also give Freddie a watertight alibi if he got it wrong. Rose had told her nephew to forget about the incident. 'Water under the bridge,' she said. Only George and his dad, Ernie, still thought the Paddy should be taught a few manners. The question for George was how much pain he was going to inflict; the solution to that came from Collier's chemist. Talking over dinner one night, he had captivated George with stories of new synthetic drugs and what they could do to the human body and mind when applied in the right locations and the right dosage. 'Send a man completely out of his mind, if you wanted to,' he told George. 'Or you could pop his heart, just as easily.'

Now that George and his boys knew what Terry looked like, they had no problem putting a tail on him. It was a Thursday night when a couple of George's most trusted helpers struck up a conversation with the Irishman in one of the West End drinking clubs. Nothing too obvious, just a couple of bad lads out for a night on the town. First it was the beers and then the gin and tonics. They were well juiced by the time Mike, a Canadian who had risen in the ranks to become one of George's right-hand men, suggested they should go on a pussy hunt.

'I know just the place in Old Compton Street, a peep show owned by a buddy of mine. Fancy a peek and a poke, then?' The three new friends struck off in the direction of Soho. The cool evening air had a sobering effect as they hit the road, but they could smell grumble and were not going to be pulled off the scent.

'Hello, Jill, Barnie around?' Mike asked the girl at the ticket booth.

'No, he ain't, but he said you might be dropping in and to make you comfy. Usual room?'

'Okay, honey. There's three of us, so send up some of your very best. We're looking to make a night of it.'

'Sure thing, Mike. Have fun, gentlemen,' she said, tossing a set of keys over to Mike. Jill opened the door to the side of the main marquee entrance and the boys fell up the stairs, staggering and giggling as they went. The staircase was dingy and dark, the only light coming from a few low-wattage red bulbs which had seen better days.

'Come on, Terry, heaven's gape awaits,' Mike said, encouraging his Irish friend, who was salivating at the very thought. Mike fiddled with the keys and the lock. He pushed the door open and signalled for Terry to enter the darkened room. 'After you, my liege!' The big Irishman started slipping out of his overcoat as he entered, which only made it easier for those who waited.

Terry never had a chance to know what hit him. A plastic bin-liner was forced over his head and his arms pinned behind him. In seconds he was trussed up like a Christmas turkey and gasping for breath. Death would have been a relief, but he feared that would be too easy. A stiletto knife sliced down the bag and the air rushed in. A man pulled the bag apart, a man he did not recognize in the poor light.

'Hello, Terry! My name is George and I'm Rose's favourite nephew. Now I gather you took some liberties with my auntie while I was away travelling and I'm here to do the same with you.' George ran the razor-sharp tip of the stiletto over Terry's face, occasionally breaking the skin with the point. Terry was still gasping for breath, but tried to keep still. George had held the tip as close as he could to Terry's eye without actually touching it. Terry felt the cold blade enter his nostril and catch the cartilage. 'I've got every reason in the world to stick this knife right up your hooter and into your brain, Terry. Can you think of one single reason why I shouldn't? . . . What's the matter, Terry? . . . Cat got your tongue? Believe me, friend, if you don't answer my questions tonight I'll be feeding more than your tongue to the cat.'

In the darkness of the room Terry could sense there were at least two others on either side of George, but he could not tell how many more were behind him. Not that it mattered, the way they had him trussed up.

'What I did was all in the line of duty, mate, it was nothing personal, you of all people should understand that. I apologized at the time . . . didn't want to touch her really,' the Irishman squirmed. 'So you're George? . . . Heard a lot of good things about you . . . You're all right, you know that?'

'Oh, that really makes all the difference, Terry. But let's get back to why we are here, shall we? Now you may be telling the truth and you may have slapped my auntie about by mistake, and I, as any of my mates will tell you, am a generous and forgiving man. So why don't you just tell me who your boss is and where I can find him, then I can go and have a little chat with him about that parcel you and your mates were looking for.'

'I can't do that, George, and you know why. I can say sorry and apologize to your auntie. Buy her a bunch of flowers, if you like, but that's the limit. I'm no grass. Do what you have to and feel a man about it, but it won't change anything.'

'I'm sorry you don't want to co-operate, because you will whether you want to or not. I'd now like to introduce you to an American friend of mine – no names, no addresses, all you need to know is that he's a whizz with the chemical substances. Sadly he doesn't get as many guinea-pigs for his work as he would like to. Government legislation and all that, that's why he's so pleased you've volunteered your services tonight.' To emphasize the point Mike pulled the Irishmen's head back by the hair. 'I'll ask you one more time, Terry. Who was your boss that day you invaded my house and where can I find him?'

'Fuck off, George. You and your pals don't scare me. Give it your best shot tonight, boy, because when I get free I'm going hunt you down and kill you. What's more, I'm going to enjoy doing it.'

'Big words from a big man! I don't think I would be as lippy as you if I was trussed up like the Christmas dinner. Okay, doctor, do your stuff.' The American, who had taken a bit of persuading to become involve in George's scheme, had not been able to resist the temptation to see if the new drugs worked the way his colleagues back home in California had promised. Mike came round the back of Terry, grabbed the Irishman's arm and held it steady. A quick pinch and run on the inner arm and the American found a good vein and shot the contents of the syringe into it. For the first time since he had fought for breath, the Irishman's eyes were wide with terror.

'Give it a few minutes and he'll sing like a bird,' the American promised. And so he did.

'Who was in charge, Terry? . . . What was his name? . . . Where do I find him?' George pressed the woozy Irishman.

'His name's Pat. Patrick . . . Patrick Green. Don't have an address . . . just a number. I leave a message and he rings me back.'

'And where do you leave the message, Terry?'

'I don't know where, but the number is 765-2290.'

'What were you looking for at my house that day?'

'The bag . . .'

'What else? The bag and the money were there. What else were you looking for, what was it?'

'A package . . .'

Terry's faced contorted in pain as he fought the effects of the drug. 'We're losing him,' the American whispered in George's ear. 'It could be a reaction to the drink he had before. Do you know what he had to drink?'

'God dammit, he's gone and shat himself,' Mike said in disgust, turning towards the door. 'Dirty bastard! God, what a stink!'

Not even the smell distracted George. 'What was it? You can tell me. Tell me, Terry, what was in the package? What were you looking for that day at my house?'

'Gems . . . diamonds . . . emeralds, I don't know. Green said it was jewels . . .' The big Irishman was a broken man. Tears rolled down his cheeks as he sat in his own stench. George went into a huddle with the American and Mike.

'Don't understand this jewel crap one little bit. You sure it makes him tell the truth?'

'That's what they wrote me, but God knows what effect the alcohol had on the mix,' the American replied.

'So where do we go from here?' George asked.

'I assume you would not want this man making a return house call on you or your family. If so, I can give him another pretty lethal concoction that will either send him totally nuts or pop his heart. Unless he's got the constitution of an ox, that is.'

'Will we have body problems?' Mike asked.

'It all depends on how long he lasts. In theory, put him out on to the sidewalk and follow him at a distance. When the drugs kick in, people around him will think he is having a heart attack. He'll be totally incoherent, so if the law are around and try and help him they'll just think he's drunk. A hobo, I imagine, in his present state ... fuck, I could market this stuff as a laxative if he's anything to go by. It's not a side effect they told me about.'

'Let's do it, then,' George decided.

Mike grabbed the Irishman's already limp arm and the American injected him with a second, far more potent cocktail of drugs. It was impossible to tell if Terry had any conception of what was going on. They untrussed him, put him in his overcoat and dragged him down the stairs. The stench was overwhelming. To Mike fell the job of shadowing Terry until he met his maker. They waited for a break in the stream of pedestrians and pushed Terry out into the night. As promised, paranoia set in quickly. The Irishman staggered one way, then the other. He looked like a rabbit caught in the oncoming headlights of a car and unable to get out of the way. At a distance Mike followed him down to Leicester Square tube station, a few minutes walk away on the corner of Charing Cross Road and Newport Street. He never made the train. His heart didn't last that long. He toppled down the stairs into a crumpled mess. The stationmaster did not look pleased.

'A little messy, but I have to hand it to you, very effective,' Mike reported back to George, who was apologizing to Jill for the smell and the mess. A wad of notes pressed into her hand, and all complaints were forgotten.

'Would you and the boys like a girl now? On the house ... a present. It's been a quiet night and they could do with the exercise.' George and the American declined Jill's kind offer, but the other boys were all for it and were led away by some attractive but slightly worn young ladies.

'Enjoy yourselves, lads,' George called after them. 'You've earned it!' George then retired with the American to the Dorchester Grill. He fancied something nice. He thought they had both earned some real class nosh. He would call Rose from the hotel and give her the good news.

London, May 1965

Freddie was far from pleased when he learned that George had taken the law into his own hands. 'You can't go knockin' off people who give your auntie a little slap. It's not on. We don't operate like that and you know it.'

George was unrepentant. 'I never laid a glove on him. He croaked from natural causes.'

'Yeah, like you'll be telling me next that the St Valentine's Day Massacre victims died from simple lead poisoning,' Freddie sneered.

Freddie was as baffled as George by the idea that the Ulsterman's boys had been looking for gems. He had heard rumours circulating that there had been valuable jewels on the train, but he hadn't seen any and he was quite sure Bruce hadn't either. That only left David Jenkins, but nobody had seen or heard of him or his wife since the robbery, nearly two years earlier. Freddie wondered where he was and what he was up to. 'Funny if he turned out to be one of our rival dealers,' George said.

'We should keep an eye out for him,' Freddie replied, 'as your Irish friends might start putting two and two together and it won't be adding up to four. Then they'll come looking for the people responsible for doing their mate.'

'And they can keep coming, Freddie. That Terry was just the start. I still want to take care of this Patrick Green fellah.'

'Now knock it off, George. We don't want a war. It would piss the law off and at the moment we don't exactly want to bring the spotlight down on us. You've had your pound of flesh with Terry. Be content and leave it with that.'

Isle of Man/London,
Thursday 8 July 1965

'Two away, Mr Jenkins!' Denise greeted her husband with a particularly affectionate hug and a big smile. It took David, who had been down with Wright studying a potentially lucrative deal, by surprise. 'I said two away, Mr Jenkins! They've just announced on the radio that four men have gone over the wall at Wandsworth. One of them was Ronnie Biggs!'

'Fuck me! Who would have put money on Ron having it away? Good on him. I just hope he's got a plan and knows what he's doing.'

Freddie had also been listening to the radio in the boys' new and palatial London office. Palatial only on the inside; from the outside it was a Camden Town warehouse, nothing special to look at. It was the legitimate front for George and Freddie's import–export operation which, much to their embarrassment, had even been cited as an example to the community. Two reformed criminals who had knuckled down to some hard work and all that. When Freddie had first heard about the citation he thought that somebody was taking the piss.

'George!' Freddie shouted down from the office to the warehouse floor. 'Ronnie's had it away!'

'Ronnie who?'

'Ronnie Biggs! Who the fuck do you think I'm talking about?'

George came bounding up the metal staircase two steps at a time. 'Nice one. Any details?' They retreated past their 'secretary' and into their private office. Freddie had the radio on as well as the television. The sound was turned down on the TV, which to anyone interested was showing children how to make a space rocket out of a squeezy bottle.

'Details are sketchy at the moment,' Freddie explained, 'but it looks as if Ron went over the wall at Wandsworth with three other blokes.'

'Do we know any of them?'

'Don't think so. Names didn't mean nothin' to me. They say they used a fuckin' removal van to spring them.'

'Bit cheeky! Serves the buggers right, though. What did they expect the boys to do, sit tight and do that kind of bird without a whisper? I'd love to get them all out, I really would . . .'

'George, don't even think about it. I know what you're like. You'll suddenly think it's your duty to spring them all and you'll end up getting nicked yourself. They are all experienced old lags who have their own contacts. Charlie and Ronnie proved that. Let them take care of themselves.'

George grabbed a couple of beers from their bar and opened them up. 'Let's drink to Ron! Wherever you are, mate, run and keep running.'

'To Ronnie Biggs!'

Although George still kept an eye open for Patrick Green, they had received far more interesting news from their informers of late. It seemed that elements of Tommy Butler's Flying Squad, who had been investigating the robber, were now pretty certain that either George or Freddie, or both, had been involved. But much to the boys' relief, however deep Scotland Yard dug, they could not come up with a single shred of evidence that linked them to the farm or the robbery. George, being the intellectually weak link, had been hauled in for some light questioning, but even he knew they were firing blanks in the dark.

'I think I'd better cancel my trip to Spain, at least until this Biggs escape thing calms down. They've got all the law in London looking for him.' Freddie was talking between sips of beer. He had his feet up on the desk and they were now watching pictures of the removal van outside Wandsworth Prison. 'A lot of people aren't half going to be pissed off now that Ronnie's had it away as well as Charlie. I pity the other poor bastards. They won't be able to break wind in their sleep without some screw jumping on them.'

'But what's your trip to Spain got to do with Ronnie's escape?' George asked.

'Well, they'll be watching all the docks and the airports, won't they? Makes sense, like, if they expect to nab him. He can't sit around here, can he? So if yours truly turns up at Heathrow with a ticket to Spain, that's not half going to set the alarm bells ringing. They'll probably think I'm some sort of scout for Ron. No, I'll sit tight for the moment, at least until we know the heat is off. Even then I think I'll route myself through Paris or Zurich. Don't want the Yard looking for reasons as to why I keep popping down to Spain, do we?'

'Should we call Juan and tell him to stall the delivery?'

'No, I don't think that'll be necessary. They'll be too busy looking at things leaving the country to worry about vans comin' in. Anyway, the van should have already crossed into France, so it's going to be safer if it keeps on truckin' up rather than send it back down to Spain.' Freddie was particularly proud of his vans. It had taken time and money, but as far as he was concerned they were the "dog's bollocks", the very best.

He had worked out the shipment plans with Juan Carlos. The journeys started on moonless or cloudy nights on the beaches of Morocco, where Juan and his crew would load up their rubber Zodiacs with the stash of dope. The bags, if they had to be dumped in an emergency, would go straight to the bottom. An informer in the Moroccan Navy gave them the green light when it was safe to cross. He kept an eye on the Strait of Gibraltar, not only on his radar screen but visually as well. Made of rubber, the Zodiacs did not show up on his or anybody else's screen unless the radar caught a signal off their large outboard motors. For safety the Zodiacs would make most of the crossing of the strait bunched closely together so that if one did give off a signal, it showed up as only a single blip on the screen. When the Spanish coast was in sight, they would break ranks for the last mad dash to the beaches, with some running a decoy if it was deemed necessary. It could only be a matter of time, Juan Carlos thought, until the Spanish authorities caught on and used their own Zodiacs to stake them out. Then it would just be a question of who had the faster boat.

Juan knew the beaches of southern Spain like the back of his hand and if he was not in one of the Zodiacs he would be waiting on the sands to give them the all-clear to land. To date, only one small shipment had been lost and that had been agreed in advance to help the local coastguard look more efficient than it actually was. The merchandise had been well past its prime.

At Collier's suggestion, George and Freddie had invested heavily in equipping their men. The boats and engines were new; the communications system was the best money could buy; they had even managed to get hold of some night-vision goggles that were being developed for the British Army. Dangerous items, they felt, if they fell into the hands of the Spanish coastguard. Happily, the dispute with Britain over Gibraltar made that highly unlikely.

Once Juan Carlos had landed the merchandise he had a choice of three safe houses around the southern tip of Spain where the cannabis would be repackaged in Spanish vans for its onward journey to the 'slaughter', a central distribution centre close to Barcelona. In Barcelona, the stuff was transferred again to Freddie's fleet of British and French vans, which would cross into France and head for the northern ferry ports. Occasionally a shipment would go straight to the port of Bilbao, on the northern coast of Spain, and pick up a freighter bound for Britain. Although this was the quickest route, it was not always the safest, because the Spanish militia in the region were intensively seeking out Basque separatists.

Juan Carlos packaged the cannabis in the side and floor panels of the vans, which had been especially adapted by Freddie for the job. An engineer in the Port of London Authority had even supplied Freddie with their customized rivets, which showed the Customs and Excise inspectors that the vehicle had been searched, cleaned and sealed by their men. At times Freddie and George thought it was easier than taking candy from a baby. It was also a lot more profitable. In just one year, they had managed to replace all the money they had spent on their American adventure, and then some.

Under Collier's tuition, Freddie had cut the risks to a minimum. Depending on the shipment he might have as many as three or four vans in a convoy. A look-out car would drive one hour ahead of the convoy to look for road blocks and other police activities. Thirty minutes behind the first car came a second, which acted as a further insurance policy. On occasions, Freddie had even given permission for a third car to follow thirty minutes behind the convoy, to make sure they were not being followed.

The reason for the Barcelona transfer was to hide the mileage on the vans. They knew that Customs and Excise were on the look-out for vans which had been down to Málaga and back. Freddie's trucks never had this problem and were always full of merchandise from the boys' legitimate import–export operations. Amazingly enough, the legitimate company was even starting to turn a profit.

London, Monday 9 August 1965

I t was no coincidence that in two different parts of London separate meetings were discussing the same topic. For some the Great Train Robbery just would not go away.

'Cream and sugar?' Sir Roger asked. William Hardwood nodded. He actually preferred his coffee black, but thought it would just complicate matters to say so. He had already sensed what Sir Roger would want to discuss. The day before, the anniversary of the robbery, the Sunday papers had been full of it and continued to ask embarrassing questions.

'It's been two years, two long years since the robbery. I just wondered where we stood. As you know, I'm due to retire at the end of the year and I would like to tie up as many loose threads as possible or bury the files, if you follow my thoughts?'

'I certainly do, Sir Roger.' If William could not follow Sir Roger's thoughts, who could? 'Unfortunately there is really nothing much to report since we last discussed the case. We are more convinced than ever that the architect of this and a number of other crimes is a figure known to us only as the Ulsterman. Sadly, neither Scotland Yard nor ourselves are any closer to discovering his real identity. We believe he was the intellectual driving force behind the Great Train Robbery and it is quite possible that if he knew about the money he also knew about the diamonds and did a separate deal with a member of the gang.'

'Reynolds?'

'Highly unlikely. Reynolds isn't that sort. If he had agreed to get the diamonds he would certainly have split the reward with the rest of the gang. A question of doing what is right, I believe. Honour amongst thieves, and all that. No, if a deal was struck it was certainly with one of the others who have never been caught. That could be any one of four or five people, as we assume that both Charlie Wilson and Ronald Biggs, who have subsequently escaped, weren't involved.'

'I'll keep the file open until the end of November, but if there are no more developments, I will leave it in your hands. My copy of the file will be sent to the archives. I don't want to leave it as a pending problem for my successor, as our interest now is purely financial.'

'I understand, Sir Roger.'

The Ulsterman was also conducting a one-to-one. He was somewhat less reconciled to the loss of the diamonds than Sir Roger.

'Two years, two bloody years and nothing,' he raged. 'It's not good enough, Patrick. I'm not looking for any needle in a haystack. I'm asking you to find two fully grown people and nearly three million pounds' worth of diamonds. People and even diamonds don't simply disappear. Not in Britain. Not yet, anyway!'

Green had decided before going into the meeting that attack was the best form of defence. 'I beg to differ, sir. The whole of Scotland Yard is after Reynolds, Edwards, Wilson and Biggs, and so far not a peep. We know where Birch and Rawlings are and we have kept an eye on them. From everything we can see, they were telling the truth. They genuinely didn't have the bag or the diamonds and that means that without doubt Jenkins is our man.'

'Now you've mentioned them, were Birch and Rawlings responsible for Terry's death? If they were I think I should make a couple of calls and get a few friends of mine at the Port of London Authority to take a little look at their import–export operation. I'm sure it's dirty, if those two are involved.'

By now Green knew very well what had happened to Terry. People talk. But at the time he had almost felt like calling George and thanking him for Terry's timely demise. He had hated Terry and his methods and as far as he was concerned it was good riddance. 'A few rumours that Rawlings was involved, but nothing concrete,' he replied. 'The killer could have been any one of a number of people. Rose wasn't the first person Terry had stepped over the line with. He wasn't a popular man.'

'Neither will I be if I ever get my hands on that little Welsh scumbag, Jenkins. If ever a man was overdue for a lesson it is him. So find him and give him one. If you can't find him, get his wife. You might even enjoy extracting information from her. That's what I pay you and pay you well for. So let's see a bit of service.'

LONDON

If David was worried that the Ulsterman would eventually find him, he never showed it. He had taken Denise out for a special dinner at one of Douglas's more exclusive restaurants on the Sunday night and then on to the casino to celebrate the second anniversary of the robbery. They had partied on into the night and made plans for the future.

'An exotic holiday, that's what's missing,' he decided. 'We'll wait for the weather to turn and then we'll jet off to the Caribbean. What do you fancy? Bahamas? Barbados?'

'How about Jamaica? That's meant to be really nice.'

'Okay, Jamaica it is. Will you check it out with the travel agent? We could go away for Christmas. The financial markets will be closed for the holidays.'

'Aren't you taking your business dealings just a little too seriously, Mr Jenkins? I'm sure Richard is quite capable of looking after our investments for a week or two without supervision.'

'We'll see. I don't want to miss the panto, though!' They both laughed.

Freddie was also thinking about travel. Collier had asked him to come over to Los Angles for a pow-wow. Both operations were expanding at a frightening pace and they wanted to be sure they were all pulling in the same direction. Moreover, Collier wanted to show Freddie a new line in designer drugs that his chemists were experimenting with. Some of the results had been outstanding. The only casualty had been Willy who had gone on one trip too many and was now, as Collier liked to put it, a 'casualty of war'.

'The lights are on, just there's nobody at home. He never really came back from that last trip,' Collier had told Freddie over the phone.

Maggie, who had signed Freddie up to the five-mile-high club, was another good reason for a trip to LA. She had come to visit him in London on a couple of occasions and had even rendezvoused with him in Spain. She had loved Marbella and been enthusiastic about Freddie's plan to build a house there. She had put him in touch with a friend who was a top LA architect. She could imagine the type of house Freddie wanted. She looked forward to being a house guest or, if things continued going the way they were, even the lady of the house.

London, October 1965

I t was not the sort of day William Hardwood would have chosen to go for a walk in Hyde Park, but Inspector Trebbin had made it sound as if it would be worth his while. The traffic up Regent Street had been appalling, so he abandoned his taxi at Oxford Circus and leapt on the Central Line tube to Lancaster Gate. He found Trebbin just through the gates of the park, sitting on a wooden bench feeding the pigeons. He did not exactly cut a figure as one of Scotland Yard's finest, but he was.

'Inspector, good to see you.' Hardwood extended his hand in greeting.

'Mr Hardwood, thank you for coming at such short notice.'

'Please call me William, Inspector . . .'

'And it's Nigel, not Inspector.'

'All right, Nigel, what have you got for me?' The two men started to stroll across the park lawns in the direction of the Serpentine.

'We've got one of your diamonds.'

'You're joking!' The news stopped William in his tracks.

'On this occasion, not. The diamond in question fits the description of one of the gems you gave me. Don't worry, I have been discreet. Only a couple of my men know what's going down.'

'So tell me more. This is fantastic! The first real break in two years.'

'The diamond was spotted by an eagle-eyed jeweller in Bath after he realized the person who had brought it in for valuation was unlikely to own such a jewel. He assumed, rightly as it turned out, that it must have been stolen and remembered the note about "pink" diamonds. I sent an officer down to Bath and we came up with a perfect match. That's the good news. The bad news, from your point of view, is that the girl who took the diamond to the jeweller is clearly not involved in the Great Train Robbery in any way. At the moment she is a very scared

184

young lady who has been very co-operative. Considering how sensitive the matter is, I don't think we are going to need to press charges. She won't do it again.'

'Do what?'

'Sorry, I was getting ahead of myself. The young lady in question is a chambermaid. She is currently working in one of Bath's better hotels, the name of which escapes me, but it's really not relevant for now. At the time she found the diamond, however, she was working at the Grosvenor in Chester. She said she found the gem in a corner of a bedroom when she was hoovering. At first she pocketed it, assuming it to be a fake. She was still almost sure that it was when she took it in for valuation, because she had stayed on at the hotel for over eight months after she found it and no guest had ever made a claim. She says she would have come forward with the stone if anyone had, and I tend to believe her.'

'Does the Grosvenor lead us anywhere?'

'Surprisingly, yes! Again with great discretion we took the young lady back to Chester to see if she could remember in which room she found the gem. She remembered immediately. I then thought we might be looking for a needle in a haystack, but started off by having a pot shot. I looked at the register at the time of the robbery and bingo!'

'My God, it gives me goose bumps just thinking about it. Please go on.'

'Firstly, I must apologize for not calling you sooner, but I didn't want to raise your hopes in case it all came to nothing. I also thought, given the leaks surrounding the robbery, that the fewer people, even in your office, who knew what I was doing, the better. I haven't even told the other officers on the case.'

'Including Butler?'

'Especially Butler and his team. Anyway, back to the Grosvenor in Chester, which for the time being is where the trail dries up. The people using the room around the period of the robbery were a Mr and Mrs David Wood. I am almost certain that this is an alias. Mrs Wood moved in a whole ten days before the day of the robbery, but Mr Wood only put in an appearance on the Saturday following it. Given the period of time that has passed since the event, there is absolutely no point in bringing in the forensic boys, because all clues and fingerprints will have been wiped clean by now. As far as descriptions go we haven't much to go on. The Woods tended to keep to themselves. Most describe them as a good-looking couple, especially the wife, whom one of the doormen described as a "right cracker, with a great set of pins".'

'He'll make a colourful witness, if we ever get them to court!'

'I have tried to involve as few of the hotel staff as possible, given that this is something of an unofficial inquiry, but those we have spoken to have been most co-operative. As I said, our trail, for the moment, peters out in Chester. The couple, the staff remember, talked about house-hunting in the region and the assistant manager thinks they said they had chosen Manchester as a base. My staff are currently looking through the lists of Mr and Mrs Woods in the region, concentrating on the Manchester, Liverpool and Birmingham areas. I think they would feel safer sticking to a big city, especially if they were used to London. On the first occasion, Mr Wood only stayed two nights at the hotel. They left on Monday 12 August and returned on the 19th, staying until the following Monday, 26 August. Strangely they then pop up again nearly a year later, in 1964, when they spent the weekend of 22 and 23 August at the hotel.'

'Registration?'

'A pack of lies, as you might expect, and as Mr Wood always paid cash nobody ever needed or thought to check the information. For what it is worth, and I believe I have it written down in my notes . . . yes, here it is, on their first visit they gave an address in Castelnau, the road that runs south of Hammersmith Bridge. It turned out to be a fish and chip shop, but perhaps it shows that they had a knowledge of south-west London. The second time around they gave an address in Manchester.'

'Another chip shop?'

'No, they went one better, the main post office in Brown Street.'

'Looks as if he's our man.'

'Certainly does. Now all we have to do is find him and hope that he's still using the name of Wood.'

'Well, if you want to make a splash you can drag in every Mr and Mrs Wood in Britain, if you like.'

'A novel idea, not one that would thrill the boss, yours or mine, but I think if we make any sudden moves it will just send him to ground. At least if Mr Wood returns to the Grosvenor we will be the first to know.'

'Do you think our Mr Wood knows he misplaced one of the diamonds?'

LONDON

'I don't think so. The scenario we have come up with, given the dates, is that Mr Wood went straight to Chester from Leatherslade Farm with his share of the spoils from the robbery, which included the diamonds. I assume that on the Saturday and Sunday they sorted through the money, which they then took on to their minders the following week. In a week, those minders could be just about be anywhere in Britain or Ireland. We also believe, or rather we now know, that Wood opened up the envelope with the diamonds in the room. It could be that in his keenness to see them, the envelope spilled open on the floor and when he picked them up he missed the vital one. He would have needed to have some extremely accurate inside information to know the pouch contained exactly fifty diamonds. However, if he is as careful as he appears to be, I'm surprised the number forty-nine didn't set his alarm bells ringing.'

'For all we know it might have. Perhaps that's why he went back to Chester.'

'Thought of that one. Doesn't necessarily fit, because they didn't ask for the same room.'

'But we have to assume he is a competent thief and so could have entered the first room at will.'

'True, I hadn't looked at it from that point of view.'

'Backtracking for a second, why did you say Ireland? What makes you think Ireland could be involved?'

'Well, as the robbery was close to London, we must assume they went north to Chester for a reason. We assume that reason was both to disappear and to launder the money through their contacts and minders. It is unlikely they would go north and then return south, but from Liverpool they had an excellent ferry service to the Emerald Isles . . .'

'And to Belfast! It begins to look as if Mr Wood was the courier for our infamous Ulsterman. It's quite possible he made the drop in Belfast and then simply disappeared into an anonymous lifestyle in the Midlands.'

'I'll have the ferry traffic to both Dublin and Belfast checked. I've some friends in the Dublin police force who owe me a favour or two, so I'll ask them to look out for any English Woods who have popped up in Ireland in the last two years.'

'They don't need to be English, they could be Irish.'

187

'I'll follow every lead. You can rely on me for that.'

'You've certainly done a thorough enough job so far.'

The two men had by now walked the entire length of the Long Water and were arriving at the Serpentine Bridge. They had only paused once, next to Peter Pan's statue. It had reminded Trebbin that he had promised his wife he would take their granddaughter to see the film.

'I assume you haven't had lunch yet, Nigel,' William remarked when he saw the restaurant by the bridge. 'My treat. I think you've earned it.'

London, November 1965

S ir Roger was delighted to hear that a real break had finally been made in the case. He pressured William to keep on Trebbin's back. 'It would be nice to file this one away before I pack my bags,' he repeated.

'I'll do my best, sir, but I can't promise anything. It won't be easy – there are literally hundreds, if not thousands, of Woods between Manchester, Liverpool and Birmingham. So far we have a list of sixty-eight couples who have taken the ferry from Liverpool to Belfast in the last two years and fifty-six who have taken the Liverpool to Dublin run. If I had more men we could process the names more rapidly, but unfortunately discretion and numbers don't seem to go together.'

'I want discretion and results and within the month. See what can be done.'

Los Angeles, Late November 1965

Freddie was pleased to be back in Los Angeles. He had enjoyed his first time there and now, alone, without George sitting on his shoulder, he would have more time with Maggie. This time he could try out the fancy restaurants with her, restaurants which George had never really liked. He always complained when he could not get his draught beer and British food. 'I want a decent pint from the tap. I don't want these fuckin' diddly little bottles of beer,' he would say. 'Don't taste the same, do they?'

Just as Collier had promised, Freddie had no problems with his passport or visa on arrival at LAX. Collier's number one driver was even there to pick him up. This time Freddie was to be Collier's house guest – no hotels for him. Collier, who was looking more opulent than ever, made it clear from the start that Freddie had the run of the house during his stay. He could invite over whoever he wanted; he could fuck whoever he wanted; and he could generally abuse his body in any way else he saw fit as long as it didn't stain the carpets. A car and driver were put at his disposal, but there was also a sporty little drop-head for his own personal use and for when he didn't want to feel his style was being cramped.

On his second day in town, Freddie went to see Willy for old times' sake. They met down by the Santa Monica pier. Collier had been right. Willy was fucked up and in a bad way. As they walked along the beach, the Scot more staggering than walking, he explained how he had finally been thrown out of UCLA after ignoring the offer of 'one final chance'. It reminded Freddie of his early days in court. With his student visa revoked, Willy was now fighting the emigration department not to be deported back to Britain. The police had yet to pin a drug rap on him, but they knew what he had been up to and how and why he had gotten himself fucked up. He was *persona non grata* in the States, unless they felt they could use him to catch some other bigger fish, like Collier.

LOS ANGELES

Behind the scenes Collier was doing everything in his power to pull political strings and speed up Willy's deportation. In his present state the Scot was a dangerous liability and in Collier's line of work he could ill afford such little luxuries, however much he had liked the liability in the past. If the decision to deport Willy did not come through soon, Collier would have to take his own steps to remove and silence him.

The business side of Freddie's visit went remarkably smoothly. Both men thought alike, Freddie's brain patterns having been moulded by the older Californian into a mirror image of his own. Collier, however, was starting to face serious competition in America for the first time, and some had been quite bloody.

'They think we're back in the Twenties and that it's Prohibition and bootlegging all over again. They think they're real gangsters, hard men, but let me tell you, Freddie, they're not. They're punks, these arseholes, punks who've got no respect for life or property. They dope themselves up on their own merchandise and then go out and shoot somebody up just for the hell of it. They should be butt-fucked all the way from here to Hawaii and back. I don't mind telling you, they scare me at times, and as you know I don't scare easily. You have to watch your back, even over in Europe.'

Collier had learnt some lessons from Willy. None of his staff was allowed to touch his more exotic merchandise any more, nor act as guinea-pigs, especially on the newer 'designer' drugs. That, he said, was strictly for the punters, whom he affectionately referred to as his 'mugs'. 'What do you do if you find a mug?' he used to ask Freddie. 'You use it.'

'I've told the staff that they can have all the weed they want for personal consumption, but not when they're on the job,' he explained to Freddie, 'and a little Charlie in moderation. Hell, I can't be a total hypocrite, can I?' As he talked he had been using the edge of his credit card to chop and spread several grammes of coke on the glass-top table of his den. The room overlooked the pool area through tinted windows and was the one part of the house that was out of bounds to everyone, including the maids, unless he specifically invited them in. Although only an occasional coke user, Freddie decided this was one of those occasions. He took a line through a pristine rolled-up ten-dollar bill. He was determined to enjoy his time in LA. He felt he needed to recharge his batteries. It had been a long two years.

191

KEEP ON RUNNING

The most pressing business matter for both men was a large-value shipment of prime-quality merchandise which was due to sail at any time from the Pakistani port of Karachi. The MS *June Star* would be carrying both Pakistani and Afghan hashish and heroin, and in huge quantities compared with anything that had gone before. The ship was bound for Liverpool, via the Cape of Good Hope, a journey of a little over four weeks depending on the stops along the way. The aim, as the ship's captain well knew, was for the arrival to coincide as nearly as possible with the Christmas holiday season, when port officials were at their most vulnerable for bribes. But such was the size and value of the shipment that Collier and Freddie had decided to unload the merchandise in stages just as soon as the ship got close enough to Europe. Juan Carlos had organized one pick-up to be made close to the island of Madeira in the Atlantic; this would then be taken to Spain and transferred by the normal route in vans to Britain. Meanwhile Freddie was scheduling another team, under George's supervision, to rendezvous with the ship in the St George's Channel, just off the Welsh coast. As they could not insure their cargo, this was the most economical method of spreading the risk. The shipment, if landed safely, would keep the European operations supplied well into the new year and allow Collier to milk the Mexican and Jamaican supply routes for his North American clients.

Freddie was a film buff, so Collier, through his studio contacts, organized a tour of one of the major Hollywood studios for him and Maggie. They were even able to have lunch in the studio canteen and meet some of the stars, many of whom were appreciative clients of Collier's. On their return to the house there was a further surprise awaiting them: a week at Round Hill in Jamaica, courtesy of Collier. Round Hill, Collier explained to Freddie and Maggie, was the Caribbean's first great resort. It had been the playground of Noël Coward, Cole Porter, Oscar Hammerstein, Richard Rodgers, Grace Kelly, Katharine Hepburn and even, recently, the late American President, John Kennedy.

Collier left the tickets on Freddie's bed. 'You two deserve it. You need the break. And Freddie, it's time you got to see where your roots are. Who knows, you might even run into your old man on the beach. It's a small world out there, as you know. You and Maggie will have a ball, that I can guarantee. I'm just sorry I can't come along as well. Round Hill is set on its own peninsula and the villa belongs to a guy at one of the studios and comes fully equipped. You won't have to do a thing, except lie back, enjoy yourselves and occasionally think of England! You can manage that, can't you, Maggie? I'll see you back here next week.'

Early the following morning, Freddie and Maggie flew out of LAX for Miami, where they connected with a flight to Montego Bay on Jamaica's north coast. On this occasion Freddie declined Maggie's kind offer to renew his membership of the five-mile-high club. He thought he should save his strength for Jamaica.

Jamaica, December 1965

Denise had won the battle. They would spend Christmas and the New Year on the Isle of Man with their new friends. She had explained to David that there was little point in having a beautiful house and lots of money if you couldn't flaunt it, and what better time to flaunt it than during the year-end festivities? David conceded the point and, giving him no time for second thoughts, Denise went straight down to their travel agent in Douglas to book their 'exotic' holiday for the first half of December. It would be two glorious weeks in Jamaica at the Half Moon, close to Montego Bay. They flew straight from the Isle of Man to London, where they joined the flight to Kingston. In Kingston, David picked up a sporty hire car and drove across the island by way of Ocho Rios and Falmouth to the Half Moon. Neither of them had seen a beach anything like the Half Moon's, nor water the colour and temperature of the Caribbean. 'Perhaps we chose to live on the wrong island,' Denise ribbed David as they stared out at the spectacular sunset. 'I could get quite used to this, especially these temperatures.'

'But that's the beauty, pet, with our money we can come and go as we please. The world's our oyster. I think we need to travel more before we decide what's going to be right for us. I want to show you the world and then some. I was thinking on the flight over, you were right, we can give old Richard his head when we get back – after all, I only ever do what he tells me to.' David ran his toes through the warm Jamaican sand and poured Denise another glass of champagne as darkness started to fall all around them. 'Now this is what I call the good life!'

Jamaica was beautiful, Round Hill was beautiful, but most beautiful of all, in Freddie's eyes, was Maggie. It was because of her that he had finally stopped running and opened his mind to the beauty that was all

194

around him. It dawned on him that they were now very much a couple. His clubbing days were over, at least for the moment. Sharing a room and a bed with Maggie certainly beat sharing with George, however much he liked the big fella. It also beat sharing a cell. As he looked around the spacious white villa a shiver ran down his spine at the thought of having to go back to the nick. He wasn't sure if he could cope any more. He was hardly reformed, he had just grown to appreciate the finer things in life and the finer things were sadly lacking in most of Her Majesty's prisons.

Freddie spoke daily to George in London. George reassured him that everything was fine on the 'Eastern Front', as he liked to call their operation. Collier was their 'Western Front'. George's only demand on Freddie was that he too could have a holiday once Freddie was back and the gear from the *June Star* safely warehoused. He had seen a brochure for a new Butlin's holiday camp and was determined to be one of the first guests and treat the family. Aunt Rose, Ernie and Albert would all be invited along for the ride at his expense. 'It's even got a fuckin' heated indoor swimming pool with a bar with beer on tap that you can swim right up to from the pool. Can you beat that?' As Freddie stared out through the French windows of the villa, which led on to the private pool where Maggie lay tanning herself topless against the dramatic colourings of the Caribbean, he realized that he and his partner now had little in common other than the fact that they still enjoyed each other's company when they were left alone. But for how long, he wondered.

Freddie made no effort to look for his father while on the island. Another time, he told Maggie. This was their holiday. They split their time between the villa pool and the beach. Lunch was normally taken at the villa, occasionally prepared by Maggie herself, and at night they had dinner in the Georgian Colonial dining pavilion or on the almond-tree terrace which overlooked one of the resort's beaches. Tonight they chose the terrace, as a typical Jamaican show of song and dance was being offered by the management. 'Not too touristy,' they promised. Freddie gave the head waiter a generous tip which guaranteed one of the prime tables – their favourite, close to the steps leading down to the beach and far enough away from the action not to disturb the two lovebirds.

Freddie and Maggie went down to dinner just after 7.30, stopping off at the bar for a pre-dinner cocktail. An hour later, they were escorted to their table where the maître d' had the Krug '64 and Malossol caviar chilling on ice as Freddie had instructed.

'I like your style, mister!' Maggie smiled across the candlelit table as they toasted their happiness and their remaining time in Jamaica. She slipped off her shoes and started playing with Freddie's legs under the table.

It was the concierge at the Half Moon who had suggested to David and Denise that for a change they might like to drive across to Round Hill for dinner. He gave them directions and made the necessary reservations.

Freddie saw David first. To begin with he was not a hundred per cent sure. The hair was different. Colour? Style? He could not pin it down, but that it was David he was almost certain. A little fatter, but David all the same. He spent the next half-hour pondering what to do. Maggie did not know of his past, not that she was likely to mind, considering her sideline as one of Collier's mules. Then again, Maggie, being American, might not even know what the Great Train Robbery was. Likewise he could not be certain that David was with his wife. The lady was pretty enough, but he had only known of Denise's reputation through pub gossip in London.

Freddie was fairly happy that he was in control of the situation. He was sure that David had not yet seen him and as his back was to their table, it was unlikely that he would. Denise, who was looking in his direction, would not know him from Adam and neither she nor David had ever met Maggie nor even knew of her existence. Freddie eventually took the bull by the horns and decided it was time to level with Maggie. He told her briefly about the train robbery and his role in it and how he was almost certain another member of the gang was also having dinner at Round Hill.

'How exciting!' Maggie said and suggested that Freddie call David and his partner over to join them. But Freddie still had his doubts. His problem resolved itself when he saw out of the corner of his eye that David was heading across the dance floor, presumably in the direction of the toilet. If there was a time and place for everything it was here and now, especially as the gents was located way at the back of the bar away from the main action. Even if David threw a complete wobbly and refused to talk to him, it would be unlikely to disturb any of the other guests.

JAMAICA

As Freddie slipped into the toilets he could see David at the urinal. A peek under the stall doors confirmed they were alone. 'Blimey, you're well made, aren't you?' he said in a soft voice, not wishing to startle his old partner in crime. David swung around, spraying himself off the side of the urinal in the process. The London voice had been enough.

'Christ!' he said regaining his composure and finishing the business at hand.

'Is that any way to greet an old colleague, then?' Freddie smiled.

'Freddie? Is that you? I can't fuckin' believe it. And in a bog in the middle of Jamaica!'

'Yeah, I'm that same silly bastard you wouldn't talk to in the car. But before you say anything, I don't blame you. I've learnt a lot since 63. Except now I've gone and broken my own rules by coming and talking to you here.'

'I'm glad you did,' David smiled and meant it. Both men had mellowed considerably over the last two years. They hugged each other in a very unBritish gesture, but they felt they needed to. They were part of history and knew it. They were survivors of the Great Train Robbery and, as such, members of one of the world's most exclusive clubs. Even more exclusive, if you counted only those who weren't behind bars.

'Well, we can't stand here rabbiting all night, people might get the wrong idea. Come and join me and my lady for a drink,' Freddie suggested. 'No business talk, no questions, just for old time's sake. That is the wife you're with, I presume? I never did get to meet her.'

'Yes, that's Denise, all right.' In the old days David would never have contemplated taking the risk of talking to Freddie in public, but if he was ever going to stop looking over his shoulder, now was as good a time as any to start. He felt a certain affection for Freddie, as well as admiration. If he had been a betting man he would have put money on Freddie's collar being amongst the first to be felt. But here he stood in front of him, obviously no worse off from the experience of holding up one of Her Majesty's mail trains.

David made his way back to his table and collected Denise. Freddie had already got the maître d' organizing some extra chairs and glasses. They enjoyed the show and danced a little before making their way up the hill to Freddie's villa. They drank on into the night, the Krug '64 flowing. The men jumped into the pool fully dressed to cool off and sober up and were followed by Denise and Maggie. When the girls got out, their dresses clung erotically to their bodies and both men could appreciate that they had done all right for themselves, all things considered. Before long the four were stripped down to their underwear and when they weren't frolicking in the water they were chatting to each other poolside.

'And George? Whatever happened to George? Never saw his name in the papers,' David asked as he puffed on one of Freddie's Cuban cigars.

'We stayed together,' Freddie explained, 'and after we realized that Old Bill had nothing on us, we set up our own import–export business to front the cash flow.'

'In the smoke?'

'Well, the centre of our operation is in London. On our old patch and all. We even got a commendation the other day, as an example to the youth of the borough. Crims going straight and all that crap!'

'So pigs might fly after all!'

'And you and Denise, did you skip the country after the job or hang around? I hear Bruce and Buster could be in Mexico.'

David carefully skirted around the first half of the question. 'I'd heard that, too. Charlie's been placed in either South Africa or Canada, but not a squeak on Ron. Who would have put money on him going over the wall and disappearing? Who do you reckon will be next?'

'Perhaps Gordon or Roy. But you can bet they will all go over the wall given half a chance.'

The girls crashed out around the pool on the *chaises longues* as the men chatted on. Dawn started to break across the Caribbean, so David put a call into the Half Moon to warn them he would be late back. He didn't need the concierge calling out a search party to look for him. The local constabulary might find more than they had bargained for, if they discovered David and Freddie together.

'Do you think it was worth it, then?' Freddie asked David out of the blue.

'I think so,' David replied after giving the matter some thought. 'Yes, I would have to say "yes" to that question. Obviously, knowing we've got thirty years hanging over our heads is not so great, but if we hadn't taken the risk we might have got nailed for something else, something smaller without the rewards. It's law of averages, isn't it? I feel sorry for the other poor fuckers.'

'Me too. Thirty years is a lot of porridge. Changing the subject, did you ever receive a visit from the Ulsterman or his mate Green after the business?'

'Green . . . Patrick Green?'

'That's him.'

'But I thought he was the Ulsterman?'

'Nah! He's just his right-hand man who gets to do all the dirty work. You met him, then?'

'Yes, I think I met Green before the job. Why?' David felt very uneasy talking openly about Green for the first time to somebody other than Denise.

'He got a bit heavy with me and George after the job. When he picked up his whack he smacked George's auntie around quite a bit.'

'That's a right liberty! Didn't George do something about it?'

'What do you think? Green said there was something else on the train besides the dough, a package full of gems that was meant to be in with his whack. Seemed we swapped bags that day when you dropped us off and that really pissed him off.'

'We certainly swapped bags – I remember that – but there was nothing there except the money. Might have made a few extra bob on the switch, but that's it.'

'If you don't mind me saying so, Dave, you're a terrible liar. But I really don't care, I really don't give a fuck. I just wish you and Denise every luck and happiness. That Green's a right shit and deserves everything he gets. All I'm saying is watch your back. He's a nasty bastard and so are his mates. I think I would prefer to have the Yard on my back than Green and the Ulsterman. But *c'est la vie*, as the Frogs would say.'

David and Denise departed around seven in the morning after a champagne breakfast. Both ladies were wilting until the boys forced a jug of fresh Bucks Fizz down each of them. David brought his car around to the front door of the villa. 'So can I give you a lift again, Freddie? Not much space for the whack in this sporty little number though!'

'Not this time, Dave, I think I'll stay at the "farm" for another day or two,' he laughed. David got out of the car and gave Freddie another hug. It was an emotional moment; an emotional release for both men.

'You look after him, Maggie. He's a very special fella,' David said as he made his farewell, 'I hadn't realized how special until tonight. He's one of the good uns.'

'Don't suppose there's any point saying we'll write,' Freddie said. 'So you two look after yourselves. You know where to find me and George if you need to. You've got my card and number. Don't worry, we won't come looking for you. I just hope that we can repeat this night again sometime in the not too distant future.'

'Luck would be a fine thing! Shit, better have a final piss before I hit the road. Not too many service stations on these Jamaican roads.' David and Maggie chatted with Denise until David's return. One final handshake and they were gone.

'Why didn't you ask them for their address?' Maggie asked as they waved to the car disappearing up and over the hill.

'It's something David once tried to teach me and only now I understand. Don't ask for information you don't need. It's better for all of us in the long run.' He had decided that this was a meeting not even George should know about. He also reminded himself to tell George to get off the Charlie. The coke was making him talk too much.

They turned and went back into the villa with their arms around one another. Freddie noticed straight away that a champagne bottle had been removed from the ice bucket and placed on the corner of a paper napkin. 'Oh no, shouldn't put wet bottles on an antique table. It'll leave a nasty ring, won't it?' He picked up the bottle and took the napkin to wipe away the condensation. As he rubbed the table he saw that something was written on the paper. He stared down as the wet blue ink started to run into the napkin. 'David and Denise,' it said, 'Isle of Man . . .' and then what appeared to be a phone number. He held it up to the light and smiled. David really had changed since that day in the car.

Two days later Freddie and Maggie were back in LA. Maggie went straight to work on the red eye out to New York, but promised Freddie she would do everything within her power to get over to see him for Christmas or the New Year.

'Quit, if that's within your power. Chuck the job in and come and join me in Europe,' he told her as he gave her one last kiss.

'I'll think about it, Freddie, I promise.' Another kiss and she was off.

After a final two days of business meetings and consultations with

JAMAICA

Collier, Freddie was back at LAX preparing to fly home, only for now he really wasn't certain where he wanted home to be. He was starting to feel that home was wherever Maggie was.

MS *June Star*, Collier reported, was making good time according to George's last report and could, if the weather stayed fine in the South Atlantic, reach Madeira as early as 15 December. 'That's a few days early for my taste. I'll have a word with the captain when I get to London,' Freddie promised Collier.

As Freddie was driven to the airport by Collier's driver, the only sour taste in his mouth was the demise of Willy while he had been away in Jamaica. An overdose, Collier had said, but Freddie could not help but wonder exactly who had applied the overdose. Willy, who was not the suicidal or careless type, had been cremated quickly in LA before an autopsy had been completed. Freddie was given his ashes and what few personal belongings he had to take back to his parents in London. The only thing of value was a cheque for $83,000 made out to Willy's old man, the total amount of his bank deposits at the time of his death. Not a bad balance for a student, Freddie thought as he settled back in his first-class seat for the flight to London. It would be a nice little nest-egg for Willy's father when he got out of the nick, but he was sure the old man would have preferred his son to be fit and well.

Whitehall, December 1965

'It is quite simple, William, the people upstairs really don't care if Mr Wood, or whatever his name is, is brought to justice or not. He must be punished, yes, but not necessarily in the courts. Too embarrassing. Could cause problems for next year's World Cup, what with the African bloc already making noises about Britain's overly friendly relations with South Africa and all that.' William had noticed that Sir Roger was getting more and more short-tempered as his retirement drew closer. 'I'm simply going to bury the file, William, but before I do I will give you a written memo for your file that Mr and Mrs Wood can be liquidated if found. That will cover you later, if anybody asks.'

'What about the diamonds? What do we do with those if we ever come across them?'

'Oh, you'll think of something, William, you always do. Plant them on one of your raids and then hand them over to the Treasury. A loss here, a find there, it all balances out on paper in the end. A few non-truths never hurt anyone, especially in our line of work, where honour and integrity are taken for granted. Still, I've rambled on for far too long. Have you got anything else to report?'

'Nothing much other than we are narrowing the field. We believe we have pruned it down to just four people, or rather four sets of Mr and Mrs Wood, all of whom fit our profile. Given the sensitivity of the case we can't exactly go in like a bull in a china shop and grab them. We are being as discreet as possible with our inquiries.'

'Where do we find these Woods or can't we now see the woods for the trees, Mr Hardwood?'

'Very droll, I'm sure, sir,' William replied with a crooked smile. 'Our main suspect is living in Birkenhead. He arrived in the area at the time of the robbery. He has made an ostentatious show of wealth, yet appears not to work. All in all not a lot is known about him. Another suspect lives

202

in Macclesfield, same profile but seems to be a genuine Mr Wood who has relatives in Manchester. Then we have our three wood . . .'

'And you accuse me of being droll, William?'

'Sorry, sir, couldn't resist, especially as you will be spending so much more time at your golf club in the coming year.'

'A bit sedentary for my liking, although not for yours, I dare say. Hopefully retirement will allow me to improve my handicap and my game so that I can finally take some money off cowboys like you.' The intercom went on Sir Roger's desk. His faithful secretary, Dawn, reminded him that he was due at 10 Downing Street in fifteen minutes for a reception for a Soviet delegation.

'Rich isn't it, William, I've spent a lifetime looking for reds under the bed and now I have to go and have a lunchtime knees-up with them in our own Prime Minister's house. I knew this new fellow Wilson would spell trouble. We live in funny times, William, mark my words. Walk with me to the lift, if you will, and tell me about the other two . . . that three wood you were talking about.'

'Number three is located on the Isle of Man. Extremely wealthy, he appears to have made his money in international trading, but we can find no record of how, where or what. Said, on the island, to have visited South Africa on a number of occasions. He has certainly played the markets since his move to the island and so far with quite remarkable results. Currently he either is, or has just returned from, holidaying with his wife in Jamaica.'

'Sounds a man of taste. Can't see him hanging around with a bunch of thieves holding up trains in the middle of the night. And number four?'

'Our four wood is to be found just south of Belfast. Lots of money. Goes backwards and forwards between London and Belfast like a yo-yo and seems fairly pro a united Ireland.'

'That sounds more like our man! Do you think the job could have been done to raise funds for the Provisionals?'

'Could be, Sir Roger. We'll keep digging and hopefully I'll have some clearer news for you by next week.'

London, December 1965

'I can't give you much more help, Patrick, without putting his head on a plate for you.' The Ulsterman was talking to Patrick Green on the phone from his study. 'I still have not got access to all the information, but they are concentrating their efforts on four Mr Woods, one of whom is Declan Wood who lives just south of Belfast. I know him, so you can cross him off your list. Nasty piece of work who hates the English and will hopefully lead our friends on a wild goose chase around the provinces for some time to come. You've got three to look at, then: Birkenhead, Macclesfield and the Isle of Man. Don't fail me, Patrick, as I will accept no excuses this time. Remember you have a huge advantage over the police: you know who you are looking for and that his real name is David Jenkins. So go and deal with him and get me what's left of my fucking diamonds.'

Spain, December 1965

Freddie spent little more than forty-eight hours in London on his return from LA. He was eager to monitor the passage and progress of the *June Star* from Spain. The weather in the Atlantic had changed dramatically since he left America and reports did not look good for the transfer off Madeira. If that was the case, he would need to double up on the transfer in the Irish Sea, as his Customs and Excise contacts had set a 'final' limit as to how much they could turn a blind eye to in Liverpool.

'Those fuckers are making far too much money for their own fuckin' good,' he had told George before heading for Spain. 'How can they turn down our offer? What difference does it make if it's one, two, three or fifteen containers? But no, they don't need the extra money for Christmas, the fat, lazy bastards. They should bloody well privatize the docks and the customs service and sling the lot of them on the dole. We might get a bit of service for our money then.'

Leaving George to organize the extra boats needed for a second Irish Sea transfer, Freddie took advantage of the trip to Spain to make sure that everything was on schedule for the completion of his dream home in Marbella. If all went well, he would be able to spend Christmas or New Year there with Maggie. It would still be a little basic, house and pool, but that was fine with him. He wanted Maggie to fix the house up for him. After all, she might be spending a lot more time there if he asked her nicely.

Juan Carlos kept Freddie informed on a daily basis about the position of the *June Star* and the weather off Madeira; the reports increased to twice daily as the 17 December rendezvous drew closer. The Atlantic storms kept getting worse, which made Juan Carlos feel a lot better. There was nothing to question or discuss. The transfer was off. It was that simple. Chances of success were negligible, at best, and Freddie had taught Juan not to gamble on these operations. As the undisturbed

KEEP ON RUNNING

MS *June Star* ploughed her way north through heavy seas, Juan met Freddie at Málaga Airport.

'It was a good call, Juan. You were right and there's no shame in being cautious. Just you remember that. I'm sure we'll pick up the slack in the Irish Sea. George is already working on it, but I would like you there all the same. You can look after the first drop as originally scheduled and George can take care of this new one.'

London, Monday 20 December 1965

'Isle of Man! I'll stake my pension on it.' Trebbin was not a betting man, so William was more than happy to go along with the inspector's hunch. 'But I want you and some of your boys along on this one. I've already stuck my neck out far further than I should. Butler's starting to ask questions.'

'I know, Nigel, and I appreciate everything you've done so far. I only hope the department and I can repay you one day. So who is our couple?'

'They say they are David and Denise Wood, although we still believe these names to be false. They fit the timing of our profile perfectly. They opened a number of bank accounts on the Isle of Man and elsewhere using an island address during the week beginning 12 August, exactly the week our Mr and Mrs Wood went missing from the Grosvenor in Chester. We can place them back on the island again as of around October 1963. We are still working on their current address, but we believe it to be a big house close to Douglas. At first they stayed in a house in Douglas belonging to their financial advisers, Stroat, Bartlett, Booth and Wright, a company which is already under investigation by the Fraud Squad and a number of financial institutions. We believe Richard Wright, the company's senior partner on the island, to be Wood's personal financial adviser and the one who, in so many words, was responsible for laundering the train-robbery money for him, although we don't actually have any proof that he knew where it came from. We have Wright under twenty-four-hour surveillance and an unofficial wire tap at both the Douglas and London offices.'

'How soon do you want to move?'

'No time like the present if we all want to be at home with our families for Christmas. If you can get yourself and your men to the island, I'll meet you there.'

'Where exactly?'

'Are you still trying to be discreet?'

'More than ever.'

'Okay, I can't promise miracles, but I'll see if I can put us up in King William's College. The school should have broken up for the Christmas holiday, so we won't be disturbed. It's also well placed for the airport, although it might be a shade chilly if they've turned off the heating!'

'I'll be over with ten of my men and my thermals the day after tomorrow!'

'Let me know your flight details and I'll have you met at the airport. Might even have the operation room set up by then and, if you're really lucky, we may even have a snapshot of your Mr Wood.'

'Talking of shots, Nigel, I think I should warn you that some of my team who will be coming over on the ferry will be armed. Wood may be dangerous and my bosses are rather keen to have him dead or alive. There are even suggestions that the former may be beneficial all round.'

'I understand. Just let me know what you want to do so that none of my boys will be around. If we get involved with your antics the paperwork will keep me busy until Easter.'

'Speak to you tomorrow and see you on Wednesday.'

Manchester, early morning, Tuesday 21 December 1965

The phone took three rings to wake Green. He could have done without having to hear the resonant tones of the Ulsterman first thing in the morning, but he knew he had no choice. He rolled over and ended up touching another body, which grunted disparagingly. The young boy next to Green snuggled up to him. 'Late night, Patrick?' the Ulsterman inquired.

'Not too late, sir, you know how it is? Have to burn a lot of shoe leather if you want to get to the bottom of things.' As he spoke he covered up the young man's torso as if he were hiding it from the Ulsterman's prying eyes, and slipped out of the bed. The boy was still only half awake. Green signalled for him to be quiet as he dragged the phone into the bathroom, where he could speak in private.

'Good to hear it, Pat,' the Ulsterman replied, oblivious to Green's sexual preferences or the fact he had company. Patrick knew he was unlikely to approve. 'I can put you out of your misery and save you some of that shoe leather; you can forget Macclesfield. I got word last night that Jenkins is on the Isle of Man. A big country house close to Douglas. His financial advisers are Stroat, Bartlett, Booth and Wright. I've done my share of favours for them in the past, so I hope to get some more information by the end of the day. You just get yourself and a few of your boys over to the island and give me a call tonight to let me know which hotel you are in. And Patrick . . .'

'Sir?'

'Time is of the utmost importance. The police will start making their moves as of tomorrow. I would be most appreciative if you had my diamonds before they started pulling Jenkins' house apart.'

'I'll do my best, sir, but, sir, if your information is correct and the police are going to move in from London, I think I would prefer to do

209

this job by myself. If what I have heard about the island is true, a group of my heavies arriving in Christmas week along with Old Bill from London might attract just the sort attention we are trying to avoid. Also, if I am going to pop him, I don't want any witnesses about, however much I trust them.'

'It's your decision, Patrick. I'll agree with anything you suggest as long as you get the job done.'

At least, Green thought, he would be able to spend the morning in bed with last night's conquest. He just wished he could remember the young man's name and which bar he had picked him up in. He would not have much time to use and abuse the lad, because he needed to be on his way to the island before mid-afternoon. He put the phone down and returned to the pleasures of the flesh which beckoned to him on the bed. Immoral, the Pope had called it, but what did the Pope know? Another good reason for Northern Ireland to remain British, Green thought to himself as he rolled the boy over. In Southern Ireland you could go to jail for it. Ironic, he thought, as that was where it was most prevalent. Like locking up an Irish drunk in the Guinness brewery!

St George's Channel, Tuesday morning, 21 December 1965

The captain of the *June Star* was far from happy and the foul weather reflected in his mood, much to the disgust of his crew. Captain Kevin Todd was not on a 'pay-to-play' package, as had first been discussed with George; his final pay-day was now strictly performance-related, with large bonuses if all the merchandise got to its destination. Freddie and George had adopted this policy after one of their captains claimed that a shipment had been seized by Customs and Excise, when in fact it had been landed safely and sold on by the captain to one of their main competitors. From that day forward, after the errant captain had had an unfortunate boating accident, there was one payment for the basic risk, with further payments made at intervals against delivery and performance. It cost Freddie and George more, but it was safer.

The missed drop off Madeira preyed on Todd's mind. His final pay-day could be affected. He, of all people, knew that they would be pushing their luck to get the extra bulk quantity of hashish and heroin through Liverpool docks without being stopped. He had a career and family to think about, so there were certain risks he was loth to take. At least they did not hang you for drug running in England, as they did in some of the less enlightened parts of the world.

Todd peered forward over the deck of the freighter. The driving rain made it difficult to see anything beyond the bow as the *June Star* drove her way up into the St George's Channel, the stretch of water separating the south-easternmost coast of Ireland from Wales and England. The radar reflected the normal heavy shipping traffic in the area, but there was only one blip on the radar screen that gave Todd any real concern. It was a ship on an almost identical heading to his own which over the last twenty-four hours, since leaving the Bay of Biscay, had been slowing

211

down as if waiting for the *June Star* to pass her by. For preference, Todd wanted nobody around when he finally made his drop.

Juan Carlos, who had flown up from Spain with Freddie to oversee the first transfer, had left Fishguard in Wales the previous night. The two trawlers had set off together and made their way out into the channel. Despite the driving rain and the cold, conditions were not too bad for their purposes, but to be certain Juan Carlos had decided to cut across to meet the *June Star* earlier and go for a daylight transfer rather than a night-time one.

The mechanics of the transfer itself were simple enough in daylight. Todd's crew would push the watertight containers off the stern of the freighter as the fishing vessels approached from behind. It would then be a relatively straightforward task for Juan and his crew to winch the containers aboard the trawlers and camouflage them in the hold with crushed ice and fish. Juan had taken the precaution of buying the fish in advance so there would be no need to put the nets out. The agreed rendezvous point was smack in the middle of the St George's Channel, at 6°W 52°N, which gave Juan a number of options if he had to run for cover, including Southern Ireland and even the Atlantic. The original plan, which Juan hoped to be able to stick to, was to return to Fishguard, the trawlers' base, where vans would be waiting to transfer the gear to the various warehouses and distribution centres around Britain. Juan was scheduled to pick up a third of the shipment. Another third would be transferred just off Anglesey as the freighter moved into the Irish Sea – a larger trawler from Holyhead, under George's command, would be involved. The final third was to be unloaded in Liverpool dock.

Juan watched the converging blips on his radar screen. One of them was the *June Star*. Only a couple of miles separated the two ships from the trawlers. Juan made radio contact with Captain Todd who made the agreed small talk about weather conditions and other maritime matters, but enough to alert Juan to the fact that the *June Star* was the trailing ship and not the first blip on his screen. As Todd cut his speed, it appeared that the other ship picked up speed for the first time since entering the channel. Perhaps they thought the *June Star* was turning in towards Milford Haven or the Pembroke peninsula.

Mike, George's long-standing right-hand man, was the first to see the other ship, the MS *Port au Prince*, which was sailing under the Panamanian flag. She was slightly smaller than the *June Star* and had now picked up speed considerably and was heading north into the Irish Sea. Juan got on the radio and in Spanish passed the time of day with the captain, who turned out to be Cuban. He seemed happy to be able to converse in his native tongue so far from home. The ship was bound for Barrow-in-Furness, which both he and Juan had trouble pronouncing. They agreed that the British had some very strange names for their towns. The Cuban captain wished Juan 'God speed and a good catch' and sailed on in the direction of the Irish Sea. Less than ten minutes later the *June Star* steamed into view. Todd had cut the speed back to the absolute limit. Going any slower would almost certainly alert the coastguard stations monitoring the shipping movements in the channel and arouse suspicion.

Juan made contact with Todd again on a pre-agreed wavelength which had a more limited range for those wanting to eavesdrop. Both men were pleased that the weather conditions were rather better than they had been off Madeira. Certainly more conducive to the transfer. The trawlers manoeuvred astern of the big freighter and followed in its wake. The crew had the containers in position and one by one they were tumbled off the deck and into the sea with a large splash. First they would sink from view, but seconds later they would break to the surface again. Spotters from both trawlers kept an eye on the bobbing containers, which were quickly secured and winched aboard. Todd was more than pleased at the way the transfer was going. He wanted to take advantage of the good conditions and drop more.

'No!' Juan commanded firmly over the radio. 'Our catch is enough for today. It would be greedy to take any more when we don't have anywhere secure to store it. There will be plenty of other trawlers around later to catch the rest of the shoal.' Todd reluctantly acknowledged the Spaniard's cryptic message and slowly increased speed as the two trawlers slipped astern and set to work storing their catch before returning to Fishguard. Juan used his ship-to-shore radio to get patched through to Freddie, who was monitoring the operation from a hotel room in Liverpool.

'Pleased to report an excellent catch today. All has been secured and we are heading for home. The shoal is moving due north and I would predict the same fine fishing conditions will prevail in the Irish Sea this evening. Over and out!'

'Copy!' Freddie replied. 'See you in London. Over and out.' Freddie passed on the good news to George, who was shacked up in a bed-and-breakfast boarding house in Holyhead and enjoying every minute of it as the landlady, a big woman by any standards, was an old flame of his. George rounded up his team and prepared to sail out to meet the *June Star*. He would rendezvous in less than six hours.

Isle of Man, Tuesday
afternoon, 21 December 1965

A s Green had imagined, once he had the name and approximate whereabouts of his quarry it was not be long before he had an exact fix and even a sighting. He had played a hunch, and after settling himself in one of the few hotels still open along the promenade, he visited a number of shops in Douglas, asking for the Woods. He claimed he was just off the boat from Liverpool for Christmas and had stupidly left his address book back home in Manchester. He was an old friend of the Woods, he told the shopkeepers, and would like to look them up while on the island. He had brought over a Christmas present for them.

Green struck out on his first two calls, to a baker and a newsagent, but at the butcher he struck gold. They had an address for the Woods in Douglas. Green thought the Ulsterman had said something about a country house, but country house, town house, what did it matter as long as he got to Jenkins? He spent what remained of the afternoon watching the house through the net curtains of a small café. He could not remember how many hot chocolates he downed, but it was at least two too many. The street was busy, which was bad for Green. If he was going to use a gun, he would need a silencer. He could resort to a knife, but that could be risky if he had to get both Jenkins and his wife. But first he had to find Jenkins. He would worry about how to deal with him when he came to cross that bridge.

'Are you waiting for somebody, luv?' the waitress inquired as she tidied away yet another half-finished cup of chocolate. 'Because you've been sitting there staring out the window for more than an hour. You hardly touched your last chocolate and it's gone cold now.'

'I am, seeing that you ask. That is, I was enjoying your chocolate, but I am also waiting for some old friends, the Woods. David and Denise

215

– perhaps you know them?' Green could be as charming as the next man when it suited him. 'I was told they lived in that house across the road. I was waiting for them to return. I just hope they're not travelling, because my visit is something of a surprise.'

'Oh, I don't think they're travelling. I don't know Mr Wood, but I know Mrs Wood, she's a lovely lady. Still pops in occasionally to buy one of our cakes. Says she can't find anything like them anywhere else on the island. But you won't find her over there, they moved about a year ago. To a big house just outside Douglas, I think.'

'You wouldn't happen to have a phone number or an address for them, would you?'

'Not here in the shop. But I could get it for you by the morning, if that's not too late. My sister's sure to have it – she's been up to the house to do some flower arranging for Mrs Wood.'

'That would be most kind. What time do you open? I'll come back for breakfast.' Green, trying to control his excitement, paid for his hot chocolates and left the waitress a generous tip. It was too late to do anything tonight anyway; he would have to wait until tomorrow. He returned to his hotel for an early night, not having had much opportunity for sleep the night before. He would eat alone in his room as his disguise was starting to bother him. He had to wear the wig and glasses because he was as certain as January follows December that once the bodies were found a lot of people would be coming forward to tell the police about the stranger who had been asking about the Woods. At least he would be adding some excitement to their drab, boring little lives, he thought. They could tell their grandchildren about the day they met the Woods' cold-blooded killer face to face. He promised himself to get the job done the next day. He did not want to run the risk of getting stuck on the island over Christmas. He called the Ulsterman and gave him the good news.

Irish Sea, Tuesday
afternoon, 21 December 1965

As trawlers went, the *Puffin* was considerably larger than Juan's boats and could manage the pick-up alone. She sailed due west from Holyhead. If she kept going she would reach Dublin by the morning. The rendezvous, however, was just ten miles out into the Irish Sea. George, like Juan, would have preferred to do the transfer in daylight but unless they left the *June Star* lying at anchor, they would just have to manage as best they could. By sunrise, at 8 a.m., she would already be tied up alongside in Liverpool dock. The *Puffin* was also better equipped than Juan's smaller trawlers had been, and had a powerful system of lights for working at night.

George was dozing on his bunk when he got the first call from his skipper. 'Could you come up to the wheelhouse, George?' Cliff asked over the intercom. 'We've got a small problem.'

George did not like problems, however small. He did not even bother to slip on his oilskins before joining Cliff in the wheelhouse. 'What's up?' he inquired.

'We seem to be experiencing a few electrical problems which are affecting both the radio and the radar. They're both coming and going in waves.'

'Know the feeling,' George cracked. He was in good spirits. This was the last big job of the year and he was looking forward to getting that January break with his family after some serious Christmas celebrations. Cliff showed George the difficulties he was having with the radar. One moment they had a signal, the next nothing.

'I don't know nothin' about these things, but if it was our telly I would say it was a loose connection and give it a bit of a thump.'

'Could be the right thing to do. I really don't know what to say, because out here I have no way of checking all the wiring. There's

217

just too much of it. That, I assume, is our target.' Cliff pointed to one of two blips on the screen as the radar came to life for a brief moment. The other point of light was the *Port au Prince*, which had slowed again and was now almost within sight of the *June Star*. 'I'm sorry about this, George, but the radar was booked in to be serviced over Christmas. You only put us on stand-by at the last moment, so a couple of things on board aren't exactly how I would like them.'

'I know . . . I know . . . no one's blaming you, mate. Just relax, Cliff, we're going to have to manage the best way we can. No sweat, like. What about the radio?'

'Much the same. We should be able to talk to the *June Star*, but I'm having trouble with calls beyond that.'

'That's okay. I hope we won't have to make any. What's our ETA for rendezvous?'

'About forty-five minutes I would say if the weather stays the same . . .'

'Okay, I'll get the lads shaped up.'

Darkness had well and truly fallen by the time George made his way back up to the wheelhouse. Like the rest of the crew he was now fully kitted out and began to understand the meaning of foul-weather gear. A couple of miles south, unnoticed by Cliff, the *June Star* had finally steamed past the *Port au Prince*, which sat wallowing in the swell of the Irish Sea, picking up speed only once the British ship had passed her by. George stared down at the radar screen, giving the machine the occasional thump. It didn't seem to help much, but it made him feel better. He felt better still whenever the radar showed signs of life, at least enough to see the converging blip. He didn't know that now he was following the wrong blip with his finger.

On Cliff's instruction the trawler doused its lights while the big ship passed about 200 yards to starboard. Cliff was already concentrating on the on-coming lights of the following freighter, which he presumed to be the *June Star*. Half a mile to the north Todd waited and waited for the trawler to make contact. He was sure he was in the right area for the rendezvous.

As had been planned, Cliff and George allowed the freighter to steam by before turning up to run astern. Cliff took hold of the radio and called up the *June Star*. Three-quarters of a mile ahead, Todd answered.

'Where are you, *Puffin*? I can't see you,' he transmitted.

IRISH SEA

'Coming around about 300 yards astern. Don't worry about the ropes, conditions are good enough for a drop. Prepare to begin on my signal.'

'Roger!' Todd alerted the crew on the aft deck to prepare to make the drop. No ropes would be needed. The crew were pleased to hear that as they squinted into the darkness for the trawler's lights.

On board the *Port au Prince*, the Cuban captain was pleased to see the stern of the *June Star* disappearing into the night. The ship had dogged him and trailed him since the Bay of Biscay. At one time he had even thought that the *Port au Prince* was the target of the *June Star*'s attentions. He had his own rendezvous to make, a far more deadly one than George's. The provisional arm of the Irish Republican Army had also chosen a trawler to make a transfer, but this time the cargo was Soviet-made weapons which were to be carried from the *Port au Prince* to the Irish mainland. The shipment had been picked up in Cuba. The Irish trawler would head west to the mouth of the River Boyne once the transfer was complete. It had manoeuvred itself along the port side of the *Port au Prince* and a rudimentary system of ropes and pulleys had been fixed up to transfer the boxes of firearms and explosives between the two boats. Look-outs had been strategically placed by the Irish on the higher parts of the *Port au Prince* to keep an eye open for the British or Irish Navy. In security terms the look-outs were armed and extremely dangerous. Their instructions were very simple – shoot first and ask questions later.

Cliff manoeuvred astern and was now closing in on the silhouette of the freighter which just showed up against the night sky. 'Okay, let's light ourselves up and get the job done.' Cliff flicked on the navigational lights and transmitted his message to Todd. 'Ready and waiting. We are in position about one hundred yards astern and closing. We are ready to take our catch on board.' Todd gave the instructions to start dumping. His crew knew better than to question the captain's orders and began dumping the containers off the stern into the Irish Sea even though they could see no sign of the trawler or its lights.

It was one of the Panamanian sailors who spotted the *Puffin* first. He pointed the trawler out to a well-armed IRA look-out. The alarm went up aboard the *Port au Prince*.

'What the fuck?!' George exclaimed. 'What the fuck's that other boat

219

doing alongside? We've been fuckin' ready eyed. It's a trap. Back off, Cliff. Let's get the fuck out of here.'

Cliff grabbed the radio. 'Todd, you arsehole, what the fuck is that trawler doing alongside? Copy!'

'What trawler?' the bemused captain replied. 'Where are you? We don't see you. Why have you not got your navigation lights on? Give us a signal, unloading has already started.'

On the *Port au Prince* only part of the radio traffic was picked up. It sounded to the Cuban captain and his Irish colleague as if they were surrounded. In the ensuing confusion, ropes were cut loose and the boxes that were in transit fell into the sea.

The Irishman on the stern had only an American World War II bazooka, but he knew from previous experience that it was more than up to the job. As he took aim he was blinded momentarily by a spotlight which shone on the stern of the ship.

'What the fuck is the *Port au Prince*?' George cried out to Cliff. His eyes froze on the figure high up on the ship's stern caught in the beam of the spotlight. The Irishman set his sights on the middle of the trawler's lights, where he assumed the wheelhouse and nerve centre would be, and fired. The rocket's trail lit up the night sky and in less than two short deadly seconds it had found its target. Neither George or Cliff knew what hit them. They died instantly. A second and then a third explosion ripped the trawler apart; *Puffin* slid into the darkness, taking the entire crew to a watery Irish Sea grave.

From the bridge of the *June Star* Todd saw the explosions to the south. Seconds later the noise reached them. The explosions and the fire on the water lit up the immediate area and for a second the silhouettes of the *Port au Prince* and the Irish trawler, now heading west, were clearly and eerily to be seen.

'*Puffin* . . . *Puffin* . . . do you read, over? *Puffin*, for fuck's sake answer, are you okay? George . . . Cliff . . . do you read, over?' The still silence, broken only by the static from the radio, confirmed Todd's worst fears. He gave the order to go to full ahead and move the *June Star* out of the area as fast as she would travel. There was nothing they could do, he reassured his crew. There was no going back. There would be no survivors. In the *June Star*'s wake the watertight containers drifted north in the cold black water.

Isle of Man, early morning, Wednesday 22 December 1965

Richard Wright got to his office early, he always did. Normally he needed to be ready to make snap decisions before the stock market opened in London if he was going to make and break the markets; today it was simply force of habit. As Christmas drew near both his workload and the tasty bits of inside information on which he based his decisions fell off considerably as the City of London got down to the far more important matter of celebrating the year end. He used the time to tidy up pending matters as he intended to shut up shop between Christmas and the New Year. No new fortunes to be made until January, he informed his clients.

Two of Trebbin's most trusted men had been watching Wright from an office above the bank opposite for the last three days. They had an illegal tap on his phone which had resulted in Trebbin calling in his friends from the Fraud Squad to take notes. By the Tuesday they had enough evidence to ask for warrants to be issued for raids to be carried out on Wright's office in Douglas and the firm's headquarters in London. From the phone traffic coming in and out of London it had become clear that Mr Wright and his colleagues were not playing the markets on a level field. They were getting inside trading information from a myriad of sources. A number of their clients were also of considerable interest to the police, including some well-positioned politicians from both major parties.

Frustratingly for Trebbin's observers, there was nothing special about the calls made between Wright and Wood. Discussions as to where funds would be placed over the year end, talk of the approaching festivities, and an invitation for drinks and dinner at Wood's house on Christmas Eve. At least they now knew for sure where he lived, but the calls had revealed very little about the man himself. After talking with London and Trebbin, the Fraud Squad decided they would make their move at half past twelve on the 22nd, when many of the staff would be at lunch. The fewer people there were around, the less chance they would have to shred or hide documents. Any of the key players, such as the partners of Stroat, Bartlett, Booth and Wright, would be followed if they went out for lunch and served with a writ at exactly the same time, regardless of who they were with. In return for breaking the case, Trebbin had asked his colleagues for one favour. All the files relating to David and Denise Wood would be turned over to him personally and, unless absolutely necessary, would not be used in the case against Stroat, Bartlett, Booth and Wright. He could also use his colleagues' presence on the island as a screen for his own and Hardwood's activities. He was certain William would appreciate this fact, not that he had ever shown any interest in Wright.

Green did not want to appear too keen, but thought that dropping in for breakfast at around 8.30 a.m. would seem about right.

'There you are, Mr Brown,' the waitress said, 'a nice plate of bacon and eggs for you and a pot of tea. I'll go and get you the marmalade and I also have that address I promised you. As I thought, they moved to just outside of Douglas. A lovely house, my sister says. Sits all alone on the top of a little rise in its own grounds.'

Green thanked the waitress and thoroughly enjoyed his breakfast. Going for the kill always gave him a healthy appetite.

Liverpool/Irish Sea, Wednesday morning, 22 December 1965

The *June Star* finally docked in Liverpool around six on Wednesday morning and Freddie was woken soon after. Chris, who was in charge of Freddie's Liverpool operations, had gone on board as soon as the freighter docked and heard the full story from Captain Todd.

'Fuckin' choker!' Freddie said sadly down the phone. 'He was like a brother to me. Me best mate. But listen, Chris, you're rambling again, stick to the point. Give me the facts, not whose fault it is. We can get to that later. You say that according to Todd, George and the *Puffin* never made contact, only by radio, but he saw an explosion in the distance which he believes to have been the trawler. He also thinks that George had met up with the wrong ship. Is that the picture? Am I right?' Chris confirmed the facts. 'Okay, now I want you to get hold of a large and fast cruiser – the cost is irrelevant – and head out to where Todd thinks he dumped the gear. I can't call the coastguard or the lifeboat service, not with all that stuff slopping about in the Irish Sea. I'm going to get hold of a plane and see what we can see from the air and then I'll call you. And Chris . . . make sure you leave the right people in Liverpool to clear our cargo. I can't afford to have that sitting around in the docks over Christmas, it's too fuckin' risky.'

After the call Freddie sat on his bed and stared out of his hotel window at the lights of a cold and wet Liverpool. The condensation on the glass ran down the inside of the window and tears welled up in his eyes. He wasn't ashamed to admit it. George had been his mate, his best mate, and they had been through an awful lot together. Good times and bad times. He started thinking about their American adventure and raised a little smile.

It took Freddie about thirty minutes to pull himself together and

223

regain his composure. He wondered if he should call Rose, but decided to put it off until he was a hundred per cent certain that George was really gone. He might have survived the blast, but even if he had, could he have survived in the sea at those temperatures? He doubted it, especially as George was not a strong swimmer, but hope is the last to die and for the Rawlings family's sake, he had to hope that George was out there somewhere. They were going to have a pretty miserable Christmas without Big George at their side to cheer them up.

As Freddie reconsidered the day's options, he managed to contact Kevin Shaw at his home just outside Manchester. Kevin, who was based at Manchester Airport, was a pilot Freddie and George had often used for special deliveries in the north of England. Kevin said he could get a plane and pick Freddie up at Liverpool Airport within ninety minutes. Freddie explained what had happened and asked Kevin to kit the plane out with a spare life raft in case it might be of use to the survivors. He grabbed his police radio and a pair of powerful binoculars and put them in his small overnight bag. He thought about packing a gun, but in the end decided against. Airfields, planes and guns did not always go well together, he had discovered, and then there was the question of the other people who might have seen the explosion and might at that very moment be showing a keen interest in any traffic, airborne or seaborne, circling in the area.

By ten Freddie was in the air and heading out over the Irish Sea. Conditions had improved and the visibility was rather better than he or Kevin had dared hope for. Chris and the cruiser were also making good speed towards the area, they reported.

On his first sweep from Carmels Head north, Freddie found what he was looking for. At least six containers were grouped together and drifting north-east. The watertight seals appeared to be holding firm, which gave Freddie hope that they would keep afloat until Chris and the cruiser reached them. He radioed the co-ordinates down to the boat and struck out across the Irish Sea to *Puffin's* last reported position. The oil slick and floating flotsam told Freddie all he needed to know. Through his binoculars he could see a number of the *Puffin's* fenders drifting in the waves. They circled for another half-hour in the vain hope of spotting something, anything, and then headed north.

Freddie stared down at the unforgiving sea. 'Goodbye, George,' he said out loud. 'I'm gonna miss you, mate. We had a fuckin' good run. No regrets and all that. Rest in peace, old son.'

Other than damage control there was very little Freddie could now do. They flew north in search of more containers. Chris had reported on the radio that they had already plucked five from the sea, with just one casualty so far, one that had sunk minutes before they got to it. The news cheered Freddie. At least George's death would not have been in vain. Rose, of all people, would appreciate that.

Because of the layout of the cruiser, Chris and his team had their work cut out bringing the containers on board one at a time, splitting them open and throwing the contents in the main cabin before dumping the remains of the container over the side to sink without trace. In the main saloon it looked like the train robbery all over again, only these smaller sacks were packed with hashish and heroin rather than five and one pound notes.

As they flew north, Freddie and Kevin spotted a further three containers below in the water. They passed on the co-ordinates to Chris. 'I'm going to have to put her down to refuel soon,' Kevin shouted across to Freddie. 'Two hours is about the maximum I can get out of this little beauty in these wind conditions.'

'Where the fuck are you going to find an airstrip in the middle of the Irish Sea? Got an aircraft carrier lined up or something?'

'Something like that. It's an aircraft carrier better known as the Isle of Man! We can put her down at Ronaldsway Airport and refuel ourselves at the same time. I don't know about you, but I'm fuckin' starvin'.'

'Good call, Kev! Small world, though, I've got a friend who's livin' on the island. I always did wonder where it was. I would have said it was off the coast of Scotland, if you'd asked me.'

'I'm glad you're not navigating then!' The normally gregarious Freddie raised a real smile for the first time since being woken with the sad news.

Isle of Man, Wednesday
afternoon, 22 December 1965

The first thing to catch Freddie's eye was the flashing blue light. Through his binoculars he saw the car turn off the main road and into what Kevin's map identified as King William's College.

'Can you take us around one more time before we land?' Freddie asked Kevin.

'It's not normal, but I'll give it a go. I'll have to have a little misunderstanding with the tower, but they'll probably slap my wrist and no more.' Freddie kept his binoculars trained on the police car as it made its way up the driveway to the school. It could be nothing, but he wasn't in the mood to take chances. Police cars with flashing blue lights made him naturally uneasy.

'Sorry, tower, say again,' Kevin stuttered. 'Sorry, I have radio interference, I'm going to have to go around again ... Do I have permission to land, tower? ... Roger, Ronaldsway, coming around again.' He flicked the radio off. 'It's okay, Freddie, with these wind conditions we'll come straight in over the college to land.'

Freddie watched the police car stop. It pulled up alongside seven other police cars, two police vans and at least ten private, unmarked vehicles. There were even a couple of police bikes and lots of movement of people coming and going. 'If I'm not very much mistaken, and I'm not often in these matters, that's Old Bill down there and I don't think he is up to much good. I just hope it's got nothing to do with us.'

Kevin landed the plane just before noon and taxied across to the hangers on the far side of the airfield where he knew he could refuel. It wasn't his first time at the island's main airport. Freddie played with his radio, going through the wavebands and frequencies until he got it tuned into the police. 'That's very strange, they seem to have one

226

channel open for normal police traffic around the island and another separate one for our friends at the school.'

Kevin organized the refuelling and went off to get them a couple of sandwiches and a cup of coffee to warm them up. Freddie listened in on the police traffic from the school and was relieved to hear nothing that tied their activities either to the explosion of the *Puffin* or to the dope from the *June Star*.

'Looks as if they're closing in on some villain, if you ask me,' Freddie said between bites of his cheese and ham bap. 'They don't have one of those maximum-security nicks here, like they have on the Isle of Wight, do they? Perhaps somebody has had it away.'

'Don't think so, at least I've never heard of one. Don't they still hang people here? They're into capital punishment and all that shit, ain't they?' Kevin was actually more engrossed in his newspaper and the sandwich than his small talk with Freddie. 'Who knows, perhaps they've tracked down one of those train robbers to the island. Aren't they still looking for that fellow Biggs and that other one, the guy who escaped from Birmingham? What was his name?'

Now it was Freddie's turn to have his mind elsewhere. 'Kev, where's the nearest phone?' he said suddenly. 'You've just reminded me that I should call somebody. Can you grab my diary from the plane? I also might need you to get me some wheels and a map.' Kevin was used to Freddie's last-minute changes of plans and asked for no explanation, just as he hadn't questioned why Freddie had needed a plane at such short notice three days before Christmas. When you were paid as well as Freddie paid him, you didn't ask questions, you just produced results. Kevin leaned into the plane as Freddie continued listening in to the police traffic on the radio. Kevin could see that Freddie was paying careful attention to every word that was broadcast.

The name Wood kept recurring over and over again. They were obviously about to move out from their centre of operations, which Freddie assumed to be at the school, to close in on Wood's hide-out, which was a house just south of Douglas. At the same time, another group of officers were getting ready to make a move on an office in Douglas which was clearly already under surveillance. 'Nobody's getting out of there,' he thought.

The Woods' house was also already under surveillance, but not from

KEEP ON RUNNING

Old Bill. Green had got there just after ten. He hid his hired car off the road in what he hoped from its general state of disrepair was an unused barn. He made his way across the fields to the house on foot. The house was a simple enough target with big windows; on one side a clump of trees and bushes came up quite close to the front of the house, which would conceal his approach. He was a patient man and would wait until the light started to fade before making his move. He would not have to wait long; it would be getting dark as early as 3.30 or four o'clock.

Green kept his small portable radio tuned into the local police frequency, more for company than anything else. Nothing seemed to be happening on the island other than the usual problems with pre-Christmas drunk drivers. He checked his Colt Commander. It would be its first outing. Other than being lighter, thanks to the use of aluminium in place of steel, his gunsmith had promised him that it was exactly the same as the trusty Colt 45 1911A1 automatic that had served him so faithfully over the years. He was only sorry that he would have to dispose of it once the job was done. It seemed such a waste.

Through his tiny binoculars he watched Denise cross the lounge to the phone. She had changed quite a bit since he had watched her in Shepherds Bush, but it was her all right. He had also seen David, but only for a second as he went into the garage to get what looked to be a bottle of gin. He could have popped him then and there, but as a creature of habit he preferred to bide his time and take him out later. There seemed no rush; the boys from London would surely not arrive until tomorrow.

Denise was worrying about Friday's dinner party and what she would serve as she crossed the thick-pile seaweed green carpet to the phone. She still had her pinafore on over her turquoise woollen dress. She had decided to avoid the obvious, such as turkey – everyone would be having that on Christmas Day. A nice piece of roast beef always went down well, she thought. She picked up the phone as she wiped her hands, expecting it to be her butcher, who had said he would call for her final pre-Christmas order. 'Hello, Denise Wood,' she said, without really thinking. She was running on auto-pilot.

Her voice cut through Freddie like a sharp knife. 'Denise? Listen, it's Freddie from Jamaica here. Is David home?'

'Freddie! It's great to hear from you!' Denise sounded genuinely excited to hear his voice. So were the group listening at King William's; what calls they had monitored so far during the day had all been straightforward and amazingly dull. All had been related to Denise and the dinner party in one way or another; this promised better things. 'David said we would never hear from you again,' she continued, 'but I said, don't bet on it. It's really great to hear your voice again. Is Maggie with you? Where are you?'

'Look, Denise, I've got to speak to David. Is he there?' His voice betrayed the urgency.

'Yes, he is. Listen, Freddie, I hope we see you soon. I'll get David . . . Send my love to Maggie.' Denise called to David, who was working in his study just off the main hall. 'Dave, a nice Christmas surprise, it's that friend of yours we met in Jamaica, Freddie. He's on the phone.'

David let his glass slip down on to his desk with a bang. It took him way back to that first day when Patrick Green had called him at home pretending to be the Ulsterman. Freddie, unless he was more stupid than David thought, would never call him at home unless there was some kind of an emergency. Perhaps he had heard something from the cops about the robbery that could affect him. David cleared his throat and picked up the receiver. 'Freddie?' As David spoke the pips began to go. Freddie's cold hands desperately fumbled with some more coins which he stuffed into the slot.

'He's calling from a phone-box, and a phone-box on this side of the island, I'm trying to get a trace,' a police sergeant told Trebbin.

'Dave? . . . Dave are you still there?' Freddie cried.

'Yes, Freddie, I am. What's up?'

'Listen carefully, David, and please listen to everything I say because there has been a change of plans and we don't have much time as there's an awful lot of interference on the line. Unfortunately the wheels have come off, so you and Denise will have to follow Charlie and Ron instead. William is already on his way around to see you, but if you don't want to take a lift with him, let me give you a ride. Grab what you can and hurry. I'll be hanging around at Maggie's office. Denise should know where that is.' There was a stunned silence from David's end of the phone. 'Dave, are you still there? Do I need to repeat the message?'

'No, Freddie, I got the message. Where did you say we should meet you?'

'I'll be hanging around at Maggie's office. And Dave, if I were you I would keep off the main road, the conditions are far too dodgy.'

'Okay, thanks, I'll see what I can do.' David's hand was shaking so much that he had trouble replacing the receiver. Denise came into the study smiling, wiping her hands on her pinny. 'Wasn't that nice of Freddie to call?' She did not get a reply. David was ashen white. 'What is it, David, you look terrible?'

'What did Freddie's Maggie do for a living?'

'What a strange question! She was an air stewardess, I think. Are you okay?'

'Not really. Where would her office be?'

'What Maggie's? Los Angeles Airport, I imagine.'

'Hanging around at airports . . . yes! Freddie must be in the hangers at Ronaldsway! Listen, Denise, I don't know what the fuck is going down, but I'm going to trust Freddie on this one and that means we've got to get the fuck out of here.'

'Are you mad? I've got a million and one things to do before Friday. I can't go out.'

'Denise, if we don't go now there may never be another Friday to look forward to. He said, "The wheels have come off", that means something's gone terribly wrong. He said we must follow Charlie and Ron. Don't you see, he's telling us to escape. "William is already on his way". He means Old Bill are on their way around here and that's why he said there was interference on the line, they've obviously got the phone tapped and the roads blocked. We've got to get the hell out of here, and now! Grab the basics, something warm. Hopefully it'll all be a misunderstanding and we'll be back by tonight, but we just can't take the chance for now. And put on some trousers, we'll have to take the bike.'

It hadn't take William Hardwood long to break Freddie's code either. He was furious that somebody else should have stumbled on the Woods the very same day he had. 'Looks like another leak,' Trebbin said. A fact that did nothing to improve William's mood.

'Did we get a trace on that call?' William yelled impatiently across the control room. The answer was negative. 'Fuck! Who the hell do you think Maggie is, Inspector, and where do you think her office is? Come on, Nigel, if we don't move quickly our bird will have flown the coop.' As they ran out the door, Trebbin turned around to those that were staying behind. 'Run a check, this Maggie might be linked to Wright. Look at the phone book for Douglas. My money says they are going to try and lose themselves in the town. Alert the Isle of Man Steam Packet Company in case they go for the ferry. And get some men down there.'

Green sat quietly chewing on an apple he had brought with him. He was wearing two pairs of gloves for warmth, though he would only wear the thin pair when he came to shoot Jenkins. Over his radio he heard the call for a car to go down to the ferry terminal. It was the first time he had heard any reference to Wood on the waveband. 'Taking their bloody time, these London boys. Christmas is coming, lads, and if you don't hurry there won't be any goose for you to find, fat or otherwise,' he laughed to himself. Green had watched Denise's comings and goings in the lounge. She was now upstairs changing her clothes. Despite his sexual preferences he could enjoy Denise's strip-tease as much as the next man. He approved of her choice of lingerie as she slipped into a pair of tight black leather trousers and a pink angora sweater. 'Must be off to the shops,' he thought. 'How fucking predictable. Wonder what she's forgotten this time. Perhaps I should pop your old man while you're out and spare you for another day. Now that would be a nice little Christmas present for you to come home to. Bitch!'

Denise was finding it hard to breathe. She grabbed a few things from her dressing table and threw them in a small bag, the largest David would let her take on the bike. They had decided to buy the bike after they discovered the island's obsession with motorbikes during the annual TT series. They had had it nearly six months, but rarely got to use it.

David opened the safe behind a picture in his study. He had two. Another was located in the floor under the doormat in the front hall and held mainly papers and the bigger valuables. David grabbed their passports as a precaution, as well as a thick wad of money which he always kept on hand for a rainy day. He also picked up the small suede pouch which held the diamonds. He fingered it for some time, rubbing the diamonds together through the cloth, wondering what he should do. If he was caught with the diamonds he would be done bang to rights, that was for sure. He put the pouch down on the green leather top of his desk and spread them out. He had only had to sell five of them so far. As he scooped them up to put them back in the pouch, one rolled against his glass. It gave him an idea. He selected the smallest and most rounded stones and swallowed hard. The gin and tonic helped, but it was not an experience he would wish to repeat. If Freddie was wrong he would make him swallow more than a couple of diamonds. After swallowing seven of them David locked the rest back in the safe. He looked up. Denise was standing by the study door.

'Are you ready, love?' he asked. She nodded. He could see she was keeping herself in control, but only just. He pulled her to him and gave her a big, long hug. 'Don't you worry. It'll be all right. It always is, you'll see. Now give me a smile!'

'But I'm scared, Dave, I'm really scared this time.'

'And so you should be. The moment we stop being scared is when we get careless and get caught. Come on, let's get out of here. I want to put some distance between us and the house. Leave the lights on. If we are being watched we don't want to attract any attention by sudden moves. Let 'em think we're still here.' David took Denise through the dining room, which was unlit, and on into the kitchen. Denise's only safety measure was to turn off the lunch. It already looked beyond salvation. They grabbed their jackets from the hooks by the back door and David rummaged in the cupboard for their helmets, which would also double as their disguise on the open road. 'Tuck you hair up,' he told Denise. He had to hope the bike would start first time. It had been some time since he last used it.

They slipped out the back door and into the garage. Green saw only one figure cross the path, and assumed it to be Denise getting her car to go shopping. He would wait till she had gone, then slip in to deal with David. It would be better one to one. Her punishment, he had decided, would be to live as an impoverished widow for the rest of her days. She might even get a spell in the nick. The 'girls' would really have fun with her, he thought.

David took the dust cover off the bike and prepared to start it. Denise slipped the latch off the garage door and waited. It took David at least four kicks before the bike roared into life. The noise took Green by surprise. He slipped back further into the bush and fingered his Colt Commander. Denise pushed opened one side of the garage door and jumped on the bike behind David. He gunned it out and down the drive. He wondered when Old Bill would put in an appearance and held his breath.

Green had little time to react. By the time he realized that there were two people on a bike they were already halfway down the driveway. He stepped out of the bushes in a firing position, but held back. He would wait for their return. He did not think they had seen him. In fact, David had glimpsed the figure in his wing mirror but, thinking it was Old Bill, he kept going.

Green decided, as time was on his side, he would check the house out and wait for his targets to return. He was sure they would be back and the noise of the bike would give him due warning. It did not cross his mind that they had done a runner.

David felt a lot happier once they were out of the front gates and on to the public highway. He headed for Douglas. At Ellenbrook he would turn right and go back along the A25 in the direction of Castletown and the airport. If the police were coming, he was sure they would use the more popular A5.

They were less than a mile from the house when David saw the first flashing blue light. He took his hand off the handlebar and gave Denise's leg a comforting squeeze, although secretly he believed this was the end of the road for them. He waited for the two police cars and one unmarked vehicle to cut him off, but they roared past without showing any interest in the speeding bike. Obviously, much to David's relief, they were not as yet looking for two people on a motorbike.

Green slipped in through the back door. Just as he had been told, the people on the island really did leave their doors unlocked when they went out. He was dressed from head to foot in black and now had on only the one pair of gloves. He kept the Colt to hand in case of any unwanted surprises.

He looked at the food on the stove. The water was still simmering. It was beginning to dawn on Green that the Woods had left in a hurry and may not be back. Everywhere there were signs of a hasty exit. A tea towel lay on the floor in the middle of the hall, where Denise had dropped it. He moved in to the study. The condensation from a glass was leaving a nasty mark on the leather top. By the pristine state of the rest of the desk, this was obviously not normal behaviour for David. Green glanced over the papers on the desk. They did not tell him much. Certainly nothing that suggested any reason for the sudden departure. A couple of bank statements, a quote from a builder for a new fence, and the bill from the travel agent for the Jamaican holiday. It had to be the phone call, he thought.

Another item caught his eye. It was a picture. A framed copy of a 'Get Out of Jail Free' card from a Monopoly set and a five-pound note. 'Cheeky,' Green muttered under his breath. He could guess where they came from.

The Irishman made his way slowly and quietly upstairs. The bedroom also showed signs of a quick exit. Denise's dress lay in a crumpled mess on the floor. He picked it up and pressed the woollen material to his face, taking a long, deep breath as he appreciated her perfume and body odours. 'Nice, very nice. Oh, the girls are going to have fun with you, Mrs Jenkins.' Denise had also left her jewel box open on the dressing table. He ran his finger through the ornaments. Most of it was costume jewellery. 'Either you have appalling taste, my dear, or the good stuff is elsewhere.'

David kept his speed within the limit. Having slipped past the police cars, he was more confident that their luck would hold and that the police were not looking for a bike. At least, not yet. It took him just under fifteen minutes, although it felt like fifteen hours, to reach the perimeter fence of Ronaldsway Airport. A signpost conveniently pointed the way to the private hangers.

Freddie had warned Kevin to have the plane ready to 'rock 'n' roll' the moment he gave the word. Kevin took the precaution of getting clearance from the tower, but said he was still waiting for a last-minute delivery. The tower told him they would be ready when he was. Their only worry was the fading light, which was also a concern to Kevin and Freddie. Kevin taxied the plane round and sat at the controls. Behind him Freddie paced impatiently back and forth at the door of the open hanger, the radio pressed to his ear. He knew the police were closing in. From first reports, the raid on Wright's office had gone like clockwork and Wright was already 'helping police with their inquiries'. Trebbin had received word that Wood's files had been separated and were on their way over to King William's College.

Freddie ran over to the pay-phone and dialled David's number again. Perhaps he hadn't understood the message or the urgency. The phone rang and rang. In the house it gave Green quite a start. He stared at the phone in the bedroom until he could bear it no longer. He picked it up and tried to hide his accent.

'Hello,' he said. The Irish twinge was still there.

'You're a cunt!' Freddie said purposefully and slammed the phone down.

Just as the police were not looking for a motorbike, neither was Freddie, so when he saw it enter the area of the hanger he paid very little heed until it was almost upon him.

'I hope you're not wanking me off, Freddie.' The voice behind the helmet and goggles could be only be David's.

'Wow, am I fucking glad to see you. No time for explanations. Get rid of the bike and get in the plane. I'll tell you everything once we're airborne.' As David propped the bike up by the hanger wall, Freddie led Denise over to the plane and helped her aboard. Kevin, who grunted a quick greeting, was already getting final clearance from the tower. David ran across the tarmac and pulled himself up and into the plane, which taxied out immediately.

'I don't know what you two have been up to,' Freddie said looking back at his two startled passengers, 'but you've certainly got somebody's back up. Old Bill and possibly the Ulsterman are crawling all over your house as we speak.'

Trebbin's men blocked off all the roads and the immediate area surrounding the house. His radio informed him that the local constabulary had found a car parked in a disused barn, about half a mile from the house. They would radio the information through to Douglas, as it looked suspiciously like a hired car.

'Well, William,' the inspector said. 'This is where my men and I take a back seat. It's your show from here on in, but don't hesitate to call on us if you need our back-up. All I can promise you is that nothing will get in or out of the grounds of the house without your permission.'

'Thanks, Nigel. We'll try and make it as clean as possible.' William gave the word for his men to move in. In the dusk, the lights illuminated much of the interior of the house. A voice in his earpiece broke William's train of thought.

'I have the first suspect in my sights,' an agent reported. 'Subject is male and located in the front, central, upstairs window. No sign of the woman.'

Green, still shaken by the phone call, thought he saw a movement down in the garden. It could have been a fox or a dog, but he was taking no chances. He daren't turn the light out for a better look in case it was David and Denise returning. He slipped out of the bedroom and made his way silently downstairs. As he crossed the main hall he had no more doubts that figures were moving in across the front lawn towards the house. He slipped into the kitchen, out across the path and into the garage.

'I've lost sight of the male suspect,' the voice reported in William's earpiece.

'Roger! Okay, lads, secure the citadel, I repeat, secure the citadel.' William's voice was drowned out for a few seconds as a light aircraft flew over. From the plane David and Denise looked down on their dream house. Visible to the naked eye were the police cars which blocked the roads in the immediate vicinity. Through Freddie's binoculars David watched as the dark figures approached the house from every angle. By their gait it was clear that many were carrying weapons.

'Fuck! That was close, too close. Freddie, how do we thank you?'

'Don't thank me, thank fate. Don't ask me what I was doing on the Isle of Man the week before Christmas. It was never part of my travel plans.' The plane flew on into the darkening sky.

Green decided to take advantage of the noise of the plane to slip away. The door to the garage was still loose, blowing open and shut with the wind. He took the Colt from his belt and slid it under David's Jaguar. If these figures in the garden were Old Bill from London, he did not want to be armed when they arrested him. It would be his only crime. He moved to the garage door. There was no real cover in the garden along his line of escape, but he weighed the options and decided to make a dash for it in the hope that he could outrun his pursuers. He rather fancied his chances – very few Bobbies he had come up against over the years had been able to keep up with him in a chase. It was worth the risk. Green took a deep breath and was gone. It was his misfortune that the nearest man to him was one of William's élite squad. The man dropped to his knee and had his rifle up in a second. 'Halt!' he yelled. 'Stop running, Wood . . . You are surrounded . . . Stop!'

'The silly fucker thinks I'm Jenkins,' were the last thoughts that went through Green's mind before everything went blank. One shot was enough. William had told his men he did not need any hospital cases – if they had to shoot, they were to shoot to kill. The gun's report was the signal needed to set the others scurrying towards the house. In seconds William got the word that the 'citadel' was secure. One casualty, a man, no sign of the woman.

'I won't tell if you won't tell,' William said to Trebbin. 'You can come up to the house if you like.' Trebbin told his men to seal off the area. He and he alone would go to the house. Officially nothing would be found. The Woods had simply disappeared.

The plane flew almost due south. Kevin had logged a flight plan to the Valley Airfield just south of Holyhead in Anglesey. David and Denise could choose to catch a train, rent a car or even take the ferry across from Holyhead to Dun Laoghaire on the Irish mainland. 'Might be the safest option for now,' David agreed. 'There are worse places to spend Christmas, in the circumstances, than Dublin.' He pulled Denise close to him. He could tell she was still in shock.

Freddie explained everything that had happened in the previous twenty-four hours, including the loss of George and the shipment, and how he had come to end up on the island. He received some good news during the flight. Chris reported that all but three of the containers had been recovered and those landed in Liverpool had already cleared the docks. Juan Carlos also reported in. He too had been successful in landing his catch and had taken it upon himself to talk to the captain of the *Port au Prince* in Barrow-in-Furness. The captain sent his sincere condolences to the families and friends of all of those who had lost their lives aboard the *Puffin*. He apologized for what had happened and explained that it had been an act not of aggression, but of defence. They had thought the *Puffin* was a naval vessel, especially when it had turned on its spotlight. Freddie and Juan were man enough to admit that they would have probably done the same in the circumstances.

David tapped Freddie on the shoulder. 'You're a hero Freddie, a real live, fuckin' hero and we can't thank you enough for that.'

'I'm no hero, Dave. I'm a survivor, just like you and Denise. We've chosen to live in our own little twilight zone and crossed the boundary of what is considered acceptable behaviour years ago. There's no going back; no apologies to be made. We made our beds and we are going to have to sleep in them, however uncomfortable they might get. Listen to me, I'm starting to sound like one of those prats on the BBC. So what are you two going to do now? Are you going to be all right? I've got contacts who can help you.'

'You've done more than enough, Freddie. Denise and I are just going to have to keep our heads down for a couple of months and start all over again. We've done it before and we will probably have to do it again. The important thing is we're still running free. I grabbed a couple of bob as we ran out the door, so that will see us through the next difficult weeks. I have a few other bits and pieces I can lay my hands on . . .'

'There is also this,' Denise interrupted, removing her gloves for the first time and showing her diamond ring. 'Might help out on a rainy day.'

Freddie looked at the ring and up at David.

'Well, you might as well know,' David started to explain, 'there was a bag of diamonds on the train that night. That is what the Ulsterman was after. I'm just sorry he gave you and George such a hard time. I really am. I never meant to take them, it just ended up that way when we switched the bags. It's all a game of chance, you know?'

'So you gone and lost them, then? That's what the Paddy was looking for in your house?'

'Probably! About half of them are sitting in my safe, which I assume he or Old Bill will find. Some, however, are buried in the grounds of the house and perhaps one day I'll be able to go back and pick 'em up.' From the look on Denise's face this was obviously news to her.

'Don't you look at me like that! You haven't heard the worst of it. I swallowed at least half a dozen of them before we left the house and you're going to have to help me find them in the morning!' Sounds of laughter filled the airplane for the first time since leaving Ronaldsway. 'You'll be a finer man than me, Gunga Din!' Freddie laughed. 'Talk about what's the worst job I've ever had!?'

William's men moved quickly and efficiently throughout the house and garden. William and Trebbin concentrated on the study. 'I wonder where the lady went?' Trebbin asked. Before he could get a reply one of William's agents put his head through the door.

'I don't think this was your man!'

'Explain?' William asked.

'It's only from some very basic tests, but the fingerprints around the house, of which there are two very dominant sets, don't tie up with our corpse in the garden. His documents show him to be one Patrick Green. Once we get the body to Liverpool I'll be able to carry out some more detailed tests. Forensic will tidy up in here.'

'Thank you.' William nodded that the agent could go.

'Well ... well ... Mr Patrick Green. Fancy him turning up in the shrubbery,' Trebbin remarked.

'You know him, then?'

'Know of him, to be slightly more accurate. Patrick Green is an alias, but is the name he mostly operates, or rather operated, under. He was considered to be the right-hand man to our friend from Ulster. We've been hoping to question him for some years, but we could never pin anything on him. But if he is here, we are yet again looking at a high-level leak. Come on, William, it can be no coincidence that two years after the event we all converge on the same house and on the same day. And that's not even counting the Freddie character.'

'Look at that!' William pointed to the framed 'Get Out Of Jail Free' card and the five-pound note. 'I think we can guess where that came from?' William went to take the picture off the wall but instead of lifting off, as he expected, it swung away from the wall, setting off an alarm in the process. It took just a few minutes for the alarm to be neutralized and for one of his team to crack the combination. The small safe contained a few cheque books and much of the information that Trebbin was certain they would find duplicated in Wright's files. But they also found the diamonds. A small pouch with twenty-eight of the most beautiful jewels either William or Trebbin had ever seen.

'So this is what all the fuss was about?' Trebbin asked.

'That's correct. And they don't even officially exist, you know that?'

'I do now.'

'Can you call off the notice to the jewellers?'

'I certainly can.'

'Good, because on behalf of my boss and the department I would like you to accept one of these stones as a mark of gratitude for everything you have done.'

'I can't possibly do that!'

'Why not? They don't exist, Nigel. They never really did. I'm going to have to plant these on another raid to get them back into the system. There's no other way to return them to the Treasury, who paid the final bill for them. Look, Nigel, my boss made it quite clear that depending on what I found here, there was one of them for you, one for me and one for him to make his retirement a little bit more comfortable. He says we deserve it. Especially on our salaries.'

'Well, if you put it like that and they don't officially exist, then they can't really do any harm, can they? Certainly help out with the grandchildren's education in the years to come.'

'Good! Our job was to get them back from the hands of the bad guys and put them in the hands of the good guys, whoever they may be. I think we just about classify as the good guys, don't we? We've done our job for Queen and country over the last two years and done it well. So has Mr Wood, or whoever he turns out to be. You've got to hand it to him, he's given us a good run for our money. I actually find myself wishing him well in a funny way. You remember that light plane that flew over?'

'Yes.'

'I bet he was on it. It would suit his style. That was probably Freddie, our mystery caller, flying it.'

'Do you want me to run a check on the small plane movements at Ronaldsway today?'

'No, I'd prefer not to know, thanks all the same. Would you?' William asked Trebbin to choose a jewel and then swept the remaining stones into the bag and placed them in his pocket. 'Well, I don't think there is much more left for us here. My team can clear up and take the body away. Then your boys can come in and do the paperwork on the abandoned house. Perhaps a boating accident would look good for the files to explain their disappearance? There were coastguard reports earlier this afternoon of flotsam in the Irish Sea from a trawler called the *Puffin*. It's apparently gone missing. Perhaps that could explain the disappearance of the Woods. I'll leave it up to you and your imagination . . .'

'That's okay with me. Looks as if I will get home for Christmas after all,' Trebbin replied.

The lights from the airport were clearly visible as they descended through the clouds. It wasn't late, but it was already dark. Kevin dropped the plane down for a smooth landing at the Valley Airfield. Freddie broke the silence. 'Listen, guys, Maggie will be sorry she wasn't here to see you. I don't think she's going to believe me when I tell her everything we've been through in the last twenty-four hours. But if you two think you'll be okay, Kevin and I will be on our way. If they start checking on the planes leaving Ronaldsway you will want them to be looking in the direction of Liverpool and not here.'

'Can't thank you enough, Freddie. We'll be all right. With a name like Jenkins you've certainly dropped us in the right part of the country. We could stay around here for a while, but I have a feeling we might take that round-the-world journey we've been promising ourselves. Who knows, we might run into Bruce or Buster, or even Charlie or Ron. The world's a small place and seems to be getting smaller by the day. Then there's always Jamaica or your place in Spain that you were talkin' about!'

'Any time, mate. Any time you fancy, you'll be most welcome . . .' Freddie gave Denise a long embrace. He could tell it had been an emotional day for her, as it had been for him. She would pull through; she was a tough lady despite her looks. The two men also embraced.

'I'm really sorry about George. I didn't know him, but he seemed all right,' David whispered to Freddie.

'It's all the luck of the draw. We had our up and downs over the years, more ups than downs, and between what he did these last two years and facing the slammer for the next thirty, I know what George would have chosen. You two look after yourselves, then, and when you're settled, you let me know. If you want to, that is.'

'We'll want to, won't we, Denise?' David gave his wife a hug and they both waved as the plane taxied out.

Within minutes Freddie was airborne and not much later he was back in his hotel bedroom in Liverpool. It had been a rough day, not one he would want to repeat. He watched the evening news. Nothing. The weather dominated the broadcast, that and the last-minute rush of Christmas shopping throughout the country. There was no word about a missing trawler or suspicious containers in the Irish Sea, and nothing about a police operation on the Isle of Man. Officially, it seemed, today had never happened.

Before he could finally put the traumatic day to bed he needed to talk to Rose. It was not a call he looked forward to making. Juan Carlos also rang. He had thought ahead, as usual, and booked them both on a Christmas Eve flight out of Heathrow to Málaga. He had also spoken to his sister, who said the house in Marbella would be ready and waiting

241

for him and the fridge fully stocked for Christmas. He put the phone down and it rang almost immediately. It was Maggie.

'Bad day, I hear. I spoke to the London office. Any news on George?' It took him nearly forty minutes, but he told her briefly everything that had happened during the past twenty-four hours.

'What a bummer for David and Denise and George's family. Still, I can't help feeling they are all survivors. Now, Mr Birch, if you are still interested I can get to Spain on Christmas Day and stay through the New Year.'

A big smile came over Freddie's face, despite his tiredness. 'Maggie, thats the best news I've heard all day. Now all we need to discuss is which New Year we are talking about!'

Kent, February 1966

'Good of you to come down to the house, William. So many people forget about you the moment you retire. Can't do any more favours for them, so they consider you expendable. You would have been amazed just how many people dropped me off their Christmas card list even before I got my last pay cheque. It's a disgrace!'

'I won't forget you, Sir Roger, as if you would let me. Anyway, I've brought you a little present. Indirectly, you paid for it from the department's budget.' William placed the diamond in front of Sir Roger.

'It's beautiful, my boy, quite, quite beautiful. I will treasure it. A souvenir from one of the strangest episodes in my long career and quite useful if I ever come up a bit short.'

'You deserve it more than anyone, Sir Roger.'

'You're probably right there, my boy. So tell me, William, what have your investigations thrown to light since Christmas?'

'Firstly, we are no nearer discovering who Mr and Mrs Wood are. We have their fingerprints and we now have photos of them, but who they actually are or were we simply don't know. I don't see them as a threat to the realm, however. In fact I'll be surprised if they are not far away by now. Britain probably won't be in their plans for some time.'

'And the money?'

'Our Mr Wood had done all right since the robbery, thanks to the diamonds and Wright's inside information. The balance of his accounts, and there could be more we haven't found yet, is a little over £150,000. We can't touch it until probate is complete, but as there are no heirs, it will find its way back to the government at the end of the day. We did, however, recover twenty of the diamonds – twenty-one if you count the one in Bath and twenty-four if you count the other sundries such as this one.'

243

'You did better than I would have expected, nearly half the total haul.'

'Thank you, sir.'

'And our corpse?'

'As Trebbin had suggested, it was one Patrick Green, a gentleman who worked for our friend the Ulsterman. His real name was Ian Stevenson and he came from Downpatrick in Northern Ireland. He worked for the civil service and local government for some time before calling it a day in 1961. We have informed what family he had in Ulster, but they appear to have had no contact with him for many years. Just like the Woods, he never existed officially on mainland Britain. Perhaps we will get lucky, one day, and some landlord will call us in because the tenant has gone missing and left a whole pile of paperwork that will unravel the mystery of the Ulsterman. But I doubt it, somehow.'

'A strange tale, William. One day I might try and tell it to my grandchildren. Although I don't expect they will believe their old grandfather.'

'I know the feeling, Sir Roger. Until people begin to accept that truth is often stranger than fiction, I doubt if anyone will ever believe what happened to those diamonds. Perhaps it's better for everyone that the public believes that the Great Train Robbery was a simple hold-up and nothing more.'

Epilogue

So there you have it. Freddie's story. I told you he had had a tempestuous couple of years!

In case you were wondering, Freddie did make an honest woman of Maggie and they have a lovely couple of kids. A boy, George, and a girl, Mary Rose, and now, thanks to Mary and her Spanish husband, a first grand-daughter, Rosa. Freddie still lives in Spain, although not in Marbella, which he says is now far too British for his taste. His operations continue to do very nicely, thank you, with Juan Carlos running the Spanish end of the business and Mike taking care of Britain for him.

Rose and Ernie are both dead, but due to natural causes, I'm pleased to report. They went into retirement on George's share of the business and lived out the rest of their days in quite a degree of comfort. Rose even came over to see me in Rio once. She had had a good innings by the time she died and I never once heard her speak bitterly about what had happened to George.

Collier, as you might expect, came to a fairly grisly end. But that is another story that only Freddie can tell. Wright, on the other hand, got off with a warning, thanks to his political connections, and was last heard of operating some scam with Lloyd's of London from his base in the Cayman Islands. Many people lost their shirts with Lloyd's, right down to the last pair of cufflinks, I'm told, but not Wright. Trebbin also moved abroad, but only to a well-deserved retirement in Florida, paid for, I imagine, by his one little jewel.

William Hardwood had a long and successful career and has only recently retired. He switched tracks, after Sir Roger's retirement, and entered the Foreign Service proper. He rose to the rank of Consul-General. There was an internal inquiry, I heard from Freddie, which questioned the lifestyle Hardwood managed to support on his salary, but he claimed his wife had inherited a large sum of money from a relative in 1966. Although this was never very well explained, it was enough to quash the inquiry.

Sir Roger has also passed on and as his death in 1969 coincided with the demise of the Ulsterman's activities, there are those who argue that they were one and the same man. I am not one of them.

That only leaves David and Denise. They're around, but I am not at liberty to tell you where. One day they promise to let me tell you the rest of their story. Then again, they say, why rock the boat?